THE
Golden
Scepter

THE DRAGON ARTIFACTS
Book 2

MIKE SHELTON

Acknowledgements

I am so excited to release this new series. Through the last few years I have found great support in the indie author community, as well as among my wife, children, and extended family.

My editors at Precision editing and my illustrator all help to bring my stories to life. Thanks to all of them!

The Golden Dragon is a work of fiction. Names, characters, places and incidents are the products of my imagination and are used fictitiously. Any resemblance to actual events, locales, or persons, living or dead, is entirely coincidental. I alone take full responsibility for any errors or omissions in this book.

-Mike-

Books by Mike Shelton

WESTERN CONTINENT BOOKS:

<u>Books of the Realm:</u>
The Cremelino Prophecy:
The Path Of Destiny
The Path Of Decisions
The Path Of Peace
The Blade and the Bow (A prequel novella to The Cremelino Prophecy)

<u>Dragon Rider Books:</u>
The Alaris Chronicles:
The Dragon Orb
The Dragon Rider
The Dragon King
Prophecy Of The Dragon (A prequel novella to The Alaris Chronicles)

The Dragon Artifacts:
The Golden Dragon
The Golden Scepter
The Golden Empire

GEMSTONES OF WAYLAND BOOKS:

The TruthSeer Archives:
TruthStone
TruthSpell
TruthSeer
The Stones of Power (A prequel novella to The TruthSeer Archives)

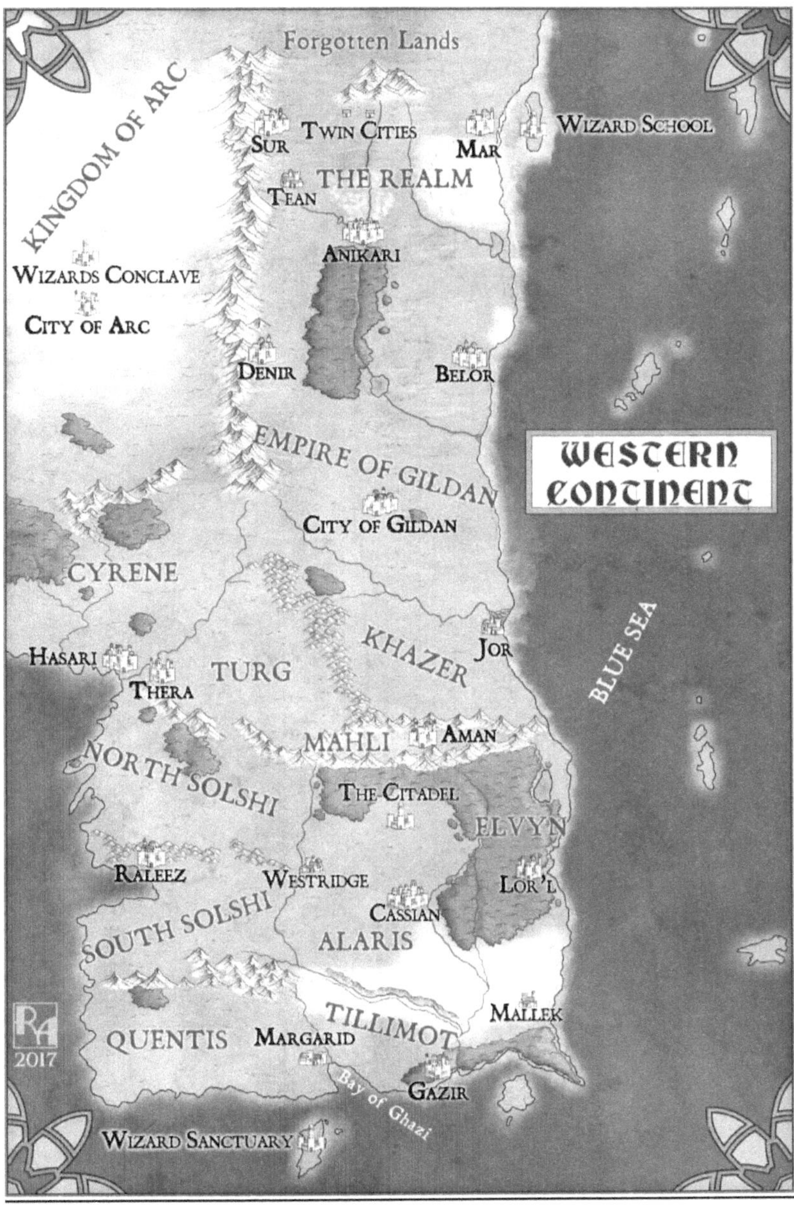

Forgotten Lands
KINGDOM OF ARC
WIZARD SCHOOL
SUR
TWIN CITIES
MAR
THE REALM
TEAN
ANIKARI
WIZARDS CONCLAVE
CITY OF ARC
DENIR
BELOR
WESTERN CONTINENT
EMPIRE OF GILDAN
CITY OF GILDAN
CYRENE
BLUE SEA
KHAZER
JOR
HASARI
TURG
THERA
MAHLI
AMAN
NORTH SOLSHI
THE CITADEL
ELVYN
RALEEZ
WESTRIDGE
LOR'L
SOUTH SOLSHI
CASSIAN
ALARIS
MALLEK
TILLIMOT
QUENTIS
MARGARID
GAZIR
Bay of Ghazi
WIZARD SANCTUARY
RH
2017

Mike Shelton

CHAPTER ONE

"Liam, watch out!" Gabby yelled from in front of Bakari. Liam's Cremelino horse swerved to the side, barely missing a splattering of rocks exploding from the side of the collapsing mountain. Bakari himself grabbed tighter around Gabby's waist as she directed their horse up and over a large boulder that had rolled down in front of them. Coming down on the other side of the rock, their horse slid on a patch of freshly fallen snow.

Bakari suddenly found himself hanging over the edge of the mountain and losing his balance. Keeping his legs wrapped around the horse's body, he tried pulling himself back upright. He had almost done so when suddenly the Cremelino stopped. That caused him to truly lose his balance, and he tumbled from the horse, hitting the rocky ground hard. The momentum of the fall carried him over the edge, and he began to tumble down the side of the mountain.

"Liam, Stop!" Gabby screamed.

Some Dragon King I am, came the thought to Bakari as he tried desperately to grab on to something. The rocks offered no handholds, and the snow-covered ground made everything else wet and slippery.

Use your powers, Dragon King.

The voice of Flash, the Cremelino horse he and Gabby had been riding, sounded in his mind. However, he was still groggy from the spell that Delia Marinos had used on all three of them—a spell that had taken away his wizarding powers for a short time.

Bakari grunted with pain each time his body hit another rock. He tried to focus his mind, but it was hard for him to concentrate as he tumbled down the side of the rocky mountain. It was all he could do to try and protect his head. He strained to take his attention away from his surroundings, and use his powers to bring up an image of a bubble of protection—the same thing he had done to protect Gabby, Jaimon, and himself from the rain the night before. But now he made it stronger, thicker, to cushion his fall.

It worked!

Well, it worked enough to keep him from being hurt, but he was still falling. Looking ahead of him, he saw a large boulder approaching. At the same moment he heard a loud *whooshing* sound, and a sudden gust of wind pushed against him and slowed his descent, eventually leaving him stopped against the rock.

Bakari lay still, trying to take inventory of how he felt. The bubbled cushion of air winked out of existence, and he once again felt the cold mountain air sweep over his skin.

"Dragon King!" Liam's voice came from up above. "Are you all right?"

Every bone in his body ached, and there was blood on his right arm and right leg. Reaching up with one hand, he pushed a few stray black braids of hair out of his face. As he did so he noticed a wide crimson gash in the back of his otherwise dark brown hand. He tried to flex his fingers but instead cried out in pain.

Looking up the mountainside, he saw Liam and Gabby with the two Cremelino horses looking down at him. He waved shakily at them with his good arm. "I'm all right!"

Well, he wasn't all right, but he was alive. Liam and Gabby must have sent the gust of air that stopped him. Both were wizards in their own right.

He saw Gabby bring a fist to her mouth and sag into the horse. He thought he could see tears of dirt running down her young olive skinned face, but his eyes were growing more blurry by the moment.

At fourteen, Gabby was the youngest child of the king of Quentis. Her knowledge of the dragon artifacts had brought her to accompany Bakari, along with Jaimon, a dragon rider from Quentis, Alli, and now Liam.

Bakari groaned as he tried to stand up. Jaimon, the only one of them without magic himself, had saved them from the brunt of Delia's attack, but in so doing had trapped himself inside the collapsed cave from where the golden dragon had escaped.

A golden dragon! Bakari shook his head at the thought and then winced in pain once again. He needed to move more slowly. The dragon hadn't been real until, suddenly, it was. It was a smaller dragon than his or the rest of the dragon riders', but definitely a dragon nonetheless.

Roland had something to do with it. In the midst of all the chaos with Delia, Bakari had heard Roland's voice through the magic stream, claiming the dragon as his own. It had shed its rocky scales and flown out of the cave, heading southeast. Much to the dismay and chagrin of Delia, he assumed.

After stealing the dragon artifact that could control all the dragons, Delia had escaped on their own horses with the wizard Korax down the side of the mountain. Using their wizard powers, they had subsequently and continually blasted at the mountain behind them, hence the exploding rocks that Bakari, Liam, and Gabby had been trying to avoid. The two offending wizards had been bent on destroying the path as they rode down the mountain side just south of Thera, the capital city of Turg.

Bakari tried to climb back up the face of the mountain, but every step brought a new crumbling of rock, and he just slid back down again.

"Climb down, and we'll meet you there," Liam yelled to Bakari as he pointed past Bakari.

Bakari looked down the mountain a hundred yards or so to where it flattened out around a copse of snow-covered evergreens. He waved his understanding up to Liam and watched the two of them mount back up and disappear from view.

Liam was a dragon rider from The Realm. He was sixteen, the same age as Bakari and a year older than Jaimon. He was a scholar wizard like Bakari—or a wizard of the mind, as it was called in Liam's land. More prone to brooding and quiet thought than the rest, Liam was still learning about being a dragon rider, but his bond to both his dragon and the famed Cremelino horses had been useful in the past and would be critical for all of them now.

Stopping for a minute, Bakari settled his left hand on another jagged boulder to keep his balance. He took a few breaths and cringed as he felt pain in his ribs. The morning clouds were lifting, and he could see the dull blue of the sea just west of the border between Turg and North Solshi. He was surprised at the lack of detail he could see and blamed it on their recent ordeal. He must have hit his head harder than he thought. He thought of flying on his dragon, Abylar, out over the Blue Sea to the east and how marvelous it had been.

His lips went tight, and he hung his head. He was a long way from his sleeping dragon in Mahli—a dragon Delia was trying to control.

Oh, Abylar!

Bakari tried to reach out in his mind to his dragon. He felt a faint spark, but nothing more. Delia had indeed cut them off. She had stolen the bond.

Moving slowly, Bakari began to limp down the mountainside once again. Having bonded to his dragon a little more than a year ago, he had only found out recently that dragons need to hibernate their first year. He had hated leaving Abylar behind. It had been hard to leave and go in search of the dragon artifacts without any of the dragons. Liam's had been left in the mountains of the Realm, and Bakari's, Jaimon's, and Alli's dragons were sleeping in Mahli—the ancient kingdom of the Dragon King. At least that's where they were. Now that Delia had stolen the bond, Bakari didn't know what would happen.

Thinking of Alli brought additional concern. Out of all the dragon riders, he had known Alli the longest. A battle wizard a year younger than he, she had become the Battlemaster of the Citadel. Although she served Bakari as a dragon rider, he knew her heart was with Roland, their friend, and High Wizard of the Citadel.

Alli had been taken when they approached Thera, the nearby capital of Turg—a city that seemed to thrive on wizard power. He had recently seen a quick vision of her suffering there when Roland had interfered with the golden dragon. They needed to find her, and Jaimon, and save their dragons from Delia. It was enough to give Bakari an additional headache. Since bonding to his dragon and becoming the Dragon King, all the leaders in the southern kingdoms had sworn fealty to him. Sometimes—no, most of the time—he marveled at that. How had he, a quiet, boring scholar wizard, been given so much responsibility? He could only do the best he could, which didn't seem like much at the moment.

Another loud boom filled the air, and Bakari looked back up the side of the mountain. Smoke and dust swirled around the peaks, and he hoped Jaimon was safe and could find a way out. He turned and carefully continued to make his way down to the spot Liam had pointed out.

Finally, he stopped on flat ground, walked a few steps, and leaned up against the side of an immense spruce. The tree was at least as big around as four men with hands held out to the side. He looked up into its boughs, sighed deeply, and for some reason thought about Kharlia.

At least Kharlia is safe!

He smiled despite the current situation. He had met Kharlia Attah when traveling with the last Chief Judge of Alaris, Daymian Khouri—before there was a king in Alaris. Kharlia had helped Bakari save the Chief Judge's life, and they had quickly grown close. He was happy that she was safe in Elvyn developing her healing abilities now. But he did miss seeing her smile and soft lips.

"Bakari!" Gabby yelled out at him from the top of one of the Cremelinos. "Are you all right? I called out to you three times, but you didn't respond. And you look all flushed."

Bakari blinked a few times to bring the two into clearer vision and felt his face grow warmer. "Just thinking. That's all."

"Dragon King." Liam, more formal, nodded to Bakari as he drew up. "Glad to see you are safe."

Gabby and Liam dismounted, and the horses wandered a few feet away in search of a tuft of grass under the dusting of snow.

Gabby walked over to Bakari and lifted his arm up slowly. "You're hurt." Sympathy showed in her soft brown eyes.

Liam drew out a waterskin from his side and held it out in front of him. "Here, use this to clean it off." He began to say, but then stumbled and fell to the ground.

Gabby ran to his side. He rubbed his leg and looked up to them in frustration. "My foot."

Bakari nodded. Liam had been born with a club foot and had always had a hard time walking. Although loved by his family—the King and Queen of the Realm—and close to his twin sister, Breanna, Liam always felt less than them. Since bonding with his dragon he had become more sure-footed and it had bothered him less.

Bakari limped over to Liam, grasped his arm, and helped him back up to his feet. Liam turned his head and wiped some moisture from his eyes.

"Our powers are weakening," Liam said softly.

Bakari's shoulders tensed at the truth in Liam's words.

"What do you mean?" Gabby asked as she took water and tried to clean Bakari's wounds.

"Liam's foot and my own eyesight," Bakari said, blinking. "I wore glasses before bonding. The powers from our dragons helped to offset those things."

"Delia can't have Ryker. He's mine," Liam said.

Bakari nodded. "I know how you feel. At least Ryker is farther away. Abylar, Cholena, and Muriel are together in Mahli, hopefully safe for a while."

"We must stop her," Liam said.

"Ouch!" Bakari pulled his arm back from Gabby.

She grabbed it back again. "The all-powerful Dragon King, and you wince at a little water on your wound?" She smiled at him to show she didn't mean the words to sting.

"Some Dragon King I am," Bakari mumbled. "Delia had this planned all along, and we walked into her trap."

"Who is that other woman with them?" Gabby asked. "She's not much older than me, I would guess. Do you know her?"

"Yes," Bakari said as he sat on a rock and let Gabby finish cleaning wounds on his leg. "I remember seeing her at the Citadel. She whispered to me that Roland had everything under control."

Bakari laughed as he thought about his friend. Charming, handsome, lighthearted, with a thirst for power—that explained Roland. But under control?

"I doubt that, though," Bakari continued. "Especially without Alli there. Roland called the golden dragon to him. I'm afraid he's getting himself into trouble again."

"More reason to get our dragons back, Dragon King," Liam said. "We can ride the Cremelinos. They will carry us to Mahli more quickly than Delia can."

"What about Jaimon?" Gabby looked up, her eyes filling with tears. "We can't leave him in the mountain."

"And Alli," Bakari added. "We can't leave her either."

Liam frowned. "So what is the plan?"

Bakari closed his eyes for a moment and tried to feel the stream of magic in his consciousness. It wasn't as clear as it used to be. Whether it was fatigue, continuing effects of Delia's spell on them, or the severing of his bond with Abylar, he didn't know. What was Roland up to?

But he already knew the choice he had to make. "First, we rescue the dragon riders, then we get to the dragons. After that we have to deal with Delia and find out what Roland is up to."

Liam nodded. "You are right, Dragon King. Jaimon and Alli should be our first priority."

"Gabby?" Bakari asked. He wasn't going to command in these things and wanted consensus of the group.

"Agreed," Gabby said, standing back up from cleaning Bakari's leg. "Though I am not a dragon rider like the rest of you."

Bakari smiled and stood. "But you do have the makings of being a powerful wizard, and you know about the dragon artifacts."

Without speaking any more, they climbed back on the Cremelinos—Liam on his own, and Gabby and Bakari still sharing one.

Happy to serve you again, Dragon King.

Bakari smiled. *Happy to have your swift legs again, Flash.* "Let's ride."

CHAPTER TWO

Roland Tyre, high wizard of the Citadel of Alaris, stood on the rooftop of the palace in Cassian and waited. A giddiness he had rarely felt filled his entire magical soul. He brought his right hand up to shield his eyes from the setting sun.

Where was it?

Only hours before he had felt the presence of the golden dragon and, with the power of the scepter, had summoned it to him. This was the third time he had come back up to the rooftop to look for any signs of its coming.

He took a deep breath and looked out over the city of Cassian—a city he had just recently saved from a brutal battle. Letting out his breath slowly, he pulled the collapsed scepter from a leather pouch on his belt. With a quick flip of his wrist the golden scepter extended out—now almost four feet long. He ran his right hand over the glass knob and drew from its power. Looking down, he marveled at the replica of an elongated body of a golden dragon wrapped around the length of the scepter. The entire thing was beautiful, but, more importantly, it was powerful. The Elvyn Ambassador Rassdurthian had referred to the scepter as the Scepter of Unification and had warned Roland about its dangerous power.

Why is everyone worried about how much magic I can handle? It annoyed him. Didn't they know by now that he was magic? At seventeen years old, and only in his first year as High Wizard, he was already the most powerful wizard in Alaris and, quite possibly, all of the southern kingdoms.

The door to the roof opened, and Roland turned. As he did so he moved his long blond bangs out of his eyes and took a deep breath. It was the Elvyn ambassador.

"High Wizard," Rassdurthian said as he approached. "The council is awaiting your direction."

Roland took one last look toward the west and followed the man down the stairs and back into the building.

At ground level, guards and others moved quickly around, trying to minimize the damage that had been done. A battle had been fought in the city—Queen Ameena Shabon from Tillimot had decided to expand her influence. And she would have won if Roland hadn't gotten there in time.

But he had.

Now as he took long strides down the wide hallway, golden cloak flowing behind him, the servants stopped and bowed low. He smiled back and with a flick of his hand beckoned them to arise.

"No need for that, my people," he said. "We have a kingdom to rebuild here."

A kingdom Roland had been born in and lived in for almost eighteen years. A kingdom that might just be the center of his new empire.

Roland shook his head slightly at the thought. *I shouldn't be thinking such things.*

Unconsciously he rubbed the palm of his hand over the glass knob of his scepter and felt the power flow into him once again—a power that augmented his already broad spectrum of abilities.

"Rass," he turned to the Elvyn Ambassador, "what is the protocol when the king dies and has no heirs, or even a wife?"

Rassdurthian took a moment to answer. The man must be decades older than Roland, but he was an Elf. His long hair fell straight down, almost to his waist, over blue silk robes that hung on his thin frame. He hardly looked like he had been in a battle at all.

"Every kingdom has its own laws," the ambassador began, looking Roland straight in the eyes. "The kingship in Alaris is fairly new—hardly less than a year since the system of judges was voted out in King Mericus' favor, so I am not familiar with its protocol."

Up ahead was the council room, but Roland stopped first and looked up at a colorful tapestry on the wall next to him and smiled. The scene was of a famous wizard fighting a battle sometime in the past. It reminded him of the tapestry in his own Citadel—the one with the powerful wizard holding the golden scepter in his hand.

Memories of finding the scepter in the protected basement rooms of the Citadel flowed back to him. He could hear echoes of Alli warning him not to go there while she was gone. He had promised her he wouldn't, but that promise had only been intended for a few days, and then she had stayed away longer. She had left him to go to her master, the Dragon King, and he wasn't going to sit around and do nothing.

As he thought of her he remembered the brief vision he had had of her lying on the ground in pain, and his heart softened. He had to help her. And he would as soon as he settled the situation in Alaris. His grip tightened around the scepter once again.

"You must be careful, High Wizard." Rassdurthian put his thin hand on Roland's arm. "The magic of the Scepter of Unification is strong."

Roland patted the man's hand. "Don't worry about me, Rass, I can handle it. I am magic."

Rassdurthian grunted. "The scepter should have never been made. It demands too much of its user. Just don't do anything stupid."

Roland laughed. "My, my, Ambassador, such words from an Elf surprise me."

Rassdurthian looked around them, and Roland could swear that the man actually blushed. "Forgive my outburst. I have been living among you humans for too long, it seems."

Roland slapped the man on the back. "No harm done, Ambassador. It just goes to show that stuffy elves can be… "

Before Roland could finish his thoughts, a man walked out from the council chambers. He was more than twice as old as Roland, his dark hair, trimmed beard, and short goatee just starting to show signs of gray. His skin was slightly darker than Roland's, but not nearly as dark as that of Bakari, the Dragon King. The man was Daymian Khouri, former Chief Judge and ruler of Alaris. Now Ambassador at large.

"There you are, High Wizard," Daymian said. "The council is waiting for you."

Roland nodded and motioned the others to precede him.

Just before entering the doorway, Daymian turned and spoke to Roland over his shoulder. "Where do you keep running off to?"

Roland smiled and thought about the golden dragon. "Just waiting for a friend to arrive."

Daymian rolled his eyes. "Roland," he whispered softly, "be serious for once."

Roland took a brief second to remember the time he had served under Daymian. As a counselor wizard apprentice, he had lived in Cassian for two years. He liked the man—and he was a good man—but one with short-sighted goals and aspirations. And Roland had grown up since being an apprentice wizard.

"I assure you I am totally serious, Daymian." Soon he would have the powers of the Golden Dragon at his disposal. Then Bakari would have nothing on him.

CHAPTER THREE

Roland glanced around the room and noticed groups of men and women arguing. The large table and chairs in the center sat empty except for two men Roland recognized but hardly knew. He was sure they were all conniving and maneuvering for a place in the new regime. Not all of them saw eye to eye with Mericus LeGrande, the currently missing king, a wizard himself. They had not heard any word from the man since the battle at Corwan, and Roland deduced he must not have survived.

Daymian, in no official capacity other than as general ambassador of Alaris, cleared his throat loudly and spoke. "Will everyone please take their seats."

Roland stayed standing while the arguments and heated discussions died down. He stood quietly by the door and observed where people sat. Remembering his training as a counselor wizard, he saw things others did not. How close the minister of trade sat apart from the minister of guilds. Where at the table the lone general sat. How all of them held their arms—some folded, some flat on the table. All were signs to be considered; all gave clues on what each person was thinking. Roland took it all in as he watched them sit down one by one.

No one, however, sat at either end of the table. No one, it seemed, had the gall—or maybe just not the support of others—to do so. But it was to one of these ends that Roland now walked.

As he did so, he smiled at the women and touched the shoulders of a few men and gave his thanks for their help to secure the city. By the time he had reached the head of the table, the room was much more relaxed and tuned to his attention. He stood and looked down the table. The king's councilors, a few of them wizards; Ambassador Daymian; the Elvyn ambassador; a general that had been left to guard Cassian; and Tam, Roland's acting battle wizard in the absence of Alli.

Thinking of Alli sent another sharp pain into his heart. He really needed to leave and rescue her. *Soon. Soon.* A voice spoke softly in the back of his mind, bringing comfort to Roland's thoughts.

Then thoughts of the dragon stirred the magic deep inside of Roland. He put his hand on the golden scepter and raised it slightly into the air, then lowered it forcefully to the floor in front of him. The building shook slightly, and the candles flickered.

Unify them.

The group at the table flinched, many of them standing back up. With his other hand he directed them back to their seats.

Lowering himself into the chair, Roland leaned forward, resting his arms on the sturdy mahogany table. "General," Roland turned his head slightly to his right, "report on Queen Ameena and the prisoners."

The general seemed surprised by the question. "High Wizard, the queen is being held in rooms fit for her station, but under guard. Her soldiers are in cells. We are arranging transport for them back to Tillimot, but we are short on men at the moment. If I may add, sir, why are we... "

Roland waved a hand of dismissal in the air and instead of continuing his conversation with the general turned to the next person at the table, the minister of housing.

"And the repairs in the city, how are they going, Minister Soren?"

"Fine, sir," was all the answer he received from Soren. With crossed arms in front of him, the man glanced briefly toward the other end of the table.

"And the people of the city," Roland asked to all in attendance, "how are they faring?"

A few counselors at the far end of the table looked back and forth among each other. Roland watched them for a moment before speaking.

"Is there something I should know?" Roland asked.

"Well, sir," one of the councilor's said. "I... well, we... "

"Spit it out, man," Roland said with a flourish of his hand, the sleeves of his robes falling down his pale arms.

"We are wondering why you are taking charge of this meeting," the man rushed on. "No disrespect to you as High Wizard, but this is an affair of Alaris, and not of the Wizard Citadel."

Roland took a moment to glance around the room. Some turned their eyes from him; others held his gaze.

He stood up and spoke quietly but with power. "In the past, in times of war or other great need, the High Wizard was able to appoint judges and raise armies. Am I correct in my understanding?"

Some of those present nodded.

"And especially of late, the former High Wizard, Kanzar Centari, appointed judges, even Mericus as one of them under that law."

Again many nodded their heads. Roland looked at Rassdurthian, and the man held his lips firm and just shook his head at Roland. Roland plunged forward anyway. "Our king is dead."

"There is no confirmation of that," spoke up Daymian.

Roland raised his eyebrows at the man. Always one for fairness and decorum. "I have been there, Ambassador Khouri, and although I agree it is not one-hundred-percent confirmed, it is very unlikely that he survived."

"Been there?" one of the councilors stood on his feet. "Pardon me, but you have been here since this morning? How could you have been there also?"

Roland smiled and remembered the feeling of summoning the power of the scepter on top of the castle rooftop. The force of the magic had taken him into the magic stream. He had used a trick that Bakari had used in the past and through the magic stream had been able to quickly visit different areas in the city as well as travel in an instant to Corwan. He was still uncomfortable spending too much time there as it wasn't a very accommodating place. But the scepter had taken him there without his own choosing and so he had followed.

He now placed the scepter on the table in front of him and held out his hands in a beckoning gesture. "I assure you, my good man, I have ways to be anywhere I want."

The man paled and sat down. Others took turns looking at each other, but no more objections were raised.

"As I was saying, it is likely that the king is dead, and in any case not able to govern at the moment. He had no heirs to the throne, so what provisions have you made for that?"

The councilors looked around at each other. A few looked at one man in particular. Roland knew the man for an ambitious councilor in his early thirties. The man's brown hair hung to his shoulders, and light stubble ran across his face. He was a handsome man and well-liked by the people.

"Symon Patera," Roland said, gesturing toward the man. "Do you have something to say?"

Symon stood with calm. "As a council we have decided—well, the majority have decided that I will lead Alaris until the king's fate is verified."

Roland glanced once more around the room. Many were nodding.

Roland turned to the scribe in the corner of the room.

"Scribe Ferrin, can you bring me the records of the law that allow Councilor Symon to assume control?"

The scribe looked up in surprise at Roland's request. His ink-stained fingers rubbed a spot on the side of his nose. "Sir, there is not any record to bring."

"Ah, thank you, Ferrin," Roland said, then turned back to the group, this time placing his hand on the scepter once again. Its power gave him boldness. He held it across both palms in front of him and let the power swirl through his mind. It spoke to him—not in words, but more in a feeling. What he was doing was the right thing to do. The people needed someone to unify them. He gritted his teeth for a moment to compose himself. The power could be overwhelming at times.

The people looked at the scepter as if trying to understand what it was. Tam rose partially out of his seat to come to his aid, but Roland shook his head at him, and his friend and battlemaster sat back down.

Battlemaster! *Oh, how I wish Alli was here!* Roland's mind briefly flashed away from his current surroundings, and he saw Alli once again—now lying almost lifeless on the floor of a dark and dirty cell.

"High Wizard," Rassdurthian called out. "Are you all right?"

The words snapped Roland's attention away from his vision. He didn't have time for all this. His heart beat fast at the frightening vision.

"Yes, yes," Roland said. "As I was saying," he cleared his voice and rushed forward, his words coming fast, "with no apparent law on your books, and with precedent on my side, it is lawful and necessary for me to name the person who will act as king until the fate of Mericus is determined."

Cacophony broke out in the room. Everyone turned to their neighbor and wondered who it would be. Symon and others stood and tried to approach Roland.

Roland slammed the full-length scepter down on the floor next to him once again. Thunder rolled through the room, and a sudden gust of wind quieted them all down.

"And who might that person be?" Symon asked in the silence.

"One who is already a proven leader, powerful, able to make quick decisions, loves Alaris, and will serve her people well." Roland said as he looked around the room.

Heads nodded to the attributes he had listed.

Daymian cleared his throat and looked at Roland. His brown eyes bored into Roland's blue ones.

Under other circumstances Roland would have smiled. But his mind was on Alli. He stood and set the scepter out in front for all to see. "Me."

CHAPTER FOUR

Allison Stenos, Dragon Rider, battle wizard, and battlemaster of the Wizard's Citadel in Alaris, couldn't find the strength to even open her heavy eyes. The hard dirt floor felt cool to her bruised face, but that was about all she could feel at the moment. She didn't know if it had been hours or days since she had been beaten in the arena. She had given up and hoped to die. It was her only way out.

"Alli, my dear?"

Alli hadn't even heard the cell door open and still couldn't find the strength to lift her head. But the voice she knew. It was Constantine Moraitis, her captor. She heard and felt him sit down next to her and then a hand on her head softly stroking the back of her hair.

"My sweet Alli," Constantine said, his voice soft and pleasurable. "You fought valiantly, but I couldn't let you give up and die. You are my special warrior."

Alli used what strength she could to slowly open her eyes and turn her head an inch or two to look up at him. He was dressed in his fine robes, short, speckled beard trimmed under hair that hung just over his ears. He smiled down at her, and she found herself smiling back at him. "I am special?" she croaked out the words.

"Of course you are, my dear." Constantine placed his palm softly on her upturned cheek.

Closing her eyes for a bit, she felt a brief modicum of power from him. It brought her such joy to feel it again. She didn't really want to die. What had she been thinking?

Another man joined Constantine. Doctor Abaddon, the man that healed her each time she was injured.

"You gave the crowd a show they will never forget, Alli," the doctor said. "And they want more."

"More?" Alli's mind was still foggy. She remembered now, being taken day after day to fight others in the arena, all without access to her wizard powers. But even at fifteen years old she had learned to fight with or without her powers and had beaten most of her opponents. Many times she had been bruised and broken, only to be healed again… and again.

She remembered the last fight when Constantine had given back some of her powers. It had been wonderful, even euphoric to feel the magic coursing through her veins once again. She had shot out fire and lightning, done flips in the air, and taken out some of her opponents. But then why had she stopped? What happened?

"Yes, Alli," Constantine's soothing voice wrapped around her. "You are their hero. They love you."

"Feel the power, Alli." Abaddon took both of his hands and placed them to either side of her head. Every time he healed her she felt that she lost a part of who she was—but a wave of pleasure also engulfed her aching body.

"Ohhh," Alli groaned with delight. The wound on the side of her head closed, her heartbeat quickened, her hearing improved, and her muscles regained their strength once again.

"I want you to be happy," Constantine said as he helped her to her feet.

She looked at the matching manacles on their wrists. It was a gift from him to her that allowed him to give her magic back to her—at least that is what he told her, and she believed him now. The silver manacle on his wrist stood out on his bronze skin. Hers was black and stood out equally on her pale skin. Looking back at Constantine, she had to look up quite far to see his eyes. He was a tall, broad-shouldered man at least a foot taller than her 5-foot, 4-inch height. He looked grand standing there. He was her master.

Something in the back of her mind told her she wasn't thinking clearly and that others would come for her, but she pushed it away. She tried to think about the past, but like always, it brought pain to her head and she had to stop. This was all there was now. Just she and her master, the doctor who healed, and those she fought. If she fought well she pleased him, and he let her use more of the magic. If she displeased him, she was beaten.

Constantine smiled at her and tapped his manacle, and Alli felt more power fill her up. It was wonderful. Had she really been this powerful before? She doubted it. It must be his power he was sharing with her. The air tingled around her, and faint flashes of battles ran quickly through her mind. Fighting in Corwan, Cassian, and Celestar. What did that mean? Then, unbidden, to her mind came the sight of a dragon flying high overhead. *My dragon!*

A beautiful dragon of yellow and orange flew through the bright blue sky with wings spread out to its side. "Muriel?" she whispered.

"What did you say?" Constantine took a step forward.

"A dragon," Alli said. "I saw a dragon in my mind. It was so beautiful. Was I… a dragon rider?"

Constantine looked at her with pity in his eyes. "Oh, Alli," he shook his head. "You are still injured and need to sit down." He led her to a cot in the corner of the room and had her sit. "You are not a dragon rider. How could that be? You are a warrior here in Thera. My warrior."

Alli tried to concentrate and to feel her dragon. Something told her she used to be able to, but there was nothing there now. No bond or link.

"Maybe you are right." She hung her head low. It would have been nice to be a dragon rider.

The doctor walked up in front of her. She could see his sandaled feet. He reached his thick arm forward and lifted her chin. "How do you feel now, Alli?"

She thought about it for a moment. Her mind still felt confused, but her body was regaining its strength. She flexed her fists and moved her arms.

"We have healed you, again," Abaddon said with a sweep of his arm to include Constantine. "You are his favorite, and we wouldn't want you to die. As his favorite, he is willing to share more power with you next time."

Alli looked up at Constantine, and her eyes watered for a few moments. He would share more power with her? How wonderful that would be. She would do anything for him if she could feel her power again. Every time he gave it to her, he pulled it back again. She knew it was to make her stronger, but she craved that power more and more.

Constantine stepped forward and patted her on her head. "Now be a good girl, Alli, and get some rest. Tomorrow will be another big day for you."

Alli smiled, scooted down on the cot, and lay on her side. Constantine and Abaddon left the barred cell, and a guard turned a key in the lock and stepped away. How could she ever have hated the man? All he wanted was for her to feel her magic again.

"Master," Alli called out.

Constantine turned around and smiled the biggest smile she had ever seen. She had pleased him, and that pleased her. She smiled back. "Thank you for healing me and for letting me feel the power."

"You are my special child, Alli," Constantine said. "You perform for me, and I will let you feel power unimaginable."

Alli's eyes went wide with excitement. "Thank you, Master."

The two men walked away, and Alli closed her eyes. Her body needed rest. She needed to prepare for the next fight. She had to please her master. That's what gave her purpose. That's what gave her joy.

As she drifted off to sleep she thought she saw two figures in her mind. In physical description they were the exact opposite of each other. One was tall, with blond hair, and extremely good-looking. A golden cloak floated around him, and when he smiled at her she felt a flash of joy. The other was shorter, with dark-brown skin. His hair hung down in long braids. The aura of a dragon floated around him for a brief moment and then disappeared. His brown eyes flashed a powerful blue, and she felt a twinkling of loyalty to this man.

"I am coming for you, Alli," said the first.

"Alli, hold on," said the second. "We'll find you soon."

A few tears leaked out of the corner of her closed eyes as she drifted off to sleep.

How nice it would be to have friends like that. But she was sure it was only a figment of her imagination. She didn't have any friends. She only had her master.

CHAPTER FIVE

Bakari, Liam, and Gabby sat on their horses a few hundred feet from the back entrance to Thera. It was the capital city of Turg; one of the three kingdoms considered part of the united territories, along with Cyrene to the northwest and Khazer to the east. The three formed a loose alliance that, along with Mahli, split the western continent from the kingdoms in the south from those in the north. North and South Solshi, Quentis, Tillimot, Alaris, and Elvyn were situated to the south, while to the north were the Empire of Gildan, the kingdom of Arc, and the Realm.

The salty brine of the sea filled a gust of wind as it swept down over Bakari. He looked up at fresh clouds that promised rain soon. The three of them had been watching the rear gate of the city for the last fifteen minutes, trying to determine their next steps.

Bakari motioned the others back behind a small hill closer to where the two Cremelino horses were enjoying a few tufts of stray grass.

"The city is more guarded than when we left," Bakari said.

"And the city's flag is at half mast," pointed out Liam.

Bakari was afraid of what that meant and voiced his thoughts. "The Oracle has died."

"Their supreme leader?" Liam asked. "I have studied about him. He holds all power over the people and is considered to be one of the most powerful magic users in the city. The Turgs pride themselves on the use of magic."

"The more powerful one is, or the more power one holds over another, the more that person is respected," added Gabby.

Bakari nodded. Both Liam and Gabby were children of royalty of their respective kingdoms and were well educated in functions and knowledge of state.

"So now Delia has her opportunity to step in and take control," Bakari said.

"What about Nicholas, the son of the Oracle?" Gabby asked.

"That may be our only hope," Bakari said as he wiped the heavy mist off his forehead. "He was friendly to us, but now that there may be a fight for the crown I'm not so sure he will appreciate us being here."

Liam stood up straight and put a hand on Bakari's shoulder. "But you are the Dragon King. They all hold fealty to you. Each kingdom declared it. You can ensure that power transfers to Nicholas and not to Delia."

Bakari thought about what Liam said for a moment. He agreed with the words in theory. For the past six months he had reigned as the Dragon King. But it was a fragile title, at best. He knew that some of the kingdoms had sworn fealty to him because there was no other choice in the matter. When he had stood with his dragon riders and the dragons and had fulfilled prophecy and rid the land of evil he had been accepted as a hero and honored as such. In practice, he really only ruled the small kingdom of Mahli as the Dragon King. And now, he didn't even have a dragon.

"I'm not so sure, Liam," Bakari let out a deep breath. "If Delia truly has stolen the bond of our dragons, how can we stand up to her?"

Liam's face darkened. "So in your first crisis you are giving up?"

"Liam!" Gabby grabbed his arm. "Do not say such things. There are many that still hail the dragons and their king."

Liam pulled his arm from Gabby's grasp and took a step forward. But his lame foot caught, and he stumbled.

Bakari reached over and stopped him from falling. Liam righted himself back up and glared at the two of them.

Bakari's first instinct was to get angry at Liam and fire back all the reasons for his own defense, but instead he offered Liam a grim smile. "You are right, Liam," Bakari said.

Liam's eyes softened a bit. "I did not mean to speak so harshly, Dragon King. Forgive me."

Gabby opened her mouth to speak, but Bakari shook his head and continued with his thoughts.

"Liam, you and Gabby have been raised in royalty. You have been trained to accept these kinds of situations. You are right to question me. When it comes down to it, without my dragon I am just a lowly scholar wizard."

"But you are not alone," Gabby said. "Even without the powers of the dragon, we are three wizards—four, if we find Alli."

Bakari pushed his doubts to the back of his mind. He was tired and hurt and not thinking correctly. "And we all know that Alli is more powerful than all of us—even without her dragon. You are right, Gabby. We need to rescue her and then we will deal with Delia."

"And find Jaimon?" Gabby asked with a sad smile.

"And find Jaimon," Bakari agreed. Once again there were too many things vying for his attention. He hated having to leave Jaimon to the mercy of the mountain. But he had to make a choice. He needed to concentrate on one thing at a time. *First, I need to find Alli.* He took a few steps forward and looked at the city gate one more time. The guards were looking a little blurry, and he wiped at his eyes to try and see better, but it did little good. He wished he had kept his glasses with him.

Bakari thought for a moment, then turned back to Gabby and Liam. "Gabby, Liam and I stick out too much here. He is too light, and I am too dark for us to move around unnoticed, and then we have the Cremelinos to think about. But with your olive skin you could move around unnoticed." He gave her a sly smile. "You up for a little covert adventure?"

Gabby clapped her hands together, and her brown eyes sparkled brightly. "Yes, I'm up for that," she almost squealed.

"Are you sure this is wise?" Liam asked. "She's just a… "

"Don't say it, Liam." Gabby put her hands on her hips. "I know what you think. But as a young girl I can go around unnoticed—I can get into places you and the Dragon King cannot."

"But… "

Gabby stood tall, long dark hair flowing around her in the wind. Her dark eyes pierced into Liam's as she poked him in the chest with her right index finger. "I have grown up in a family that leads the southern followers of the dragon, and my wizarding powers are growing. I assure you I can handle myself."

Liam took a step back and let out a loud breath. "You remind me of my sister."

Bakari laughed. "Liam, we do seem to surround ourselves with strong women." Unbidden, his mind went briefly to Kharlia. He had missed her terribly lately and wished more than once she was with them. Shaking his head to clear his thoughts, he finished speaking. "Gabby is perfectly capable of handling herself."

"I can see that," Liam mumbled, clearly convinced but still not happy. "So what is your plan?"

"You and I don't like to call attention to ourselves, Liam, but you are right in the fact that, as the Dragon King, I need to take charge." Bakari began to share his plans. "You and I will ride into the city on the Cremelinos in all our splendor." He looked down at his own dirty clothes, then over to Liam, and laughed. "Well, maybe we need to get some new clothes first."

As if on cue, they heard the sound of wagons and horses on the road in front of the city gate. To the west and then south was a little-used coastal road that went down to North Solshi and the rest of the continent. Most people going that way took ships. But to the east was the road they had come into originally from the mountains of Mahli. It was from that direction they spied a long wagon train.

"Traders," Gabby said with a smile. "Gypsies, most likely."

Liam frowned and tilted his head in an unspoken question.

"They should have clothes for sale; at least, whatever is left after their travels through the smaller towns," Bakari said with a grin. "Almost as if I called them to us."

Maybe you did.

Bakari turned to look at Flash as the horse spoke to Bakari's mind. The Cremelinos, who usually only bonded to one rider for life—though they did make exceptions for him it seemed—had been unusually quiet on their trip so far. They were secretive, magical creatures who seemed to know more than they let on.

Surely I don't have that kind of power, Bakari answered back in his mind.

You would be surprised to know the potential for power you have, Dragon King. The wizards of old could do much. Such a power is gathering now in many places, in many people.

Liam, noticing the silent exchange, turned to Bakari. "Liberty said they are feeling extreme powers to the east and south."

"Flash said somewhat of the same."

"Any idea what they mean?" Liam asked.

Bakari chuckled. "No, their thoughts seem to always be layered in secrets."

"Don't I know," Liam said but put his hand out and rubbed his Cremelino's nose with affection. "Their magic and abilities are hard to understand."

"Just like the dragons," Bakari added with a frown. "I am afraid Delia may be waking them early and taking their power."

"Bakari!" Gabby, who had gone closer to the road, came jogging back. "The traders are slowing down before the city gates. Now is the time."

Bakari nodded, and leaving the Cremelinos still in hiding, the three made their way to the wagons.

One of the traders walking beside a wagon jumped in surprise when the three came out from behind a tree. A strange trio they must make, Bakari thought.

The trader instantly pulled a knife from his belt. "Hold it right there."

"We are not thieves," Bakari reassured him, but the man was now joined by two others, who had also pulled their knives.

"We would like to see some of your wares," Liam said. "We are looking for a change of clothes."

The men still looked at them suspiciously, and when Liam reached to his side one of them jumped closer to him, knife ready.

Liam's eyes went wide, and Gabby stepped forward. Bakari didn't want to make a scene or to tip their hand yet with any magical abilities. He gave a slight shake of his head to the other two.

"I'm just reaching for my coins," said Liam.

The man stepped back a step. "We'll see about that. Bring your hand out nice and slow."

Liam proceeded to pull out a leather bag with a drawstring and shook it in front of the man.

"Maybe we should just take it," said one of the other men with a laugh.

"We are not thieves, Gaden," said an older lady coming around one of the wagons. "All of you, put your knives away. These children aren't big enough to do you any harm. Looks more like three runaways to me."

Bakari smiled inside. If the gypsies only knew…

Gabby stepped forward. "Ma'am, my friends here only want to buy some new clothes. They were coming across the mountains and were caught in a storm."

The woman turned to Bakari and Liam. "Obviously not from around here." She looked them over suspiciously.

"Their parents came on a ship to enjoy the hospitality of Thera and Hasari, but they went on a little adventure in the mountains, and now look at them. They can't show back up dressed like this." Gabby nodded her head to the flag at half-mast and then back to Bakari and Liam, waving her hand in front of her nose as if to dispel their stink.

The three men and woman hadn't seemed to notice the flag until Gabby pointed it out.

"The Oracle?" Gaden said as he turned to the other three.

The woman motioned them toward the gate. "Go see what's happened. I'll take care of these three." With that, she pulled the three after her. "I don't know if I trust your story or not, but you do seem to have money, and we do have clothes for you—fit for a king."

"That will do nicely," Bakari said with a wink to Liam.

CHAPTER SIX

A half an hour later, Bakari and Liam had changed and now stood next to the two Cremelinos. With all the commotion of the traders entering the city, Gabby had sneaked in unnoticed. They had agreed to meet her sometime later that night.

Liam smiled at Bakari—a rarity for him. "A little overboard, but they'll get the idea."

Bakari looked down at his black breeches, white frilly shirt, and long, flowing red coat with a golden cord cinched around the waist. He rolled his eyes at Liam and laughed. "Not my normal style."

Liam himself had on blue-dyed breeches, a brown shirt, and a fur-lined cloak that had bright purple silk on the outside. "Me neither, but we will get their attention."

Both young men fastened a sword to their side and hopped up on the Cremelino horses. Liam stumbled for a moment getting up, but his horse knelt down for him.

"Liam," Bakari said to his lastly named dragon rider. "It'll all work out. We'll get the dragons back again."

Liam only grunted. Bakari understood his frustration. His own loss of eyesight was beginning to be annoying for him. He had worn glasses most of his life until bonding with his dragon. He pushed the depressing thoughts from his mind, and they rode out. Reaching a hand to his hair, he tried to smooth out his obviously messed up braids—but he did the best he could do, given the circumstances.

Per their plan, Liam jumped out in front of Bakari and galloped toward the city gates. "Hail the Dragon King!"

The guards at the gate came to quick attention, and others just inside poked their heads out. Bakari came riding quick on Liam's heals and stopped just in front of the city gate.

"Sir," said one of the guards, bowing low to Bakari, "we were not informed of your arrival." He then turned to another younger man and barked out orders. "The Dragon King needs an escort. Prepare the mounts."

Bakari moved up next to Liam and gave him a sideways look. Liam cocked his head to the side, as if asking if this is what Bakari wanted.

"Sometimes the show is what counts," Bakari whispered. "Especially with these people."

Somehow, within a matter of moments, a full contingent of guards lined up just inside the gate and awaited Bakari's direction.

"I am the Dragon King." Bakari amplified his voice with his powers so all nearby heard. "I offer my condolences to the city for the loss of the Oracle and come to greet his son, Nicholas Marinos, the next Oracle."

This brought a rumbling throughout the gathered crowd. It is what Bakari had intended. He knew many of the people wanted Delia, the granddaughter of the Oracle, as their next leader. By stating the opposite, Bakari, as the Dragon King, had stirred the pot of Thera.

Bakari urged his Cremelino forward and let a glow envelop him. His powers were almost back to full strength once again. This brought the expected gasp from those who had gathered, and they went down on their knees.

"Hail the Dragon King," rang out a high voice above the crowd.

Bakari looked back over his shoulder at Liam, who smiled. It was Gabby, playing her part well.

"Hail the Dragon King," echoed others in the crowd.

Bakari waved his hand. Pointing back to Liam, he introduced him to the throngs that were gathering.

"And welcome Liam DarSan Williams, prince of the Realm, dragon rider, and wizard of the mind."

"Hail, Dragon Rider," Gabby yelled out from a different position this time. Others echoed her sentiments.

However, Bakari noticed a group in the back of the crowd eyeing them with less enthusiasm.

"Where are your dragons?" shouted out one of them.

Bakari cringed at the question but thought quickly. "Today our dragons rest while we ride the famed Cremelino horses."

A murmur of *oohs* and *aahs* drifted through the crowd. The Cremelinos were rare in the southern kingdoms. Suddenly the horses' blue eyes brightened, and a soft glow of powder blue enveloped them, leaving trails of wispy magic in their wake.

The crowd began clapping and cheering.

Show off. Bakari sent a message to Flash.

These people need to learn to respect the Dragon King, came the answer back.

The guards moved along with Bakari and Liam, lining both sides of the street. The crowds gathered thicker as they proceeded through the city. The main streets were in good shape: solid cobblestone, whitewashed cement homes and businesses able to withstand the salt air and harsh winds, and colorful banners adorning the street corners. Down the side streets, as with any major city, Bakari noticed and even sensed conditions that were more harsh, poor.

"I wish we could do something to help all the people," Bakari said over his shoulder to Liam.

Liam nodded his agreement. "These people place too much emphasis on magic, and those who don't have it are pushed to the bottom of the pile. It's not right."

Bakari agreed, though he was using the people's worship of magic himself right now for his benefit. He felt somewhat ashamed for playing into their hands.

"Hail the Dragon King!" came another lone voice again as the group turned onto the main thoroughfare leading to the castle.

Soon they arrived at the gates, and the castle guards bowed low to Bakari and Liam. Word of their arrival obviously preceded them. They dismounted, and a few stable boys came to take the reins.

"Don't try to ride them," Liam said. "They are only bonded to one at a time. Feed them well. They have had a hard journey from the Realm."

The stable boys nodded and looked up at the creatures with awe.

Bakari and Liam were led into the castle. Faded marble floors, light, worn wood, and a humongous candled chandelier adorned the entrance way. Walking down a circular staircase came Nicholas Marinos, son of the Oracle and father of Delia. He looked like he had aged since Bakari had last seen him. His dark hair framed a face that was lined with worry, and his broad shoulders were drooped as if holding up a large weight. The passing of the Oracle was a time of change in the kingdom of Turg.

"Dragon King," Nicholas said as he fell to one knee. Others in the entryway followed, some more slowly and less enthusiastically than others. "Welcome back." Looking up at Bakari, he asked, "Did you find what you were looking for?"

Bakari nodded. "But it did not turn out as we hoped."

Nicholas arose. "My father has passed away, and by law, a new Oracle must be chosen within twenty-four hours."

Bakari wondered how much of this plan Delia had orchestrated herself. Events appeared to be favoring her rise to power.

"High Minister." Bakari addressed the man by his current title. "We need to speak in private. This is Liam DarSan Williams, prince of the Realm and a dragon rider. He will accompany us also."

Nicholas bowed his head to Liam. "Prince Liam. Welcome to Turg. I'm sorry it is not under better circumstances."

Liam gave a grim nod. "I bring greetings from my father, Darius DarSan Williams, King of the Realm. He has always enjoyed your salted salmon, though it is rare to get up in

Anikari." Liam smiled more than Bakari knew he was feeling, but he, too, had been raised to play a part.

"I welcome your father here to Thera in the future, and we will dine together," said Nicholas. "I've heard he is a powerful wizard of the heart."

"Yes," Liam said. "One of the most powerful in the western continents."

Nicholas motioned the two forward. Bakari took a step, but then Liam stumbled on his club foot and fell into Bakari. Bakari grabbed him quickly and tried to resume walking as if nothing had happened. He spared a sideways glance at Liam's red face. The dragon rider's head hung low, and he shuffled forward as best as he could.

Bakari let out a deep breath. The strength lent to them from their dragons was indeed lessening. *Oh, Abylar!* He reached deep into the recesses of his mind. *Stay strong.*

But there was no reply.

Fear for his dragon coursed through Bakari's veins, and he stumbled, catching himself on a wall. He took a deep breath, trying to regain his composure.

"Are you all right, My Lord?" Nicholas asked with concern.

"Yes," Bakari lied. He had to help Abylar and the other dragons, but he didn't know how to do so. When the others weren't looking he wiped a tear from his eye and tried to focus on finding Alli.

Nicholas led them into a study—the same one they had met in before leaving to search for the dragon artifacts and Delia.

Bakari took the next half-hour telling Nicholas what had happened and getting his thoughts about Delia.

"A new Oracle must be chosen within twenty-four hours—that is the law. It's now been nine hours since my father passed away."

"So, if Delia doesn't return in time, then you will become the Oracle?" Liam asked.

"Even if she does return in time, you are next in line," Bakari added.

Nicholas shook his head. "Next in line does not always mean most powerful. Delia has a lot of followers and power." He hung his head low. "I'm afraid she has been more powerful than me for quite some time."

"And now maybe even more so," Bakari said. "If she truly is able to get the power of the dragons even I may not be able to stop her."

A servant brought in some refreshments, and the conversation lulled for a few moments while they took a few bites of bread, dried fish, and juice. Bakari was about to ask something about the coronation of a new Oracle when yelling and power blasts sounded outside the castle and carried into the entry way of the castle itself.

Nicholas shared a worried look with Bakari and Liam and headed toward the door.

Before he got there, the door crashed open, almost pulling off its hinges.

"What is the meaning of this, Father?" Delia yelled at Nicholas. "Why were there not guards to escort… "

Her tirade died out as she noticed the others in the room. Her dark hair hung disheveled around her lightly tanned face, and a fur-lined red cloak encircled her tall body. She brought her hands out in front of her as if preparing a spell.

"Delia!" Nicholas swatted her hands back down.

Liam stood and took a careful step forward, a scowl covering his face. "Guards were not there to escort you because they escorted the Dragon King. It is his right. You will bow to your high king."

Delia opened her mouth and then closed it again. Wizard Korax and Tabitha, a young wizard from the Citadel, came into the room behind her. Korax's eyes went wide when he saw Bakari standing there. Tabitha raised her eyebrows at him, but then lowered herself to the ground on one knee.

"Dragon King," was all she offered.

Nicholas stared down Delia and Korax. "Bow to him who is most powerful."

The two gave grave looks, but finally they bowed and offered a quick greeting before standing back up.

"What are you doing here?" Delia spoke to Bakari.

"Making sure the crown of Turg gets transferred peacefully. What are you doing here?"

Delia smiled. "I am here to take the crown of Turg from my father and become the next Oracle."

CHAPTER SEVEN

Roland Tyre, self-proclaimed king of Alaris, once again stood on the roof of the castle and waited. He felt the presence growing in his mind by the hour, and now by the minute. It was powerful, beautiful, and incredible. He hadn't felt this giddy since Kharlia had brought him back from the dead after the ancient evil wizard king had tried to take control of his body. He hadn't been ready to die then, though he had been prepared to do what needed to be done. But now the scepter he held and the visitor he awaited would ensure that his name would be held in reverence for centuries. The most powerful wizard of them all!

"Roland!" Rassdurthian said next to him. "Roland, are you listening to me?"

"Rass?" Roland turned to the ambassador. "When did you get here?"

Rassdurthian rolled his eyes. "My Lord, I was saying I need to get back to Elvyn. I need to inform our King and Queen of matters at hand."

"Give my regards to Lan and Breelyn," Roland said.

"They will not be happy that you are using the scepter, Roland. It was made by the Elves long ago and… "

"Rass!" Roland looked across at Rassdurthian. With a flick of his hand he could have the man flying off the top of the building. He shook his head to clear such thoughts—not knowing where they had come from. Rassdurthian had done nothing to harm him. But he was trying to take the scepter from Roland. "I can handle the magic of the scepter. The elves do not have a corner on powerful magic or control over who uses it. I am the High Wizard of the Citadel and now acting King of Alaris. I am magic!"

Rassdurthian only shook his head. "It will only bring you trouble, my friend. It was made to help unify the lands centuries ago when men first came from the east and settled the southern kingdoms. It never should have been crafted. The lure of power it holds is too tempting for one so young as you. My people live longer and are able to handle the temptation of power better. I plead with you once more to give it up."

Unify them.

"I will not," Roland said. There was so much power coursing through his veins. He rubbed his hand over the glass knob and felt distant voices of power flicker through his mind. He closed his eyes and took a deep breath and basked in the glory of it all. Opening his eyes a moment later, he wished Rassdurthian could understand. "I cannot give it up, Ambassador. I must unify the people. Tell your queen and king they have no right to take it from me."

Rassdurthian's face grew hard, and his elderly wrinkles seemed to grow more pronounced as his shoulders slumped. "I will inform them of your decision, High Wizard, but they will not be happy. And beware, for things of such power usually extract a high price from the user. Are you prepared to pay its price?"

A commotion down on the ground took Roland's attention away from the Ambassador before he could answer.

The man would do what he had to. But the Elves had better not get in Roland's way.

Walking to the edge of the building, Roland looked down at the courtyard below. His troops marched Queen Ameena Shabon and her men to a ship back to Tillimot.

Something far away caught the edges of his attention. He looked up into the clear winter sky and saw a speck far, far away. Lifting his scepter up with both hands, he heard a voice in the back of his mind.

Embrace the Power.

Roland cocked his head as if trying to understand. He had felt promptings and heard voices from the scepter before, but this was different. The voice was softer; more like a woman. He looked back down at the Queen of Tillimot.

Unify them, came the original voice he now recognized as the scepter.

Thoughts raced through Roland's mind like lightning, and he knew what to do.

"Ameena Shabon!" Roland yelled down from the three-story roof. The queen, along with the rest of the men and women in the courtyard, looked up at Roland. He stood on the edge of the building, scepter in hand, golden cloak blowing in the breeze around him. With barely a thought, he lifted himself off the roof and over the side. He felt everyone's eyes as he lowered himself through the air and landed with a soft touch on the ground directly in front of the former queen.

Roland ran a hand over his blond hair and smiled broadly. He leaned over and, taking the queen's hand, leaned down and gave it a kiss. For a lady twice his age, she held her grandeur and beauty well.

"Your Highness," Roland began, "I just realized that you have afforded me a great opportunity."

The queen frowned. "I don't understand."

Roland waved his left hand in the air as if to dismiss her lack of understanding. "Many do not understand me, my lady, but that's neither here nor there. I do what I must do to keep peace in a fractured land. By attacking Alaris for no reason, you have showed me… "

"No reason?" The queen's cheeks reddened. "Alaris has been a thorn in the side of her neighbors for hundreds of years. The wizards of Alaris have always thought they can control the world."

"Ah, I see," Roland said with another flourish of his hand. "Your grudges go back a long time. However, I will clarify myself. Nothing has been done by Alaris in the recent years, since… " Roland raised his voice for emphasis, "since we have been behind a magical barrier for 150 years."

The queen and those around her stepped back as Roland slammed the scepter to the ground. Sparks of yellow and gold flew out of the cracked ground.

Roland took a deep breath and lowered his voice to a mere whisper. "Since you chose to attack us without any recent provocation and lost, it is my duty and the law to now inform you that I am relieving you as Queen of Tillimot. By my grace and mercy I will allow you to retire to an estate of your choosing with a contingent of servants worthy of your station."

The crowd stood speechless. Roland turned around and noticed that the council, including Ambassadors Rassdurthian and Daymian Khouri, stood with stern faces and looks of amazement on their faces.

"My son rules in my absence," the queen stated after regaining some of her composure.

Roland flicked his hand again. "His services will no longer be required either."

The queen staggered a bit, but a guard held her up. "Then who will rule Tillimot?"

Roland held up the scepter. "I will assume leadership of Tillimot for the time being."

"Roland!" Daymian whispered loudly. "Are you mad?"

"Quite the opposite, my good Ambassador. I am the Unifier."

"By what right?" Ameena said with a gasp. "You are only the High Wizard of the Citadel, not a ruler of a kingdom."

"And that is where you are incorrect. I am High Wizard of the Citadel, King of Alaris, and Monarch of Tillimot." With that he slammed his scepter in the ground again, and a bright golden light shot up high into the air.

The crowd looked up as one and watched with Roland. The light in a stream only a few inches wide streaked straight up into the sky until something large above them moved to intercept it. As it did so, a giant array of golden sparks and fire burst out from the sky, so bright that the crowd had to cover their eyes.

When they opened them again a golden dragon glided softly down toward them. People scattered away from the center of the courtyard as the dragon continued to soar back and forth, dropping lower and lower with each turn.

The crowd shielded themselves from the wind of its wings. The magnificent creature dropped down in front of Roland and bellowed a loud roar, shooting fire off away from the crowd. The force of the roar shook its golden scales—hard-plated sheaves of gold that glittered in the evening sunlight. Its long tail slithered around, while its menacing head turned back and forth on a spiked neck, taking in the gathered crowd and eventually settling on Roland.

Roland waved a hand in greeting and laughed. "And now, I add Dragon Rider to those titles. Orelia, come forth!"

The dragon took a few steps forward, then went down on her knees. Roland moved slowly and put his hand to the dragon's snout. The scales were smooth—more so than any of Bakari's dragons. She was beautiful! And she was his!

Not yours! Came a faint but firm female voice to his mind.

Roland took a step back, confusion flickering across his face. What did the dragon mean, not his? Isn't this what he had been waiting for?

I summoned you. I gave you life. Roland wasn't going to let this dragon spoil his moment.

The dragon roared, and many in the crowd ran off. Those who stayed scooted back as far as they could. Roland could barely keep from falling to his knees in the wake of the dragon's immense power.

You are mine. I will give you your *life,* came the firm voice again into Roland's mind. *A life you have dreamed of. Delia of Turg has stolen the dragons' powers and will come for you soon. But we will defeat her, and kingdoms will bow to you in reverence. They will love you and chant your name for centuries. The scepter of unification and I will lead you to your glory!*

"Yes, yes, yes," Roland said out loud and in his mind. *Together we will have glory. You and I and the scepter. Yes.* It was all he had ever wanted. He would be all powerful. Not a tyrant, but a benevolent ruler. He would no longer bow to Bakari, and Alli would… would… A scene of Alli once again flashed through his mind. She sat on a dirty cot in a tiny and dirty cell and looked up at another man. He was older than she, broad shouldered and not bad looking. Roland turned his focus back to Alli and gasped in surprise. Her eyes, they… they held admiration, maybe even love for the man in front of her.

Nooooooo, his mind screamed. *Alli, you belong to me. You will rule by my side!*

The scene shimmered, and Alli looked around in a bit of confusion. Then she shook her head as if to clear the unwanted thoughts, stood up and was led out of the cell by the man.

No, what have they done to her?

I will take you there, High Wizard. We will save her.

Yes, Roland spoke to the dragon in his mind again. *Yes, we will save her. You will take me to her!*

Another deafening roar and Roland looked around. By the position of people, he believed the previous thoughts had raced through his mind in a matter of moments.

You. Do. Not. Command. Me.

Roland was taken aback by the force of the dragon's words. *Very well, it doesn't matter, as long as you deliver what you promised.* He would deal with who commanded whom later. His powers were growing, and soon even the golden dragon would not control him.

He walked to the side of the dragon and mounted. Again the crowd gasped. The dragon stood regally.

Turning back to the crowd of those they had captured, Roland spoke to them for the first time since the dragon had arrived. "Men and woman of Tillimot, since your attack was only following orders of a queen—a good woman, I assume, but one with misguided priorities—you will not be held responsible for what you have done. In fact, you are free to return to your kingdom and to take up whatever occupation you would like. If you want to stay in the army, I will appoint captains over you, and you will be a part of *my* army. If you desire another occupation I will pay for your training or apprenticeship. Those are my conditions."

The soldiers cheered and clapped.

One yelled out. "Hail Roland Tyre."

"Hail the dragon," the chant continued as Orelia and Roland rose up high into the sky.

"Daymian!" Roland called down to the ambassador and former ruler of Alaris. He stood next to Rass and a few others, not chanting Roland's name.

The man brought his hand up to shield his eyes from the brightness of the golden dragon.

"You will accompany the soldiers and Ameena back to Tillimot. I trust you to be my eyes and ears there and to rule in my absence until I return from Turg."

Daymian was not one to be left speechless very often, but Roland knew he had caught him unaware. The man had little imagination and was filled with little ambition, but was fair, level-headed, and had a knack for ruling with compassion. He would do until Roland could return.

Daymian shook his head slightly at first and mouthed an exasperated sigh while mumbling a few curses that include Roland's name. But Roland smiled at him, and Daymian finally nodded his acquiescence to Roland's wishes.

Roland rose higher and waved at the mostly-adoring crowd, then ran his hand over the smooth golden scales. The dragon felt more mineral than flesh. Something didn't feel quite right to him, but he ignored it for the time being. He was flying on a dragon!

"To Thera," he said to his dragon out loud. "The Battlemaster needs our help."

The dragon banked right and soared up higher into the sky, soon disappearing from the cheers of the soldiers of Tillimot and the citizens of Alaris.

CHAPTER EIGHT

Bakari, Liam, and Nicholas stood facing Delia and Korax. Tabitha stood off to the side. Bakari thought that Delia would attack her father right there in front of them, but she seemed to come to her senses and lowered her hands.

"The people will choose, Father."

Nicholas nodded but didn't say anything. He had aged even more since his daughter had returned.

"Sir?" Bakari asked. "What can I do?"

"Nothing, Dragon King," interrupted Delia. "Or should I call you former Dragon King?"

Liam jumped forward, sword in one hand, wizard fire instantly in the other, but stumbled on his bad foot ruining the valiant effort. Wizard Korax stepped out in front of Delia.

"Your first strike will be your last, young man," Korax said. His voice was low, and his hair and clothes seemed to hardly even shift as he moved.

Liam looked at Bakari, and Bakari shook his head and put his hand out for Liam to stand down. Then he caught Nicholas' eyes and saw a barely perceivable nod. Within a matter of moments both had transported to the hall—a trick Bakari had learned from Nicholas during their first encounter. It was similar to using the magic stream, but for only short jumps. With three other jumps they stood in another room, empty except for a few ancient tapestries on the wall and two chairs and a low table in front of a window.

"Where are the dragons?" Nicholas spoke first.

Bakari shook his head. "I don't know. She has an artifact that can control them, and I barely feel my bond anymore. My dragon is in trouble, but that's all I know. She is planning something."

"Always. Delia is always planning something, Dragon King," Nicholas said. "She's been paying bribes, gathering supporters, giving gifts, and amassing powerful friends for years in anticipation of this day. Today, I am the high minister, last son of the Oracle. Tomorrow, I will either be the Oracle or be dead."

"No," Bakari said with surprise. His braids smacked him in the forehead as he looked around the empty room. "You can't mean that. She wouldn't kill her own father?"

Nicholas' laughter boomed off the walls. "Bakari, I know my daughter. She wants power and nothing will stop her. Not even me."

"I can't believe that."

"Oh, it will look like an accident, I am sure." Nicholas walked to a window and pushed back an old curtain. The castle looked north over the city. Bakari joined him and could see the faint ribbon of a broad river on the other side of the city—leading to the western Blue Sea. "First the city will vote. Each district will then send a representative to the coliseum in the morning. There the votes will be counted and the new Oracle announced. By tomorrow morning it will all be over, one way or another."

Bakari blew out a breath of air. "Maybe something will change between now and then."

The high minister nodded, then quickly the two of them travelled back into the study. Their entrance back into the room caused the others to jump in surprise. The members of the room had barely moved and an uneasy feeling filled the room. Liam stood alone on one side of the room. Tabitha looked up at Bakari as they came back into the room, then resumed pouring drinks for Delia and Korax on a small table by the window.

After a few moments of uncomfortable silence Delia, sitting now in a comfortable stuffed chair, brought her legs up and over one of the armrests. She finished off her drink, wiped her mouth, and handed the cup to Tabitha.

Delia reached into a pouch at her waist, drew out a finger size carving of a dragon head and lovingly ran her hand over the wooden artifact. "Do you know what this does, Bakari?"

Bakari had read only a little about the dragon artifacts. Gabby was the expert, and she was out in the city.

When Bakari didn't answer, Delia continued. "Too bad your little friend isn't here. Where is Gabrielle?"

Liam limped closer and joined in the conversation. "It's of no concern to you."

Delia laughed, her lips forming a nasty grin. "Bakari, where did you get this one from? Is it his Cremelinos I saw in the stable? Such nice creatures—someday I may control them also."

Liam pulled his sword and lunged toward Delia, but with a flick of her wrist she sent him flying backward and landing hard on his backside.

"Delia, enough," Nicholas said. "Everyone knows you are powerful, no need to provoke others."

Delia pouted. "Oh, Father, how are you the son of the Oracle and my father?" She shook her head a few times. "You are too lenient and worried about others to make a good Oracle. It is good that I am here to save our kingdom and keep it from falling into softer hands."

Nicholas' face reddened.

"Tabitha," Delia called, "help the poor wizard to his feet."

Tabitha began to walk forward, but after only a step, Delia yelled out at her.

"No, not with your hands," Delia instructed. "With your magic. If you are going to serve me you must learn to realize that magic is the answer to everything. What can be done with magic should be. It's only the pathetic ones that have to rely on their own physical strength and senses."

Bakari watched Tabitha closely for her reaction, but the young woman only smiled, brought her hand out in front of her and summoned her powers. Of an age for an apprentice, she nevertheless exhibited strong powers. *So did Roland and Alli at that age.*

All in the room observed Liam rise from the ground and resume standing on his own two feet. Tabitha lowered her hand, and Delia clapped her hands with delight.

"Wonderful, wonderful," Delia said. "You really do have good control. I chose right having you for my servant."

Bakari walked over to Liam. "Are you all right?"

Liam glared at Delia and then turned back to Bakari. "For now, yes. But if she insults my Cremelino again, she will be sorry."

Bakari felt a burst of pride come from both of the Cremelinos. By the look on Liam's face, he felt it also.

Delia cleared her throat and brought Bakari's attention back to her. "Tabitha tells me that this artifact will help me feel more of what my dragons feel. It will strengthen the bond."

"They are not your dragons," Bakari said with force and took a step toward Delia.

Korax stepped between the two, and Bakari only glared up at the tall man.

"Now, let's not get testy here, Bakari," Delia said. "Even as Dragon King—a title that might very well be short-lived— you are honor-bound to abide by the laws of each kingdom, are you not?"

Bakari's mind raced through all the books he had read on each kingdom. There were differences in law among them all— some he agreed with, others he did not, but she was right. It was not his place to question their protocol of choosing their own leader.

"Yes," Bakari acknowledged.

"Then any interference by you in the election and appointment of the next Oracle is forbidden by your own rules of morality." Delia walked around him and toward her father as she spoke. "With the power now at my disposal you know I could take the kingdom on my own, however, a legitimate vote will strengthen my position with the other kingdoms. I expect everyone in this room to abide by the voice of the people and honor the laws, rights, and traditions of the Kingdom of Turg.”

Delia crooked her finger at Tabitha and Korax—the latter had a look for her that seemed to not enjoy being beckoned along with the servant. Bakari wondered if that may be a future key to minimizing Delia’s influence.

“Delia,” Bakari called to them as they exited the room. His voice was firm and strong, and he surrounded himself with his power. “I will abide by the laws of your land, but that does not include your treachery with the dragons. They do not belong to you.”

Delia waved a hand in the air. “We shall see.” The three of them stepped through the door frame. From out in the hallway she raised her voice. “I expect to see you at the coronation ceremony tomorrow morning. Your presence will lend legitimacy to the proceedings.”

As their footsteps receded down the hallway, Nicholas spoke for the first time in a while. “Dragon King, you must be careful. It will not be safe for you at the coliseum tomorrow. You should stay away. I’m afraid Delia has lost all sense of decorum and respect for our laws and traditions. She means to have this kingdom either way, the vote will just give her an opportunity to gloat even more.”

“He is right, Dragon King,” Liam added.

“But I must be there,” Bakari sighed. “I must show the people I am still the Dragon King.”

But am I?

CHAPTER NINE

Alli ducked as a broadsword swept so close that it caught a few hairs from the top of her head. Swinging out a leg, she caught the attacker around an ankle and forced him to stumble backwards. She jumped high in the air and kicked the man in the chest with the bottom of her foot. As soon as she landed she dove to the side and grabbed a pair of knives lying on the arena ground. Bringing them up in front of her, she began to circle around the second attacker, this one a woman ten years her senior.

Two other opponents circled around her, and she took time for a quick glimpse at Constantine. He sat in the first row of the arena with his hands folded and hanging over the edge of the railing. A nearby torchlight reflected off the silver bracelet he wore—the bracelet that controlled how much power she was allowed to have. He had been more generous lately. She gave him a pleading look, and he responded with a smile.

In an instant she felt her magic flow through her veins once again. The darkness around her became lighter, her hearing increased, her muscles strengthened, and her reflexes quickened. The blades in her hands began spinning faster and faster in front of her in a mesmerizing figure-eight pattern. Colors of green, blue, and yellow flew from the tips, and the crowd's energy grew to a frenzy.

Cheers, claps, and excited yells blasted forth from the crowd, and Alli rose to the challenge. While her first opponent watched the spinning blades, Alli used her new reserves of power to jump up in the air and side-swipe her leg around the woman, knocking her to the ground. Suddenly, she heard a swoosh of air and instinctively fell to the ground and rolled— noticing a blast of fire scream by where she had just stood. *So, the others have been given their power also.*

With a quick flip, Alli was back on her feet, facing now only two remaining fighters. Even in the cool night-time air she wiped sweat from her forehead and backed up a few feet. Taking a deep breath, she thought about her next move. This had been her third fight that day, and she was tiring, but her benevolent master had given her more of her powers today than at any time since she had been fighting for him. How long had that been? She wasn't sure at the moment. She knew she had to have had a life before, but only bits and scraps flitted through her mind. Mostly she just fought now. That's who she was. And she was all right with that.

A man in front of her slammed a staff to the ground, and the vibrations caused Alli to stagger a moment. The other attacker took advantage of her seemingly precarious moment and lunged forward, sword in one hand and a ball of blue fire in the other.

Suddenly Alli's body filled with power and moved on instinct of a trained fighter. In a blur so fast that she knew others could barely see her, she moved to the side, then rushed toward her attacker. Letting the blast of fire go by her, she moved up inside the sword arm of the woman. Grabbing the blade by the hilt, she tore it from the woman's hand and flicked it far across the arena. It flew end over end, sticking into a wooden wall just inches below the crowd.

Chants of frenzied and bloodthirsty minds filled the air once again and roared for Alli to finish off her attackers. Grabbing the larger woman by the wrist, Alli brought the woman's arm behind her just as the last man threw a knife toward Alli. The sudden change of position brought the knife into the shoulder of the woman. She screamed in pain, and Alli dropped her to the ground.

Readying a last blast of fire, Alli rushed toward another man, but suddenly stumbled as the power was pulled back from her once again. She hated it when the master did that, but she was told it was for her own good. Too much power made her rely on her magical abilities and not on her physical prowess. She grunted with frustration and changed tactics mid-stride.

An old shield sat upside down on the ground between them, and with increased speed Alli jumped on the back of the shield and used it to propel herself forward. She rode the shield, skimming across the hard-packed dirt until she was a few feet in front of the surprised man. He lifted a sword in front of him, preparing to skewer Alli as she slid into him, but Alli was smarter than that. She leaned back on the sliding shield, then jumped off the back of it, kicking the shield up into the man's face. It knocked the sword out of his hand and smashed into his head. The man instantly fell to the ground. He moved for a moment, then groaned and lay still.

The spectators' yells filled Alli's ears, and she actually smiled. She had beat off four attackers at once. All larger, stronger, and bigger than she. Constantine beamed a smile back at her, and she felt his adoration. She had pleased him. There would be no need for additional beatings or healings this time.

Walking back to the arena door, she was met by Doctor Abaddon—though she knew his title must be contrived. He was like no doctor she had ever known. He was always her escort and healer, but today she didn't need healing.

"You did well," Abaddon said. "Constantine will be pleased with you."

Alli nodded. "And I don't need healing this time." She was tired, but otherwise felt good.

"A good night's sleep is what you need," Abaddon said. "Tomorrow is a big day."

"What is tomorrow?" Alli asked.

Constantine came around a corner in front of her. "Tomorrow, my dear, is what we have been training and fighting for." He wrapped his arm through hers and led her forward, the doctor dropping back behind them.

Alli looked around and noticed they were going a different direction; away from her usual cell. Soon they exited the underground lair, and she found herself in a small alley behind what she presumed was the arena. From what she remembered, this was the first time she had been taken outside in a long time.

Suddenly she felt conscious of her looks. Her leather pants were torn, and there were blood stains on her tunic. She brought her hand up to smooth down her hair and found small pebbles and dirt mixed in.

"Where are we going?" she said.

Suddenly she felt the sting of a whip from behind her and winced.

"Where are we going, master?" she repeated.

The surroundings had caused a momentary slip on her part. She had disobeyed the rule of not showing respect to her master by speaking to him out of turn and Abaddon had caused her to be whipped. It was her fault. It always was. The welt on the back of her leg would just be healed before the next fight. It was what she was used to.

Constantine ushered her into a waiting carriage. She was directed to a cushioned seat opposite Constantine and Abaddon. It was so soft. She sighed as she settled into it. The carriage lurched softly, and then they were traveling down the road. Curtains hung over the windows, but a slight sea breeze swayed them, and Alli was offered glimpses of the street, buildings, and people as they rode farther from the arena.

A large wall loomed up beside them, and a young, long-haired woman skirted out of their path. Alli saw a glimpse of two other young men in the shadows, and a flicker of recognition seemed to flit around the edges of her tired mind.

"Do you know how special you are, Alli, my dear?" Constantine's voice took Alli's attention away from the streets outside.

"Master?" Alli asked, intrigued by the softness of his voice.

"You have made it to the finals," he said.

Alli sat waiting for more, but Constantine offered nothing else. She knew not to question him again, or she would feel the sting of Abaddon's whip.

Soon Abaddon moved over next to her and placed his hands on her head. She looked at him questioningly. She didn't feel hurt. She didn't think she would need the healing this time. But he didn't ask her opinion, and soon she felt the familiar tingle. Her mind went blank for a moment, and her body filled with strength. Then she could think of nothing but how grateful she was for these two men who took care of her.

Not much time later the carriage stopped, and Alli was ushered out. She looked up at a three-story mansion. Two doormen stood ready to greet them at the double-sized ornately carved door. Alli found herself in the tall foyer of one of the most beautiful homes she could remember ever being in—of course, she couldn't remember much before she had been Constantine's prize fighter. When she tried, it only brought pain.

Artwork and tapestries adorned the dark wooden walls around her. Vases and other trinkets sat on glass tables and a curved staircase at least five feet across rose up in front of them. It was up this staircase that she was brought. The doctor went off in another direction, but Constantine, along with a young female servant, walked up with her.

"It's amazing," Alli whispered, then winced, waiting for the whip to hit her. She had spoken out of turn.

"It's all right, my dear," Constantine said with a gleam in his eye. "I understand. You are the first fighter I have ever taken here. This is a great privilege for you."

Alli nodded.

She was taken to a bedroom that was four times as large as the cell she had been staying in. The top of the bed was three feet off the ground, full of blankets and pillows that looked soft and inviting.

"Mara will be caring for you," Constantine spoke to Alli as he waved his arm to Mara in introduction. "She will help you bathe and get ready for bed. Then in the morning she will help you dress and get a grand meal for you. You have a big day tomorrow." He reached up and ran two fingers down her cheek and chin.

Alli stood still, not knowing what to feel inside at his touch. It both repulsed and excited her. He was her master and cared for her so much.

"Tomorrow you will fight for the championship, in front of our new Oracle in the grand coliseum itself," Constantine continued. "It will make both of us famous, my dear. Our lives will never be the same after tomorrow." His face darkened a bit, and he grabbed her wrist and held tightly, moving his hand over her manacle. "But you have to win. No more games this time. Do you understand?"

His eyes bored into hers, and she could see the murderous intent if she didn't please him. Alli swallowed hard and had but one question on her mind. She didn't know if she should ask.

Constantine must have sensed her hesitancy. He dropped her wrist and smiled at her. His teeth showing white against his tan skin. "And yes, Alli, I will give you all the power you need. For this fight you shall have it all."

Alli staggered a bit at the thought of him allowing her to have it all. She put a hand out against the bedpost and tried to calm her stomach. "Thank you, master."

"Just make sure you win." Constantine shook a finger at her, then turned around and walked out the door. "I will see you in the morning."

Mara came to her side. She was a few inches taller than Alli, but most likely not much older. She had shoulder-length black hair, tan skin, beautiful large brown eyes, and a quick smile. "Come, Alli, let's get you out of these clothes and cleaned up. The master wants you to have a good sleep tonight."

After a quick bath and a change of clothes, Mara was walking Alli back to her room. Alli heard voices floating up from the foyer to the second floor where they walked.

"She is magnificent," Alli heard Constantine's voice say with pride.

"And she is broken?" said a female voice that Alli thought she recognized. "She remembers nothing of her past."

"The doctor has taken care of that," Constantine said. "She is a fighter, and that is all she knows."

"Good. Good," said the woman. "I will look forward to seeing her win."

Alli's chest swelled with pride on hearing the two adults speak about her.

"Then the deal will be finalized," the woman said.

"As you wish," Constantine said. "I will return for her in the morning."

Alli and Mara rounded a corner and entered Alli's bedroom as the front door closed in the distance. Mara pulled up the sheets, and Alli slid in between them. She sank deeply into the soft bed and pulled a warm comforter over her. She didn't think she had ever felt so comfortable before in her life. Thankfulness for her master surged through her as her eyes drifted closed.

She heard Mara blow out the candles and walk to the door.

"Mara," Alli called out softly. "Who was the woman my master was speaking with downstairs?"

"Oh, that is Delia, the granddaughter of the Oracle," Mara said in a hushed voice.

For a moment Alli thought the name meant something to her, but then she only sighed. "She seems like a nice lady."

Not more than a few minutes after Mara closed the door, Alli felt herself drift off into a deep and relaxing sleep full of pleasant dreams.

CHAPTER TEN

After the confrontation with Delia, Bakari and Liam left their rooms in the castle and walked in disguise down the streets of Thera. The disguise wasn't much more than hooded cloaks pulled up over their heads. But in the early-winter dark, it was enough.

They currently sat in the common room of The Tides Inn—a small place filled mostly with locals. They sat quietly eating a late supper of broiled fish and bread baked earlier that day. Bakari's ears were attuned to the conversations going on around them in the room. The talk was all about who the new Oracle would be. Many were rushing to their neighborhood centers to vote and were planning to attend the event the next morning.

In the far corner of the room voices were raised, and Bakari and Liam looked in that direction. A big man pulled up on the collar of a small man, jerking him to his feet.

"Don't disrespect the dead like that, Willie," said the large man. "You'll bring a cursing down on all of us."

Willie tried to pull away from the other but was not very successful. "I didn't mean any disrespect. I was just saying that maybe he'd become a little too obsessed with power and that his son might be more reasonable."

"Said by someone without any magical abilities, I would guess," said a woman walking over from another table. Her demeanor, dress, and age, reminded Bakari somewhat of Delia.

The woman pushed long, wavy brown hair back behind her shoulders as she approached the other two.

"I don't need your stinkin' magic to make something of myself." Willie pulled away from the large one, turning his head to speak to the woman.

The woman waved a hand in the air, and the man jumped.

"Hey," Willie yelled out, reaching back and rubbing his back side. "What'd you do that for?"

Bakari looked at Liam, and his fellow dragon rider gave a quick smile.

"Looks like he has his hands full now," said Liam.

Bakari turned back and watched as four others stood up behind Willie, followed by three behind the woman. This was going to get ugly.

"We need to get out of here," Bakari said to Liam as he stood up.

Liam nodded and followed suit.

To get out of the room they had to pass close to the woman and her supporters. Liam moved to go in front of Bakari and squeezed himself between two people in chairs at different tables. Suddenly Liam's lame foot didn't lift properly, and he kicked the edge of a chair and then proceeded to trip over it. Trying to regain his balance, he grabbed the back of one of the woman's supporters.

The man turned around. "Hey, what's your problem? You with him?" He pointed to Willie.

"No, sir," said Liam. His hood slipped down, and his face reddened.

"You're not from around here, I can tell." The man stood in Liam's face. "What business do you have in our city?"

"My father's... a... a... trader," Liam stumbled. "We came in on a ship yesterday."

The thinner man took the time the diversion offered him and pushed the larger man who had bullied him backwards. On his way down, his foot kicked the woman who had been harassing Willie, and she stumbled but stayed upright as the larger man crashed against a table.

With no warning, the woman clapped her hands, and a loud boom echoed throughout the room. Customers held their hands over their ears as a wind followed the sound. In the wind, plates, cups, and silverware gathered together and swirled around. Metal knives moved to the outside of the gathering wind tunnel and moved toward the thinner man.

"No!" Willie said. "Stop this! I didn't say anything wrong!"

Bakari had helped Liam up and was pulling him toward the door.

"No," Liam said. "We have to help the man."

"Liam, this isn't our fight," Bakari said.

Liam didn't listen, but began walking in Willie's direction.

Bakari shook his head, not wanting to get into the fight, but realized that Liam understood full well about being picked on and bullied.

"Leave the man alone," said Liam, by far the youngest of the group.

All around there was laughter. Liam shuffled closer.

"Are you a mighty wizard coming to save a non-wizard?" said one of the men.

Again the crowd laughed, and Bakari had a bad feeling in the pit of his stomach.

Liam kept his cool. "Let the man eat in peace. He meant no harm." He spoke evenly. Bakari could sense the tightness in the dragon rider's balled fists, but Liam kept them at his sides.

A flare of light surrounded a man behind the tall woman, and a ball of light sped toward Liam. "Let's get this non-magic riffraff out of here."

Liam's hand came up, and a white glow surrounded it and blocked the ball of light coming at him.

"You're one of them?" Willie said and tried to push away from everyone.

Someone behind Liam pushed him to the floor, and Bakari saw a heavy boot swinging toward Liam's head. He couldn't let Liam get beat up. With or without dragons, the dragon riders were still his responsibility.

Looking around him, Bakari let his mind work quickly. Thrusting a hand out in front of him, he shot a line of fire, not at the crowd, but at the base of a chain hooked to the wall closest to the group. The chain was hooked up to a tall, multi-candle light fixture above them and was used to lower it to change or light the candles.

When his burst of fire hit the hook on the wall, the chain released, and the chandelier crashed to the floor. Someone screamed, and a few men pushed others trying to get to safety. Hot wax flew everywhere from the falling candles. Bakari jumped into the fray, grabbed Liam, pulling him back to his feet.

"Hey, where do you think you're going?" shouted a man who grabbed the back of Bakari's cloak.

Bakari twisted and turned, and the cloak and hood came off. The man who had grabbed him was obviously the innkeeper. He glowered hard at Bakari for a moment as if trying to figure out what he was seeing. They obviously didn't get many visitors from Mahli. And especially not ones dressed as lavishly as Bakari was at the moment. Even though it was the next kingdom to the east, Mahlians tended to stay to themselves.

"Get your hands off the Dragon King," Liam yelled out.

Suddenly everything went quiet, and Liam blushed for his mistake. Bakari took a deep breath and pulled away from the innkeeper. Everyone stopped fighting and turned to look in their direction, waiting for him to say something.

Pulling himself up as tall as he could, which was still under 5'10", Bakari looked over the group and determined what to say.

"I am Bakari, the Dragon King," he began. "I am here to observe your election of the new Oracle."

A few people fell to their knees and bowed their heads. Most of them remained standing and didn't seem to believe him.

"Prove it," someone from the crowd said. "Where is your dragon?"

Bakari felt a hollow pit in his stomach. *Yes, where is my dragon?* If he were in their shoes and watching a sixteen-year-old stand up and declare he was the Dragon King—would he believe?

Liam and Bakari looked at each other.

"Our dragons are resting," Bakari said.

The crowd laughed.

"Oh, are your dragons tired?" said a lady from the back. "Poor boy."

"This isn't going well," Liam whispered. "Let's leave."

"That's what I said before." Bakari gave Liam a hard look.

Liam looked down in shame.

The crowd began to move forward. So Bakari grabbed Liam's hand and took a deep breath. He hadn't ever jumped with the magic before while holding anyone else. In his mind's eye he saw the magic stream, and rather than jumping in—as he didn't know if he could escape without the power of his dragon—he only skirted around the edges. Everything around them blurred, and it was as if everyone else stood still as they moved deftly through them.

Heading toward the door, they pushed it open and tumbled out into the street.

Bakari stood up and then leaned over and helped Liam to his feet. They turned to run and instead ran into someone else, all three tumbling to the ground in the middle of the cobblestone street.

"Bakari!"

"Gabby!"

"Liam!" Gabby said, untangling herself from the two men.

Once they sorted themselves out they began running back toward the castle. Light from the tavern doors spilled into the street, but they soon left the ruckus behind them. Bakari rubbed his arms in the cold, having lost his cloak in the inn. It was getting late, and few people were out, but they stayed in the darkest parts of the street as Gabby began to tell them what she had learned.

"These people are crazy, Bakari."

Bakari and Liam shared a smile with each other.

"What?" Gabby asked.

"Nothing," Bakari laughed. "We understand."

"Everything they do, every decision they make, every friend they have is based on the amount of magical power they have," Gabby continued. "And below it all is a very dangerous underground of criminal activity and slavery."

"What?" Bakari questioned. "Slavery is outlawed in all the southern kingdoms."

"Magic-users are kidnapped and used as gladiators by more powerful users. It's watched by thousands, and a lot of money passes hands, betting on the fights."

A few night guards passed by but paid the young people no concern. The lights of the castle loomed ahead of them.

"But what does this have to do with finding Alli?" Liam asked. "I want to get out of this city as soon as possible."

"I'm getting to that, Liam," Gabby said with a flip of her head.

"Go on," Bakari said to Gabby.

"There are rumors in the city of a short female warrior who fights like no one else—one who has been beat up over and over but keeps returning." Gabby stopped and grabbed both Liam and Bakari by the arms. "I think it's Alli. She's being held as a slave and forced to fight."

Bakari sucked in a cool breath of night air. "Do you know where she is?"

"Not yet. There are many of these places of fighting throughout the city." Gabby's dark brown eyes went wide. "But there is talk of a championship fight tomorrow in the coliseum."

"The coronation," Liam muttered.

"What?" Gabby asked.

"Tomorrow the new Oracle is chosen and ordained. It's happening at the coliseum."

"Delia?" Gabby asked.

Bakari nodded. "We've seen her. She is determined to be the next Oracle."

"And the dragons?"

"I don't know." Bakari shook his head. "She doesn't seem to have them, but the bond is weakened to the point that we can't feel them, either."

The three approached the castle gates and tried to walk in but were stopped.

"We are guest of the castle," Bakari said. "Nicholas has rooms for us."

The guard, muscled and firm, looked them over. "Nicholas is not in charge."

Bakari's stomach fell. Had Delia already disposed of her father?

"Delia has said no one is to enter the castle until her coronation is held tomorrow," the guard said with a flurry of his hand.

"This is the Dragon King!" Liam said to the man.

The guard bobbed his head, but then smiled grimly and put a hand on his sword. "Dragon King or Mermaid Queen, doesn't matter much to me. Orders are orders!"

Liam took a step closer, but Bakari pulled him and Gabby back with him. Once they were a dozen feet away and around a fenced corner, he let go of their arms.

"Things are definitely changing with Delia around," Gabby said. "Suddenly their protocol and respect toward you and those of power seem to be skewed in Delia's direction."

Bakari agreed. "We don't know what other wizards Delia has with her," Bakari said. "We can't storm in. Obviously they have orders to keep us away."

"Sorry," mumbled Liam.

"You've got to get control of your temper, Liam," Bakari said. "You can't keep jumping into things."

Liam glared at Bakari for a moment, then lowered his eyes. "It's just so hard, Bakari… "

Bakari's heart softened. He knew what Liam meant. The bond with their dragons had been all encompassing. It was like a limb had been cut off—or like a best friend had been taken away. He put a hand on Liam's shoulder.

"I know, Liam, but we have to keep cool heads, or we'll never get them back." Bakari tried to give some level of comfort.

Liam looked up and wiped a few stray tears from his eyes. "I understand." Suddenly he tilted his head to the side as if listening to something.

At the same time, Bakari himself felt a message of panic well up in his mind.

"The Cremelinos!" Liam shouted and took off running.

"What?" Gabby asked. "What's going on?"

Bakari grabbed her hand and caught up to Liam, who now was stumbling on his lame foot. They ended up at a quick walk along the side wall of the castle complex. All castle walls had stable doors in the back.

"We need to get to the Cremelinos," Bakari explained to Gabby. "There's trouble."

"What kind of trouble?" Gabby said as she jumped out of the way of a carriage.

The windows parted slightly in the carriage, and Bakari saw a faint outline of a woman for only a moment. The coloring of the woman's hair reminded Bakari of their need to find Alli. Where could she be? He was worried sick and, without their dragon bonds, didn't know what else to do. He feared the coronation the next day would bring more problems than answers.

"Come on, hurry!" Liam shouted. "Someone is trying to ride the Cremelinos!"

CHAPTER ELEVEN

Bakari stood with Gabby and Liam behind the stable door and looked inside. Liam let out a relieved sigh, and Gabby put her hand over her mouth to stifle a laugh. Two young stable boys were trying to get on each of the Cremelinos. One boy got up on the rail of a fence and slowly moved his leg over Flash. With a triumphant grin he reached his hand over to the horse's mane to pull the rest of his body over. Flash took a brief sideways step that was just far enough away to allow the boy to fall on the ground between him and the railing.

Liam shook his head and relaxed. "You don't know how many times I've seen this."

Bakari turned toward him.

"It happened all the time back in Anikari and even at the wizard school."

They watched the other boy trying to get on Liam's Cremelino, Liberty. This time he had his friend try to hold the horse still while he jumped from a crate behind the horse. Mid-air, Liberty kicked up her hind legs and caught the boy in the stomach. The boy tumbled to the ground with a grunt.

"Stupid horses," said the boy who had just fallen.

Liam stepped forward with a dark look on his face. "I told you not to ride them."

The boys scrambled up and tried to wipe straw and dirt from their clothes. One had the decency to bow and apologize. "I'm sorry, sir. We were just… "

"A Cremelino only bonds to one rider, and that is all who can ride him." Liam turned and looked at Bakari and Gabby and amended his statement. "Unless they are wizards."

The boys looked from Liam, to Bakari, to Gabby, then back to each other. When they turned to Liam again their faces were more grim.

"You are all wizards?" the first boy spoke, then bowed his head. "We are your humble servants. Please don't harm us."

Bakari stepped forward. "We're not going to harm you, but we could use your help."

"Help?" asked the second boy. "Of course. Of course, anything you desire."

Bakari rolled his eyes. The people were too quick to defer to those who had magic. He reached a hand into a pouch, brought out a few coins, and handed them to the boys.

"You watch our Cremelinos here tonight and make sure no harm comes to them. We will come for them in the morning."

The boys bowed and looked happy to have the coins.

"And don't try to get on them again." Liam wagged a finger at them as the three wizards turned and walked back out of the stables.

"Now where?" Gabby asked.

"I guess the castle is out of bounds for tonight, so we need to find an inn and prepare for the coronation tomorrow." Bakari pointed toward the city center. "Any ideas of where we can stay?"

Gabby smiled. "I have one. An ambassador from Quentis lives nearby."

"And he will let us stay?" Liam asked.

"Of course," Gabby said. "He is a cousin of mine and a follower of the dragon."

Bakari sighed. "Oh great."

Gabby laughed. "Cheer up, Dragon King. You still have plenty of supporters."

* * *

The next morning, Bakari sat with Liam, Gabby, and the ambassador's family, eating a delicious morning meal of eggs, ham, and fresh-baked rolls.

Before leaving, Bakari gathered up his few belongings. As he grabbed his pouch of coins, it dropped to the ground, spilling its contents. A ring dropped out of the pouch and began to glow. It was the ring that Gabby brought with her from Quentis. She had given it to Bakari to help them find Delia and the cave with the dragon artifacts.

"Bakari?" Liam pointed at the ring. "What does that mean?"

Bakari picked it up. "It means there is a dragon artifact close by."

Just then, Gabby walked in and saw what Bakari was holding. Her dark eyes went wide, and she turned and walked back to where the ambassador stood before a fireplace, warming his hands.

"Cousin?" Gabby called his attention. "Where is it?"

The ambassador turned around and with feigned innocent shrugged his shoulders. "What do you mean, Gabrielle?"

"The artifact. Where is it?"

"I'm not sure I know what you mean," said the ambassador with downcast eyes. His wife walked over next to him and nudged him in the ribs.

Liam took a step forward, but Bakari put a hand out and held back his impetuous friend. "Sir," Bakari held out the glowing ring. "If you have something that could help us we need to know."

Varying emotions flashed across the man's face, but he finally relented. "Very well, Dragon King. If anyone but you would ask for it I would not give it up. It has been in the family for centuries."

The ambassador reached up high on a shelf to the side of the fireplace, pushed two books to the side, and pulled out a thin, flat board about six inches square. He held it in front of the group. A familiar outline of the western continent was carved on one side.

"What does it do?" Bakari asked.

"Is this the dragon map artifact?" Gabby said with excitement. She grabbed it and ran a hand over its face. "How does it work?"

The ambassador hung his head. "That is the problem; we do not know."

Bakari felt a power from the board that was not unlike what he felt from his dragon and, to a lesser degree, from the Cremelinos. He held his hand out for the artifact. Gabby reverently handed it over. Bakari ran his hand over the polished wood and felt a powerful surge. He thought about all he knew about magic, digging back through the many books he had read. The magic of earth, mind, heart, and… "Spirit," he whispered.

"What?" Liam asked. "What do you feel, Bakari?"

"The power of the spirit," Bakari said.

"The power of the Cremelinos and the dragons?" Liam said with wide eyes. "The fourth wizard power?"

Bakari nodded and closed his eyes for a moment. He tried to find his dragon bond, but it just wasn't there. At all. He was tempted to dive into the magic stream to find answers. Maybe he could meet Wizard Danijela of Arc, or Emperor Mezar of Gildan, or even Liam's father, Darius, King of the Realm. They had more history and knowledge of these types of things and had helped him in the past. But without his dragon powers he hesitated to do so. But he felt another source of magic closer by, and he smiled. *The Cremelinos.*

Hello, Dragon King, came the mirth-filled voice of Flash.

You hold the same powers of the dragon—the power of spirit.

Yes, the power to bind all other powers. A power not to trifle with. This time it was Liberty who spoke.

"Bakari, are you speaking to the Cremelinos?" Liam asked.

Bakari opened his eyes. "Yes, I think I know how this artifact works—it works off the power of the dragons—the power of spirit."

"But we don't have the dragon bond anymore," Liam said.

"You're right," Bakari said with a smile. "But we do have the Cremelinos. They allow me to ride them, but I am not bonded to them. You, however, have the bond."

Bakari held the dragon artifact between him and Liam. "Take it and call on the power of the spirit through your bond."

The Ambassador looked around the room. "Are you sure this is safe to do here?"

"If this will show us where the dragons are, Ambassador, this could be a great help," Bakari said. "I think it is safe to use, but if you would rather us leave, we can do this elsewhere."

The ambassador shook his head. "No. Stay here. It has been in our family for a long time. I am curious to see it work."

Bakari nodded to Liam, and they both took hold of the board and closed their eyes to concentrate. Bakari could feel Liam's presence in his mind, then the flare of both Cremelinos' presences.

I need your power, Liam spoke to his Cremelino. *We need to find the dragons.*

Brace yourself, dragon riders, came a soft reply.

Then Bakari felt a surge of power, and his hands grew warm. Without knowing why, he ran his hand over the board. It felt like pinpricks stabbed at his palm. He felt Liam waver a bit, and the board sagged from his end.

"Liam!" Bakari said out loud. "Hold on."

Bakari opened his eyes and removed his palm from the face of the board. Kingdoms and countries became more defined on the map, and then before his eyes, small dots of light appeared. Liam opened his eyes, and all around gathered in closer.

Bakari took a moment to orient himself with the map. There were three larger white dots moving in their direction from the east, and one other from the north. "They're almost here," he said with excitement. "Our dragons are almost here."

"But I don't feel anything," Liam said.

"Because Delia is controlling them with her artifact," Gabby said. "They aren't coming for you."

Bakari almost dropped the board with Gabby's words. The lights on the board dimmed for a moment. "Liam, keep the power coming."

Liam grunted, and the lights resumed.

"What is this bright mass?" The ambassador pointed toward the northeast of the board.

"That is White Island, where the Cremelinos are raised," said Liam. "And here," he pointed around the map, "are other Cremelinos that have been given to the most powerful wizards in the land."

Bakari saw one in Arc; Danijela's, one in Gildan; Mezar's, and three in Anikari; belonging to the king and queen there, and Liam's twin sister.

Bakari studied the map for a moment. Something bright and colorful burned down south. *Are there other magical creatures that we don't know about?* The thought excited his scholarly mind, but he pushed it aside as something to think about later. Something else caught his eye. It was a moving dot, very bright, and it was coming northwest across northern Solshi. It soon would be crossing the mountains there and coming into Turg.

"What is this?" Bakari voiced out loud as he put his finger on the spot.

Suddenly his mind flared with light, and he was transported somewhere to the edge of the magic stream.

Bak? came a voice Bakari recognized immediately.

Roland? Bakari asked.

How are you here? Roland asked. *Where are you?*

I'm in Turg. Are you on a dragon?

Bakari heard Roland laugh.

Jealous, my friend? Roland said. *The Dragon King doesn't have a dragon, but I do.*

Roland! Bakari was getting frustrated. *Be serious. Things are dangerous here.*

I am quite serious, Bak. Orelia and I are coming to save Alli—something it seems that you haven't been able to do.

Bakari sighed. His friend was more frustrating and arrogant, it seemed. *Delia has stolen the bond of the other dragons and intends to name herself as the new Oracle this morning. Be careful of her, Roland. This is not a game.*

Oh, I assure you, I know this is not a game. But I am more powerful than she.

She has dragon artifacts.

I have a golden dragon, Roland said with pride.

Through their magical connection, Bakari heard a loud roar. The sound made him sick for his own dragon. But the feel of Roland's dragon felt strange and different from his own.

Are you all right, Roland? You're not into something you're not supposed to be in again, are you?

Suddenly, he lost the connection with Roland. "Liam!"

"I can't hold on any longer, Bakari," Liam said. "I can't take any more of the Cremelinos' power."

"Just a moment more, Liam," Bakari encouraged him. "Just a bit more."

Just be careful, Roland, Bakari sent one last message to his friend.

Why does everyone think I can't handle things? Roland said viciously. *You will see, Bak. You will see.*

Liam let go of the board and the connection with Roland was lost.

I must unify them. Roland's final words flitted through Bakari's mind.

Liam sagged to the floor in exhaustion.

"Dragon King, what's wrong?" Gabby said. "You look like you've seen a ghost."

Bakari shook his head a few times to clear his thoughts. "No, not a ghost, something possibly far worse."

The ambassador reached down and helped Liam back to his feet. They all looked at Bakari for more explanation.

"Delia may not be our biggest problem," Bakari said to a startled group.

CHAPTER TWELVE

There were two ways that Bakari could attend the coronation—in disguise, among the throng of people, or as The Dragon King, with all the pomp and circumstance he could muster. After a brief discussion with the ambassador and Gabby and Liam, they decided that their best chance at both rescuing Alli and stopping Delia from becoming the next Oracle would be from a position of power.

The ambassador found new changes of clothes for the three of them, ones that showed off the royal stature of each of the three wizards but would be serviceable in a fight. Gabby wore a skirt, but it had a slit to allow her to move around and held a few secret pockets to hold knives. Both Liam and Bakari had black leather pants, loose-fitting shirts, and warm cloaks over their shoulders—Bakari's blue, and Liam's red. Through his network in town, the ambassador also found Bakari a small crown to wear.

After retrieving their two Cremelinos and securing a third horse for Gabby, the ambassador mustered up a group of men to serve as their escorts. An hour before the coronation was to begin the three rode abreast down Thera's main thoroughfare.

One of the guards rode out front and shouted to the people, "Hail the Dragon King. Hail the Prince of the Realm. Hail the Princess of Quentis. Make way for the three wizards!"

The streets were thick with crowds, and the guards had to push people out of their way. Those of high status rode in carriages and palanquins, while others walked. The side streets leading to the coliseum flowed like winding streams into the main river of people walking forward. Suddenly the crowd was so thick and loud that the group had to stop.

"You wanted to enter with power and authority, Dragon King," Liam said. "Now is the time."

Bakari took a deep breath, still not liking that he had to show off his power at times. But this was one of those times that might make a difference. He knew he didn't have the power of his dragon behind him, and in reality before becoming the Dragon King he was a relatively weak wizard. But he did have Liam and Gabby—both of whom were stronger than he in base wizard strength. And he had the Cremelinos; a power unto themselves.

Bakari drew Gabby and Liam in closer, and with a nod of his head all three held out their hands in front of them. Fueled by the Cremelinos, a bright-white light shot out from the three of them and down onto the ground in front. It pushed forward down the street, and as it did so it pushed people softly out of the way to the left and the right. People yelled and screamed, then stopped and stared in wonder and amazement.

Wide enough for all three horses and running from the three riders to the front of the coliseum itself appeared a road of white and gold. It shimmered in the overcast winter day and flared brighter as it went along. Bakari led, and Liam and Gabby came up on either side, just a few feet back. Their contingent of guards now walked proudly in front of them. Someone had found a bugle and now blew it with all his might, signaling that royalty approached.

Gabby waved a hand in the air, and colored streams of blue, green, and yellow flowed around the three of them as they walked. The people cheered and yelled and bowed their heads to the three wizards.

Whispers ran ahead of them down the street, and by the time they had arrived at the coliseum another group came from the side to meet them.

"Dragon King," spat Delia, who rode out in front of her own group. "I wondered if you would come."

"Delia," said Nicholas beside her, "have some respect."

"I will respect others when they respect me for my power," Delia said through clenched teeth.

"Power you have stolen," said Liam from Bakari's right.

Wizard Korax rode up next to Delia and then prodded his horse closer to Liam, his face dark with murderous intent.

Bakari smiled and used the situation to his advantage. "Korax," he called out.

In surprise, the wizard looked over at Bakari.

"I didn't think protocol allowed you to precede Delia."

The wizard's face flushed, and Delia's eyes bulged.

"Delia, are you already acquiescing your power to others?" Bakari asked.

"Korax!" Delia called her wizard back in line.

"Well, let's go inside," Bakari motioned to everyone and pulled out in front.

Delia kicked her horse hard and jumped up next to Bakari, trying to take the lead as they entered the coliseum.

"You have no right to go first," Delia said to Bakari. "Before this day is over I will be more powerful than all of you."

Bakari put on his best smile. "Since it is your kingdom I will allow you to go in first."

Delia grunted and jumped ahead. Korax tried to follow, but Bakari, Liam, and Gabby blocked him. He entered fifth in line, just ahead of Nicholas. As they entered, grooms came up to take the horses.

Not knowing where to go, Bakari had to follow Delia. By now Korax had wormed his way back up to her. Soon they walked through a narrow tunnel and then out into the seating area of the coliseum itself.

"Wow!" said Gabby to his left.

Bakari echoed the sentiment. The coliseum was one of the largest structures he had ever seen. "There must be seating for twenty thousand," Bakari murmured.

"Almost thirty thousand, to be exact," said Nicholas, coming over to him. "It is one of the largest gathering places in the southern kingdoms."

Bakari let his eyes wander. Large columns held up a roof over the entire seating area. Down at one end were colorful tents full of vendors selling food and other wares. In the center of the circular building was an open-sky arena with a dirt floor. At both ends of the area stood racks of weapons.

This is where Alli will be.

Delia began walking to a covered boxed area high up in the coliseum. It had plush chairs, and the flag of Turg was draped down in front of it. Bakari, Liam, and Gabby followed.

Coming to the box, another group of people joined from the other side. One of them opened his eyes wide upon seeing Bakari.

"Dragon King," the man bobbed his head. "I had not heard you were attending the coronation."

"King Abbas," Bakari smiled. "Nice to see you again." Bakari had met the King of Cyrene twice before. Once at the Elvyn King Lanwaithian's coronation and later as Bakari had made his tour of all the southern kingdoms. The man was slightly taller than Bakari and twice his age, but his arms and neck were thick with muscles.

"I had not seen your dragon," he said with a sly look at Delia.

So the two were in cahoots. It did not surprise him. However, he hoped that King Abbas knew what he was getting himself into with Delia. The two countries shared a border and a long heritage. Khazer, far to the east, was the third kingdom in the united territories.

"They will be here soon, from what I have seen," said Bakari.

The comment caught Delia off guard, and she coughed, trying to cover up her surprise.

King Abbas waved over another man to him. This one had lighter skin and wore a flowing, colorful robe. "May I introduce you to Prince Ender, from Khazer. He happened to be here visiting Cyrene."

Liam grunted his disbelief.

Bakari extended a hand to the man, and they shook. "Give my well-wishes to your father, Ender."

The man's eyes went wide with apparent surprise. "You know my father?"

"Not well, but we have met," Bakari said. Something else bothered Bakari about Prince Ender. He had never met the man, but there was something he had heard about him recently. Shuffling back through his mind he finally remembered. "Ahh," he said out loud. "I thought I had heard you'd been in an accident, Prince Ender."

Ender's eyes darted right and left and then focused back on Bakari. He tried to smile, but it came out more of a sneer. "My demise has been greatly exaggerated. I assure you I am doing well."

Bakari motioned Gabby and Liam over, and introduced them as if they, too, were representatives of their own kingdoms for the coronation ceremony. "This is Prince Liam DarSan Williams, of the Realm, and Princess Gabrielle Von Wulf, of Quentis. We are looking forward to a pleasant ceremony." He looked from Ender, to Abbas, to Delia. "I would hate to explain to the kings of these powerful nations that something happened to their children."

Delia glared at him but said nothing. The others all bobbed their heads in greeting one to another. She ushered all of them to the royal sitting area. She sat next to Korax, with her father, Nicholas, on her other side and King Abbas and Prince Ender just below her. Suddenly Tabitha appeared behind them ready to serve Delia and do her bidding.

Delia motioned for Bakari and his two guest to be seated to her left, just on the other side of a small barrier.

"Prince Ender and King Abbas are both wizards," Gabby whispered to Bakari as they sat down, though there is something different about Ender.

"We are definitely outnumbered here," Liam grumbled. "I don't have a good feeling about this."

After sitting for almost an hour, letting the coliseum fill to capacity, Delia signaled a trio of trumpeters. After a few short blasts the crowd grew quiet, and Delia stood. Using her power, she amplified her voice out over the crowd.

"Before the votes are tallied and the coronation is held, we have a show," she began.

Cheers and whoops and hollers rang out through the crowd but soon quieted back down.

"Let the festivities begin!" she yelled.

A gate opened on one end of the coliseum, and Bakari held his breath, waiting for Alli to appear. But instead a group of rare animals—leopards, elephants, and lions included—came into the arena area with a group of acrobats, jesters, and trainers. For the next thirty minutes the crowd watched amazing spectacles.

In his mind, Bakari continued to calculate where he had seen the bright dragon dots on the board. His stomach sank as he realized that Delia was timing this perfectly. The dragons would arrive as she was crowned the new Oracle. With them so close, Bakari hoped that Alli, Liam, and he could somehow get through to their dragons and break through the bond. *And what about Jaimon?* His stomach sank again. *One thing at a time.*

The show ended, and the performers left through the same door they had entered. Anticipation filled the air. The gate at the opposite end opened, and Bakari held his breath and tried to see better. But without his glasses or his dragon sight, he could barely see who came through the large gate. But as they did so, he knew once again that it wasn't Alli. Music began to play as a group of musicians marched around the inside of the coliseum.

Delia leaned over and caught his eye. She smiled and winked, then turned her head back to the show.

"Where's Alli?" Liam said. "Delia's playing us here, Bakari. We're going to be lucky to get out alive."

"When Alli sees us, she'll know we are here for her, and with her powers and ours we should be able to hold our own in a fight," Bakari said, letting out a slow breath. "Let's hope it doesn't come to that, however. I'm still hoping for a peaceful solution."

Liam grunted.

"But someone has been holding her," Gabby said, "or she would have escaped by now. It might not be so easy."

Bakari nodded. Nothing was easy these days. He thought briefly back to his time growing up in the Wizard Citadel and then as a scholar in the castle in Cassian. Reading books, studying, preserving history, answering a few questions once in a while; that was a relatively simple life. Boring, he admitted, but simple. Nothing was simple anymore.

The musicians left and the crowd starting cheering and clapping. Some rose up on their feet. One of the gates opened, and out came a bulky man—twice Bakari's size and ripped with muscles. He stuck a fist up in the air, and a flash of lightning crackled from it. The crowd went crazy.

"Oh, Bakari," Delia called his attention, "I think you're going to like this show."

"Is that one of your champions?" Bakari said, pointing at the large man. Delia sorely underestimated Alli's abilities if the woman thought that man would stop her.

"Oh no, Bakari," Delia almost purred. "*That* is my champion." She pointed to the other side, and the gate opened.

Out walked a petite young woman with dark hair framing her pale face. She wore a tight red leather outfit that hugged her body, and she walked as if she feared nothing.

Bakari squinted his eyes, gasped, then turned back to Delia, who nodded her head.

"She's mine, Dragon King," Delia spat. "All mine."

CHAPTER THIRTEEN

Alli felt stronger than she had in a long time. Today was a new day, and she felt as if nothing in her past existed. Today she would prove her worth. The good night's sleep in the soft bed, and a morning meal of sausage, potatoes, and toast had filled her stomach and given her renewed strength. And her blessed master, Constantine, had already allowed her access to her incredible powers. She stood dressed in red leather and bouncing on the balls of her feet, ready for anything to come her way.

She entered the arena and looked up and around. It was the largest gathering of people she had ever seen. Tens of thousands of spectators lined the awesome structure around her. Built of wood and cement, it rose up a hundred feet in the air on all sides. As she stepped through the gate a deafening roar met her ears, and she smiled. As a fighter, there wasn't much to smile about. But these people cheered for her and loved her—as did her master.

Alli's eyes scanned the nearby crowd and found him—Constantine. After waking up this morning she had felt an increased fondness for him, with hardly even a flicker of memory of life without him. He had given her life, through Abaddon's healings time and time again. She was strong now because of him. She was who she was because of him.

Constantine smiled at her, and she gave him a quick solute and then raised both fists in the air. She wasn't going to be outdone by her opponent's display of lighting in the sky. Twin bolts of lightning leaped from her raised fists in a show of colors. She opened the palms of her hands and clapped them together once, and a loud boom erupted over the coliseum. Then another clap and another boom—in a rhythmic nature, spaced a few seconds apart. It brought the crowd to their feet in a frenzy. They joined in the clapping. Soon their claps overwhelmed her magical booms of power, and she brought her arms back down in front of her.

Then a woman high up in the stands stood up, and with a few blasts from the trumpets the tumult around the coliseum quieted down.

"Citizens of Turg, today is a historical day in our great kingdom. A day in which a new Oracle will be confirmed and ordained as the next leader of our kingdom. A kingdom that relies on the magical strength of its leaders to keep us a pre-eminent kingdom. Today our greatness will be expanded, and the kingdoms of the world will know our might. As a show of that, might I introduce the culminating event of this year's tournaments. We have the people's champion, Pantheras." Delia swept her arm to the right.

The crowd cheered loudly, and Pantheras shook his fists in the air and then glared over at Alli, letting out a wailing growl. She rolled her eyes at his demonstration.

The woman continued speaking, pointing now to her left. "And his opponent, my personal champion, Allison Stenos."

The level of the crowd's cheers rose to a higher pitch as Alli took a step forward.

Delia. The woman Constantine was talking to the night before. Mara had said Delia would be the next Oracle. Alli's chest swelled with pride; the obviously powerful woman had called Alli her champion. If her master had chosen Alli to fight for Delia, then she would prove herself worthy of such an honor.

Alli looked up at Delia, and the woman smiled down at her. Something tickled the back of Alli's mind. A faraway thought that she had met the woman before. She squinted her eyes up, trying to remember, but finally shrugged it off and looked back at her opponent. Men always underestimated her in a fight. Fighting wasn't always about brute strength. It was about finesse and agility. It was fractions of inches, slight movements, and almost imperceptible changes in stance that won fights. And as she pushed the sounds of the crowd further back in her mind she took a few more steps toward the rack of weapons afforded her.

"Let the championship fight begin!" Delia yelled out over the crowd.

* * *

"Something's wrong," Gabby said, leaning over to Bakari. "Something's wrong with Alli."

Bakari agreed. Something in the way she stood and then had looked up at Delia. "It's as if she didn't recognize Delia."

"She's just focused, I'm sure," Liam offered, but his eyes said he didn't even believe what he was saying.

"Let's just watch and wait and see what happens," Bakari said as he leaned forward in his seat. Squinting his eyes to see better, he watched Alli take up a pair of curved swords and begin walking toward her oversized male opponent.

The man picked up a larger broadsword and took off at a dead run, his powerful legs kicking up dust around him. His sword arm bulged with toned muscles as he roared loudly.

Alli didn't look to be phased and only continued walking. She swung one blade in the air, and then the other. They began to spin faster and faster, becoming a silver blur in the air around her. As the larger man approached, a wind picked up around Alli and began to kick up dust and dirt into the air in front of her. The man skidded to a stop and had to cover his eyes with one hand.

In that moment, Alli came in and brought her two knives up toward the man. Somehow, in the midst of the dirt and wind, he brought up his broadsword and blocked Alli's spinning blades. The force of his hit threw one of Alli's blades in the air. The man brought his sword around again, in a speed that belied his size. Alli went into a crouch and slid under the blade and through the man's legs.

Coming up behind Pantheras, she hit him hard in the back of the head with the hilt of the blade she still held. He stumbled forward, and Alli followed him closer to the ground. But he feinted and came up to the side and around her.

"She shouldn't have fallen for that," Bakari grunted. "She knows better." He gripped a railing in front of him hard, and his knuckles grew white.

"Maybe we should help," Gabby offered.

"And get all of us killed?" Liam said. "Who knows how many wizards are here and how many are on Delia's side."

Gabby put a hand over her mouth and gasped. Bakari turned his head from his friends back to the fight below them. Pantheras had grabbed Alli from behind and held her in a headlock. Alli's eyes bulged, and she kicked and struggled to get away.

Use your powers, Alli. You are the Battlemaster. Bakari pleaded for her to do something.

Bakari turned and looked at Delia, but her attention was elsewhere. She was staring intently farther down in the stands to a broad-shouldered older man. Alli looked up from her grip in the same direction. Her eyes pleaded for help. The man stood up, and it was then that Bakari saw something metal on his wrist. He brought his attention back to Alli, who seemed to have a similar-looking one on her own wrists, although Bakari couldn't tell for sure.

"Gabby?" Bakari pointed toward both the man and Alli. "What's on their wrists?"

Gabby stood up to see better.

"Hey, sit down!" yelled out a spectator from behind.

Liam turned around and pulled out a knife, and the heckler quieted down with a mumble.

"He's controlling her with manacles; they're powerful artifacts I'm sure." Gabby nodded her head and turned to Bakari. "It looks to be similar to what stopped her magic last year in Quentis when she had been captured. But look!"

Bakari turned back and saw a golden glow surround Alli, emanating from the manacle. Suddenly a flame erupted from it and raced toward the man's face. He bellowed in pain, covered his eyes, and staggered backwards. Alli fell to the ground, panting for breath. But only for a moment.

A second later she turned and faced Pantheras again. And the crowd came to its feet and cheered.

"We need to get closer," Bakari said and motioned for the other two to follow him. "We need to find out who that man is."

They got up and began pushing through the crowd. Bakari caught Delia's eyes. She only smiled at him, then she looked up into the sky. When she brought her head back down she mouthed the word "soon." Bakari knew what she meant. They had little time to rescue Alli.

Trying to get lower down through the crowd was difficult at best. At one point the crowd stood and cheered again, and Bakari poked his head through to see what was going on. Alli stood over the man with a sword in her raised hand. The fight was about to end.

But at the last possible moment, the man turned to his right and caught someone's eye, and then with speed that only came from magic he rolled to the side and came up in a crouch with his hand in front of him. A ball of fire flew from his raised hand, and Bakari noticed that he, too, wore a bracelet. Alli ducked just in time and, grabbing a handful of dirt, flicked it in his direction. The distraction gave her time to get into better position. Before Pantheras could recover from the dust in his eyes she jumped up and, in her signature move, twirled in the air and came down with a foot to his chest. The force of her kick threw him a dozen feet in the air, landing hard on the ground.

Bakari, Liam, and Gabby continued to push through until they were at the bottom seats, not far from the man Alli had been looking at. They watched a grin of pride spread across his face as Alli turned and looked at him. Bakari waved in the air and shouted her name, but Alli only had eyes for the man. She smiled at him, and he held up the manacle for her to see and touched it again.

Out on the floor of the arena, Alli lifted her head and shrieked, an otherworldly sound escaping her lips. Bakari could physically see her swell with additional power as she turned back to her opponent. With a flick of her wrist, the man jerked upwards on his feet. His head hung low, and he couldn't stand on his own. With swirls of her hands in the air she lifted the man off the ground ten feet.

"Alli!" Gabby cried out.

But in the sea of spectators what was one lone voice?

Alli then screamed, and a barrage of colors swirled around her lithe body. With a push of her right hand into the air in front of her, Pantheras flew through the air a hundred feet, hit the side wall of the coliseum, and slid to the ground without moving.

The crowd yelled and clapped and chanted her name for minutes before the trumpets blared again and Delia stood back up. The crowd quieted down and turned attention back to her.

"Behold my champion!" Delia beckoned Alli closer to her side of the coliseum. Before consenting, Alli looked once more at the man who now stood only a dozen feet away from Bakari. He nodded, and Alli went forward.

"The manacles didn't stop her magic," Bakari said to Gabby.

Gabby shook her head. "No, but I think they control her somehow."

"We need to get the other manacle from that man," Liam said.

Bakari agreed, and they tried to move closer to him as Delia began to speak.

"The votes are tallied, and the decision has been made." Delia raised her hands high in the air. "I, Delia Marinos, am your new Oracle!"

Delia let the crowd cheer, then continued speaking.

"Worthy citizens of Turg. Long have we stood in the shadow of the southern and northern kingdoms. Long have they regulated the united territories as unworthy of the recognition we so deserve. But this day I declare that no longer will this be." Delia paused a moment for cheers. "This day I declare that the great united territories will rise up and rule those who previously have looked on us as powerless. Today we rise as a united people—Turg, Cyrene, and Khazer—and declare that we are a people deserving of their attention. With me as the new Oracle of Turg, no longer will we be a depressed people. Today is the day that we rise and take control. Today is the day we show the world what real power is!"

Bakari stood only a few feet behind the man with the manacle, but his attention was on Delia. This was more than an acceptance speech; this was a play for power.

Side by side with the king of Cyrene and the prince of Khazer, Delia raised her arms with theirs, and powerful thunder filled the skies around them. The morning fog parted, and blue sky and sunlight covered the coliseum. Flashes of lightning touched down outside the coliseum, and suddenly from the eastern skies flew four large, beautiful dragons, in their lead a stunning blue dragon.

"Abylar," Bakari whispered.

"Ryker," croaked out Liam at the same time, looking at the red one.

Bakari drew all the power at his disposal and tried to reach his dragon, but to no avail.

Bakari felt a tiny speck of recognition far at the back of his mind, but nothing that would allow him connection through his previous bond.

"This is enough!" Bakari growled and jumped up on a bench. He thrust his own hands in the air.

"Delia!" Bakari shouted out through the thousands of people, his voice carrying on the wind of his power to every corner of the coliseum.

Delia turned his direction, and with a flick of her wrist, the dragons came lower and began to circle around the coliseum. Ryker's red, Abylar's blue, Cholena's green, and Miriel's orange and yellow churned faster and faster.

"I am the Dragon King," Bakari shouted out. "You have no right to these dragons!"

Delia held up a small chain attached to her wrist. "I have all the right. She who holds the power holds all the right of that power. The united territories are now called Drakena—the land of the dragons—and I declare myself the Dragon Queen and ruler of the western continent. We will bow to no one."

CHAPTER FOURTEEN

Roland took that moment to make his entrance. "I take exception to that declaration, Delia Marinos," he said from high above the crowd.

Above the clouds and behind a spell of invisibility shared with him from the Scepter, Roland had watched Alli's final act, Delia's announcement, and the summoning of the other dragons. The woman had obviously let too much power go to her head.

Removing the spell of invisibility, Roland appeared above the other circling dragons, sitting atop his own marvelous golden one.

Delia had lowered her arms and stood staring up at Roland. "You are not the queen of the dragons," he said with a loud voice. "As all can plainly see, I have my own dragon, which you do not control—and I daresay I would rather have my friend Bakari in control of them than you."

"They are mine now, High Wizard." Delia cried out, obviously not enjoying Roland's interruption to her plans.

Roland dropped lower and landed in the middle of the arena floor. The scales of his dragon caught the morning sun, and a dazzling display of gold twinkled around the crowd. With one hand he smoothed down his blond hair and with the other straightened his golden cloak around his shoulders.

"I am more than the High Wizard of the Citadel now, Delia Marinos," Roland said. "I am King of Alaris, Monarch of Tillimot, and now rider of the golden dragon."

Delia seemed to hesitate a moment. "I, too, am more than when we last met, Roland Tyre. Heed my power!"

All eyes in the crowd went back and forth between the two. Roland's eyes roamed the crowd for a moment until he found Bakari.

He nodded in greeting to his friend, but Bakari didn't look happy. Voices in his head told him to be careful of his old friend. Bakari would be jealous of Roland's new powers and of his dragon. Roland didn't want to hurt his friend, but Bakari had better not get in his way.

Roland jumped down from his dragon and strode across the dirt floor toward Alli. "Alli, it's me, Roland. I'm here for you."

Alli turned around and looked at Roland. She tilted her head and pursed her lips. With a flick of her eyes to the crowd, she turned back to Roland and shook her head.

"Who are you?"

Roland stopped midstride and felt like he had been kicked in the gut. Standing about ten feet away, he noticed how well the red leather fit Alli's body. It was a good look for her.

"Battlemaster?" Roland asked, trying to appeal to her title. Maybe she was playing some type of game. "Are you ready to return to the Citadel?"

"The Citadel?" Alli said with a confused look. "My place is here with my master." She turned to the crowd, and Roland watched a man just in front of Bakari smile and take a step toward her.

"But, Alli?" Roland didn't know what to say. "Are you still mad at me? I know you told me to stay away from the artifacts in the basement. I tried. I really did. But when you didn't return, I just couldn't wait." Roland brought the scepter out in front of him. "I found this golden scepter, and I have saved Alaris, brought back a golden dragon, and now come to rescue you."

Alli acted as if she hadn't heard anything. She peered up at where Delia stood. Delia smiled at Alli before Alli turned back to Roland. "My master needs me now. I serve Delia, the Oracle of Turg."

Roland took another step forward but stumbled at Alli's words. What did she mean? What had happened to her? He came as fast as he could. Did she really hate him this much to make a spectacle of this in front of such a considerable crowd?

"Alli?" Roland whispered, his heart pounding hard in his chest. "What have they done to you?"

Roland's hand rubbed the glass pommel of his scepter and let anger fill him up. "Bak, what have you done to her?" He whipped his head around and glared at his friend. With power filling him, he leaped in the air and landed mere feet in front of the first rows of benches in front of Bakari.

"I have done nothing, Roland," Bakari said. "But somehow this man controls her." Bakari pointed toward the man with the manacle.

The man took off running as fast as he could through the crowd in the other direction.

"The manacle, Roland," Bakari yelled out. "He controls her with the manacle."

Roland leaped toward the man, but others blocked his path.

"Get out of my way!" Roland brought his hands up in front of him, and people in the crowd flew to either side as Roland made his way toward the man.

"Enough!" came Delia's voice from above.

Roland paused to look up at her.

She pointed to her dragons, and Abylar dived toward Roland, mouth open wide and shooting flames.

Roland put up his hands and with a shield of air deflected the fire. "I am not someone you want to trifle with Delia," Roland shouted across the coliseum. Turning to Bakari, he yelled out again. "Stop your crazy dragon from eating me!"

Bakari brought his hands out in front of him and shrugged his shoulders. "I don't control them anymore, Roland."

Roland sighed. "Do I have to do everything?"

With a flick of his wrist, his golden dragon came forward and crashed into the side of Abylar.

The crowd began to yell and scream and run for exits. A battle between dragons was not something anyone wanted to be in the middle of.

Roland continued running toward the man, but before he could reach him someone hit him from the side and knocked him to the ground. When he rolled back over, Alli stood over him, glaring down with a murderous look on her face.

"Alli, it's me, Roland," Roland pleaded with her. "I am your friend, remember?"

"I don't have friends," Alli said with a sneer. "I am a fighter."

"Yes, you are a fighter. You are my battlemaster," Roland said, trying to get her to remember. "You must remember." He stood back up and walked closer to her.

Alli's eyes went unfocused for a moment, as if she might remember, but then a voice called out.

"Alli, help me," the man with the manacles yelled out.

"Constantine!" Alli shouted and turned toward him.

Bakari and Liam grabbed Constantine from behind and held him down. In a blur, Alli raced toward them. Before she got there, though, Gabby intercepted her with a considerable wind of air, knocking her off course.

Roland took the opportunity to reach the man she referred to as Constantine. He grabbed the man's wrist and held it up. "What did you do to her?"

Constantine laughed. "Turned her into the champion of Turg." Then he added with a whisper, "and made a lot of money doing it."

Roland slugged him in the jaw. "Give me the manacle!"

The man shrugged. "It won't matter now."

Just then Alli barreled into all of them and pulled out a set of hidden knives. First, she leaped toward Roland, trying to free his hand from the grasp on Constantine's wrist.

"Alli!" Bakari pleaded. "This isn't you."

Alli looked up at Bakari for a moment.

"I'm your friend, Alli, as is Roland." Bakari tried to get through to her, as Roland had done. But nothing seemed to work. "You are one of my dragon riders."

She kicked out toward Bakari, and Liam moved between them. But he moved too slowly and was only able to deflect the kick somewhat. Taking most of the brunt himself, Liam crumpled to the ground, holding his leg.

A roar behind them turned their attention back to the arena. Ryker now joined Abylar in attacking Orelia. Roland ground his teeth in frustration.

"There are too many of them," Bakari said to Roland.

"Shut up, Bak!" Roland said. "This is all your fault!"

"*My* fault?"

"If you wouldn't have taken Alli away on your foolish trek to find dragon artifacts, none of this would have happened!"

Bakari's eyes burned into Roland's, but then his head dropped a bit. "I didn't mean for any of this to happen, Roland. You have to believe me. Let's save Alli, and we can talk about this later."

Roland grunted. The scholar wizard did make some sense.

Constantine lay on the ground next to him, and Alli was leaning over him. The man had fallen and apparently hit his head. A pool of blood spread beneath him. Roland moved over closer and put his hand on the manacle around the man's wrist.

"When he dies, the manacle will stop working," a young woman with Bakari said. It was not someone he recognized. He looked up at her.

"Gabby, are you sure?" asked Bak.

Gabby nodded her head. "Yes, all artifacts stop working for a holder upon his death."

An idea came to Roland as he looked up at Delia—still standing next to Wizard Korax. Coming out from behind them was Tabitha, the young woman he had sent to become part of the Oracle's household. He was happy to see she was still around. He nodded to her, and she nodded back. He would have to take care of Delia later. Bak was right, he couldn't fight her right now.

"You killed him!" Alli yelled up at Roland. "You killed my master."

She cradled Constantine's head in her lap. Most of the crowd around them had left, and they stood alone.

"You are free now, Alli." Roland reached a hand toward her soft check, now streaked with dirt and tears.

She flicked his hand away. "Don't touch me. You killed my master."

"But, Alli?" Roland tried to get her to recognize him. "It's me, Roland. You are free from the manacle's influence now."

"More must have been done to her," Gabby sighed from behind Roland. "Alli!" she called out. "Remember me, your friend, Gabby from Quentis. Remember my brother Kaspar. You helped us in Quentis with Jaimon and his dragon."

Obviously, Gabby and Alli had more of a history than Roland knew about. He did know who Kaspar was—the heir to the throne of Quentis.

Unify them, the voice came to Roland's mind again. He pushed it away for now and turned back to Alli.

Alli stood up and faced the rest of the group in front of her. Her hands were balled and her eyes flashed wildly around. "I don't know who any of you are! Leave me alone!"

"Alli?" Tears filled Roland's own eyes. "Please." He knew they bickered and she didn't understand his obsession with magic, but he cared deeply for her and wanted her to rule by his side.

"I said leave me alone!" Alli repeated, and she put her hands out in front of her and threw them all back over a dozen rows of benches.

As Roland tumbled backward his heart broke. But then as his back hit the benches, it hardened.

They would all rue this day. He would make sure of it.

CHAPTER FIFTEEN

Bakari tried to stand back up. When he reached over to offer a hand to Gabby he winced. Looking down, he noticed a thin scrape running from his wrist to his elbow. Small drops of blood dripped from his arm onto his cloak, but he hardly noticed. Standing now twenty feet away from them was Alli. Fire crackled from her fingertips as she stood in her red leather outfit. The whites of her eyes swam with flecks of red and orange.

Liam stood next to Bakari but leaned on him for support. Roland drew himself up from the ground a few feet away. He stood glaring at Alli for a moment, then turned to Bakari with hatred in his eyes.

Suddenly his eyes darted around and he looked to be in a panic.

"Where is my scepter?" he roared.

Bakari's mind barely even registered that Roland had been holding a scepter earlier.

Gabby reached down and grabbed something under one of the benches. "Is this what you are looking for?" She held it reverently for a moment, and then a look of recognition flooded through her mind. "The Scepter of Unification."

"That's mine!" Roland reached over and snatched it back from her. Instantly his visage calmed, although he still looked to be in a barely controlled rage.

"A very dangerous artifact," Gabby said. "You should be careful."

"Why. Does. Everyone. Keep. Saying. That?" Roland roared and slammed the scepter down against a bench.

The bench collapsed, and a rumble grew louder and louder. Sparks and flashes of lightning grew out of the point where Roland still held the scepter to the structure.

"It's going to collapse!" Bakari shouted. "Roland, stop!"

Screams of the remaining spectators sounded behind them as the entire structure began to shake.

"Alli!" Delia called to her. "Come to me."

Alli turned and took off running toward Delia, Korax, and Tabitha. Nicholas still stood at their side, but he had moved a few steps away.

"Bakari, we need to get out of here!" Liam yelled. "Before we are buried alive!"

With Bakari on one side and Gabby on the other, they helped the limping Liam up the stairs, trying to find the closest exit. A loud roar sounded around them, and they turned to look.

Roland had jumped in the air and was now sitting on Orelia's back. Golden flames roared from the dragon's maw, enveloping part of the coliseum. Bakari grabbed a rail to keep from falling as the structure shook again. The exit was not far away.

"Liam, the Cremelinos!" Bakari said. "Call them to us."

Liam nodded, and Bakari felt the calling in the back of his own mind.

Alli had now reached Delia. Bakari felt like he had disappointed everyone this day. He had not saved Alli, Delia was now the Oracle, and his friend Roland hated him. And to top it off, his own dragon didn't even recognize his presence.

"Alli, come with us," he shouted at her. "We will help you."

She turned around at his voice, and her face was void of emotion or recognition. How could he reach her? What could he say? Finally he thought of one last-ditch effort he would try. He pulled all the power into him that he could manage and reached out to her both with physical voice and trying to reach her mind and heart.

"Alli, I am the Dragon King—and as a dragon rider I command you with all the authority I possess to return with us. Come, now!" Bakari stretched his hand out, and lightning sizzled around him. It was the call of the Dragon King to his riders, a call that couldn't be ignored or disobeyed. He never had liked that kind of power, but he used it now in desperation.

Alli staggered with his call and took a step forward. But Delia grabbed on to her. For one brief moment Bakari thought he saw recognition come to Alli's eyes. Her hand rose a half a dozen inches in the air in his direction. But Delia pulled her in closer and whispered something into her ear, and Alli stiffened and turned back to Delia.

"What did you say to her?" Bakari yelled across at Delia.

"Bak!" Liam pulled at him. "The Cremelinos are here."

"I told her the truth, Bakari," Delia said. "I told her she was still a dragon rider."

For a moment Bakari didn't understand what she meant. Then Miriel, the bright orange and yellow dragon that had been Alli's, left the rest and flew to the air to where Delia and her group stood. She stood precariously on the edge of some rows of benches. Debris crumbled below her.

No. No. No. Not this way.

"I am the Dragon Queen now, and she responds to me," Delia said. "Hail the Dragon Queen!"

"Hail the Dragon Queen," echoed Alli, Korax, Abbas, and Ender.

Miriel came close to Alli and with a snap of her jaws bit off the manacle around her wrist. For a moment hope grew in Bakari's breast. Without the manacle maybe Alli would respond to them; maybe she would remember who she was. But the hope died almost as quickly as it had come. Alli mounted her dragon.

Nicholas scrambled to get away from the group, but just then a portion of the coliseum collapsed under him. He nodded to Bakari, and just as he fell, Bakari saw him flicker and disappear. Looking around for him, Bakari hoped he had survived.

Delia motioned the others with her, and they each jumped onto the backs of the four dragons. Delia took Abylar, with Tabitha behind her. King Abbas of Cyrene took Ryker, with a growl from Liam. Prince Ender jumped on Cholena, with Korax on the back, and all four dragons lifted up in the air.

As they did so, something dropped from Tabitha's hand, and before Bakari could think of what it might be, Roland flew down atop his dragon and scooped it up.

The rest of the structure began collapsing. Bakari scrambled up the last remaining steps with Liam and Gabby. Standing in front of them were the two Cremelinos. Bakari helped Liam on his, and then Gabby and he jumped on the other. Thousands of people still filled the streets around the coliseum, trying to get to safety as it continued to fall around them. The two Cremelino horses pushed through, trying not to trample anyone. With their renowned speed, they rode down the main thoroughfare and out through the southern gate of Thera.

Bakari heard a loud roar and looked up.

"Stay out of my way, Bak!" Roland shouted down at them from atop his golden dragon. The golden scepter hung from his right hand, and his still-intact golden cape flew behind him. "I *will* destroy Delia."

"Roland!" Bakari shouted up at him. "You're angry and hurt. Let's work together."

"I'm done working together," Roland said. "I'm done sitting on the sidelines. I will unify the kingdoms and then destroy Delia and get Alli back."

"That's not the way to do it," Bakari said as Roland rose higher. "We can help."

"All you want is my power. But you can't have it," Roland yelled from higher up. "The golden dragon and the golden scepter are mine!"

Oh, Roland. Bakari's heart went out to his friend. The power of the scepter and dragon were not natural. They had somehow played to Roland's vain ambition for power and glory.

"Roland!" Bakari shouted one last time, not even knowing if he was heard. "You can't do this."

A moment later, more in his mind than through a voice in the air, came the faint reply. *I **can** do this. I am magic!*

With the full speed of the Cremelinos, the city quickly receded behind them. Trees blurred by, and the coastal mountain range south of Thera where they had found the cave of artifacts loomed up in front of them.

Gabby patted Bakari on his back softly and whispered. "It's all right, Bakari. We'll fix things."

Bakari smiled at Gabby's eternal optimism. Had he been like that at one time? The last year or so seemed to have given a lifetime of wear to him. Who had he been to think he could be a dragon rider, or even the Dragon King? It had always been inevitable that someone would challenge him. Delia had. And she had won.

Lost in his melancholy thoughts, he was letting his Cremelino follow Liam's, not caring for the moment where they went. The cold wind whipped his braids back from his face as the two horses skirted the edge of the mountains.

Suddenly, without warning, Liam yelled out, "Stop."

Flash skidded to a stop, and Gabby grabbed around Bakari's waist to keep from being flung off the horse.

"Liam!" Bakari called out. "What are you doing? We need to get as far from Thera as we can. Delia will be looking for us."

"Look!" Liam pointed up about a fourth of the way up a foothill in front of the mountains.

Bakari and Gabby turned and did as Liam beckoned. Abruptly Gabby leaped from the back of the horse and went running up the side of the mountain.

"Jaimon! Jaimon!" Gabby shouted as she ran.

CHAPTER SIXTEEN

Bakari jumped off jumped off his Cremelino and then helped Liam dismount as Gabby came running back down the side of the mountain, pulling Jaimon stumbling behind her. He carried a sack with him, but Gabby didn't seem to care.

Bakari couldn't keep from smiling. Seeing Jaimon again was indeed a sign that maybe not all hope was lost.

"Jaimon!" Bakari gave him a slap on the back, and Jaimon and Liam gave each other a hug. "How did you get out?"

"Are you hungry?" Gabby added. "Do you need water?"

"I'm so sorry we had to leave," Liam said with a serious face. "Are you really all right? We saw the cave collapse and wanted to come for you, but the entire mountain seemed to be falling apart."

Jaimon laughed, and his long, dark pony tail swung around behind him. His clothes were dirty and torn, and his face looked a bit gaunt, but he didn't seem too worse for the wear. Gabby reached up and wiped a dirty smudge from his light-brown skin and gave him another hug.

Bakari smiled at the two. Jaimon was barely fifteen and only a few months older than Gabby herself. He was the youngest dragon rider and the only one without the use of his own magic—an attribute that had actually been beneficial in helping all of them escape Delia in the mountain.

"I'm fine. I'm fine," Jaimon said. "Just a little tired and hungry." He looked at the group expectantly.

Bakari shook his head. "Sorry, Jaimon. We don't have any food on us. We had to leave Thera in a hurry."

Jaimon's countenance fell. "I saw the dragons, Bakari." His voice caught for a moment. "I saw Cholena. I called to her, but she wouldn't come. What happened?"

Gabby started to explain, but Liam interrupted. "We need to get farther away. Delia and her dragons will be searching for us."

"The smaller villages will be more likely to take us in," Gabby said. "I can find us some followers of the dragon that will help."

Bakari thought a moment before speaking. "I don't want to put others in danger."

"We can ride faster and farther on the Cremelinos than Delia would think," Liam said.

We will protect you, Dragon King, Flash spoke to Bakari's mind.

"Not much of a king anymore," he mumbled.

"What did you say, Bakari?" Jaimon asked.

"Nothing. Nothing." Bakari waved their inquiries off. "Just talking to the Cremelinos."

"I think Gabby is right. If we can find those that still support you we can begin to fight back," Liam said as his Cremelino knelt down, allowing him to mount more easily. He motioned Jaimon over. "Hop on behind me."

Jaimon swung a small leather bag up in front of him and then joined Liam on the back of Liberty.

"What's in the bag?" Gabby asked as she and Bakari mounted back up on Flash.

Jaimon gave off an impish smile, and his eyes sparkled in delight. "Just some gifts from the dragon's lair."

"Artifacts of the dragon?" Gabby said with excitement.

Jaimon nodded and opened his mouth to say more, but just then Liberty took off and Jaimon grabbed hold of Liam's waist to keep from falling off. Bakari sent a quick thought to Flash for him to keep up, and they, too, took off galloping at full speed once again.

The four travelers on the two Cremlinos rode in a southeasterly direction, keeping the mountain range to their right. The farther from the coast they went the colder it became. Heavy clouds hung over the tops of the mountains, and at the speed they rode the wind became numbing.

After hours of riding, Gabby cried out. "Bakari!" and pointed back behind them.

Bakari looked up to where she was pointing but couldn't see anything. "What?" He squinted more, but his eyesight was growing worse by the day. He would need to find another pair of glasses.

"Liam, Jaimon, stop!" Gabby called out to them. Liam's Cremelino skidded to a stop in front of them and then circled back around and moved under a canopy of trees.

Gabby pointed up in the sky again behind them.

"Delia!" Liam spat out, leaning over to see through the branches better.

"Or at least one of them," Gabby said. "I can't tell which dragon it is."

"I wish I knew the land here better," Liam said.

"There's a break in the mountain range not far up ahead." Bakari pointed in front of them. "Just around that rock. There's a gap that leads down into North Solshi."

"I thought you couldn't see well," Liam said with a frown.

Bakari tapped his head. "It's all in here. I've got the maps in my head. I've flown over here before."

A loud roar tore the air behind them.

"Hurry, before they see us," Gabby yelled out. "Liam, ride!"

Liam scowled at her, obviously not liking her telling him what to do, but he did so anyway. Bakari's Cremelino followed closely behind. As he had said, around the next rock was a gap between the coastal range and the larger Mahli mountains to the east. A valley opened up below them, and they cautiously but quickly made their way down a steep incline.

Fenced-off pastures, barns, and a few homes littered the valley floor.

"Over there!" Jaimon pointed to a grove of thick evergreens. "We can hide there."

Liam turned his horse in that direction, and Bakari followed with theirs. He was sure Delia would not be happy until all the riders were dead. Another roar sounded overhead, and just as they entered the trees a large green dragon flew overhead, its wings spread out to either side. The dragon screeched a strange sound and flew down lower.

The four dismounted from the Cremelinos and pulled themselves and the horses back under the thick trees.

"He's hurting her," Jaimon said with a cry of anguish.

Jaimon moved a step, but Bakari put a hand on his shoulder and pulled him back. "We can't help her right now." Memories of riding his own dragon flooded his mind, and for a moment he was overwhelmed with emotion. But using all the strength he had, he pushed the thoughts away.

"Who's riding her?" Jaimon said, turning around and facing Bakari.

"Prince Ender of Khazer," Bakari whispered.

"Khazer!" Jaimon said. "What happened back there?"

"The united territories have united even more under Delia. They call themselves Drakena. Each of the kingdoms now controls a dragon," Bakari said, ending with a deep sigh.

"Who has the fourth?" Jaimon asked.

"Alli," Gabby said.

Hope formed on Jaimon's face, but Bakari dashed it with his next words.

"She's one of them for now," Bakari said, then closed his eyes for a moment. It was hard to face and comprehend. Alli had been his responsibility. The things Roland had said were all true. It was entirely his fault.

"It's *not* your fault," Gabby said, as if reading his mind.

Bakari gave her a questioning look.

"I'm not using my family's power of *seeing* on you, Bakari," Gabby said. "It's written all over your face."

"She's right, Dragon King," Liam said. "It's not your fault."

"I am no king anymore." Bakari spoke slowly. "Just Bakari or Bak will do."

"You're still King of Mahli," Liam said, his mouth held tight. "You took a lame prince and gave me so much more when you gave me Ryker. You are my dragon king until *I* say you are not."

"Mine too," Jaimon said. "You found me—just a young boy in the mountains of Quentis—and offered me a dragon. I will never forget that."

Gabby put her hand on Bakari's arm. "My family has led the followers of the dragon for hundreds of years. I know all the prophecies and all the histories. The Dragon King is not an easy title to gain. But it is not solely based on whether you ride a dragon or not; it is based on your heart. And you, Bakari, have the heart of a dragon king."

Bakari's heart pounded with emotion. His shame didn't go away, but he was touched by what his friends thought of him. Was he still the Dragon King?

"We will have to fight Delia and maybe Roland to get our dragons back, protect all the kingdoms, and bring peace to the land again," Bakari said. "Are you willing to do that?"

"I thought I already signed up for that when I became a dragon rider," Liam said. He couldn't hold back a smile.

A faint screech from the dragon drifted through the trees, and the four of them crept slowly to the edge and looked about. Bakari spotted the dragon flying northeast.

"Seems like we are safe for now," Gabby said. "Let's see if we can find lodgings for the night down there."

They emerged from the trees and looked down into the valley. A half dozen homes had smoke spiraling out of their chimneys. Jaimon's stomach growled.

"And some food," Liam said with a slight grin.

The four walked with their horses down a thin, but well-maintained trail down into the valley.

"There are many that still support you, Bakari," Gabby said as they made their way down. "We will find them and gather them."

"Alaris is now ruled by Roland, it seems," Bakari said. "And Tillimot also, if you believe him."

Jaimon raised his brows at that. "I have missed a lot. What is the High Wizard's plan?"

"His intentions are to unite all the kingdoms and go after Delia," Gabby said.

"His thirst for more power has always been his motivation," Bakari said. "He is a good man but gets distracted."

"Then where do we go for help?" Liam said. "With that golden dragon of his, his arm stretches far, and no offense, Dragon King, but the kingdom of Mahli is not in a position to take him on. And with Delia controlling the untied territories with our dragons it will be hard for the northern kingdoms to offer any help."

Bakari thought for a moment and then smiled broadly. "There is one land in the south that will not bow to his or Delia's power."

The three others looked at him, awaiting his answer.

"The elves," Bakari said with a surety he hadn't felt in a while. "We begin our ride to Elvyn in the morning."

CHAPTER SEVENTEEN

Roland flew away from the coliseum in Thera with a burning rage. *How dare they all defy me?* Alli had played with his heart and now spurned him, Bakari had always thought he was smarter than anyone around him, and now Delia—she was the worst. How dare she declare herself Queen of the Dragons? She had no right to that title.

He directed his dragon south over the coast range that divided Turg and North Solshi—his next destination. His scepter hung at his side, and Roland rubbed his right hand over its glass orb and thought about his plans.

Unify. Unify! came the throbbing voice in his mind.

Who was that young girl named Gabby to tell him what he could and couldn't handle? What could she know of such power?

Roland took his hand from the scepter and moved it slowly over the golden scales in front of him, a sudden feeling of adoration welling up inside of him. *Are you all right?* He asked Orelia. *Did they hurt you?*

No. I cannot be hurt. I am made differently from other dragons.

But you are a real dragon, right? Roland didn't like the idea of riding up so high in the sky with something that wasn't real.

I am as real as the scepter you hold.

Well that was a cryptic answer. *Are dragons always so ambiguous in their answers?*

As a creature of magic, I am what you make me to be.

Roland thought about that for a while as he flew over a valley between two mountain ranges. Off to his left he thought he saw one of the other dragons receding. He thought about his first time on a dragon. It had been with Alli. They were all attending the coronation of the Elvyn king, Lanwaithian Soliel, and the marriage to his wife, Breelyn. That was when Alli had been given the dragon bond, and she had offered him a ride—his first one.

He now thought back about the first time he had met Alli—coming into the castle in Cassian. That was almost a year and a half ago. He was stricken immediately by her—and not just in a superficial way like he was with all the other women he met. She was beautiful in her own way, but it was more her wit, spunk, and fierce loyalty that had attracted him. And now!

Roland slammed his fist down onto the hard scales of his dragon. *And now Delia has taken her from me!*

Unify!

The thoughts throbbed through his mind and heart. This is what he was meant to do. To unify the kingdoms. They would love him and bow to him with glory. Their eyes would be filled with adoration for their king and protector—just like in the vision he'd had when he had first touched the scepter.

The people needed him. They all did. Bakari, Alli, the other dragon riders, the kingdoms of the south. They needed Roland Tyre and his golden scepter.

Roland took a deep breath and looked around him. The sky had cleared, and bright afternoon sunlight sent slanted shadows across the land. He could see the great shadow of his own dragon on the brown winter fields below. He took in a deep breath and blew it out. And did it again. And a third time. He closed his eyes and put his arms out to his sides and became one with the dragon.

He dug deep inside and felt the presence of the dragon there. He melded with it, and soon he was seeing the world through his dragon's eyes. It was all so clear, and he could see so far. Off in the distance he could see the faint outline of the city of Raleez, capital of both North and South Solshi. He knew those of Solshi to be fierce warriors, and soon they would be his warriors.

Unify!

He pushed all his angry thoughts deep inside and thought about how best to gain the loyalty of the kingdom below him. A few ideas came to him. Maybe he could wrap in both North and South Solshi at one time—two kingdoms for the price of one. The thought lifted his mood. He was not a tyrant. That's not how he did things. He saved people, and for that they loved him. But he wasn't above a little trickery to get the job done.

He directed Orelia west toward the coastline. Using his dragon's eyesight, he saw the fishing villages much earlier than they could see him. A grouping of hills caught his attention, and he took Orelia down to the ground behind them.

Sliding down off his dragon, he paced around a few times, trying to loosen up his legs. He had done a lot of riding the last two days, and his body was stiff. He walked over to the saddlebag that hung over the side of his dragon and stuffed his golden cloak inside. He wasn't ready to draw attention to himself yet. From an outside pocket he drew out a few bags of gold and hung them from his belt. He looked at his sword and wondered if he needed it. Between the scepter and his magic, he hadn't used his sword much lately. But he needed to blend in.

After he strapped his sword around his waist he donned a long, thick coat that hung down to his knees. Wrapping a scarf around his neck completed the look.

Now he stood and stared at his scepter.

Unify them.

The voice came to his head again. He didn't know if it truly was the scepter that spoke to him or his own mind. But he couldn't bear the thought of leaving the scepter behind.

Holding the scepter out in front of him, he placed a palm against each end. The glass orbs felt cool on his skin. He squeezed, and the scepter collapsed on itself. Shortly the scepter reduced in size until it fit nicely in the palm of his hand—or in an inside pocket of his jacket.

Whistling a tune he had heard at an inn in Alaris, he grabbed a brimmed hat off the side of the saddlebag, bade his dragon goodbye for the time being, and began walking toward the nearest town.

* * *

An hour later, Roland entered the outskirts of a typical fishing village. A cool wind brought the salty air to his nostrils, and his nose twitched. Having grown up in landlocked Alaris his entire life, he had not seen much of the sea other than a few visits to Lor'l, the capital of Elvyn—which sat on the opposite shore of the continent.

Pulling his coat tighter around him, he wasn't sure he liked the sea much this time of year. Up ahead of him, near the docks, he saw a gathering of men. Some seemed to be arguing. He walked up slowly. A few people turned to look at him and gave him strange looks, but Roland only surmised it was because he wasn't recognized in the area—and looking around realized his hat didn't really fit the décor of the fishing village. Most of the fisherman had woolen caps pulled tightly over their heads.

Besides initial looks, the people didn't seem to care enough to look at him again. So he removed his hat and moved in closer to see what was going on. Standing next to a two-mast ship with the flag of North Solshi was a middle-aged man in an official uniform.

"This is the second delay," the man said, his cheeks ruddy and his jowls shaking with frustration. "Queen Esmaralda wants her taxes. They were due months ago."

Roland new North Solshi had a newly crowned queen. The king had recently fallen prey to an overambitious general and had had to step down to save face. He had abdicated the throne to his daughter, Esmaralda. It was rumored she was taking a firm hand with her people and trying to prove herself as a capable ruler in her own right.

"The fish were scarce this fall, Commander Luis. Storms kept driving them farther out to sea," said an older man with a white bushy beard and black cap. A black wool coat didn't hide the fact that he was as thin as a rail.

"The queen is tired of excuses, Henry." Luis spoke firmly but his shoulders dropped a bit. "You know how hard she can be. I'm just doing my job. Villages up and down the coast continue to give me the same excuses. I have to bring something back or… "

"Or what?" said a younger man, stepping forward. "Or she'll come here herself?" He laughed. "I doubt that very much. We can't give what we don't have."

"I don't know what she'll do," Luis said. "And I don't want to find out. Now give me something, or I take some of the children back with me."

"What?" screamed out a lady off to Roland's side. "You can't take the children."

Luis spread his hands out to the side. "They will be taken care of in the castle. They'll be servants for Her Highness. It might be better this way."

"How is it better to lose our children?" Henry asked. "The answer is no."

A half a dozen men suddenly appeared behind Luis. They carried long swords, and who knew how many knives lay hidden within their uniforms.

"This will not solve anything," Henry said.

"Then give me something," Luis pleaded for what looked to be the last time. The soldiers with him moved in closer.

Roland pushed through the crowd, collecting dirty looks as he did so. He pulled one of the pouches of money from his belt and thrust his hand inside. "Will this do?" He held open a hand in front of Commander Luis.

He looked up at Roland, then over to Henry and the rest of the crowd. "Who are you?"

"Just someone who wants to help." Roland kept his hand out. In it sat a dozen large coins of pure gold. "Is this enough?"

Luis looked down at Roland's hand and laughed. "Son, that will be more than enough."

Roland emptied the contents of his palm into the commander's hand.

The commander saluted, then motioned for his men to follow him to their boat.

Henry and the others crowded around Roland.

"Thank you, young man," said a woman.

"What is your name?" asked Henry.

"Where did you come from?" asked another.

Roland just laughed. "Just consider me a good neighbor looking out for your best interests. My name is Roland."

The crowd cheered and slapped him on the back.

"You're welcome here anytime," said one of the women. "Have you met my daughter?" She shoved a young, dark-haired girl about Alli's age in front of Roland.

"Join us for a meal," motioned Henry, and Roland followed.

He smiled. *Step one, done.*

CHAPTER EIGHTEEN

Bakari led his group east across North Solshi, crossing the Mahli River two days later. It had taken them some time finding the best place to cross. In the end they had used their magic to fell some trees and move them across the river, forming a crude bridge. Coaxing the Cremelinos across had been the hardest part, but by sunset they had made camp on the Alaris side of the river along the edge of the Northern Forest.

Liam built a fire, while Jaimon and Gabby caught fish. Bakari brushed down the horses and fed them oats they had purchased earlier that day from a rancher in a small village.

They were much nearer to Elvyn, and Bakari felt an increase of excitement growing inside, followed by trepidation. Kharlia would be there. Just the thought of seeing her again brought a smile to his face.

"What's so amusing over there, Dragon King?" Liam called over the fire. "Cremelinos entertaining you?"

"No, just thinking of Elvyn," Bakari said.

Liam laughed. "Or a certain young woman there, maybe?"

"Liam!" Bakari felt his face flush.

He finished with the horses and joined Liam by the fire. He put his hands out in front of him to warm them.

"I've only met her twice," Liam continued, "but from what I can see you should be excited to get to Elvyn."

"But it's been awhile, and, well, you know," Bakari stumbled on his words.

"Hey, I'm obviously no expert on these things," Liam said. "Girls never pay me much attention, but that girl really likes you."

"You think so?" Bakari felt like an idiot grinning, but he couldn't help it. "But I lost the dragons, war is coming again, and… "

"And she liked you before you were the Dragon King, from what I recall."

"Yes." Bakari's eyes brightened. "Yes, she did. We met when she helped me cure poison that had been given to our last Chief Judge, Daymian Khourri."

"She saved Roland's life once; maybe she can get through to him."

"Maybe who can get through to Roland?" said Gabby as she and Jaimon joined them at the fire with a string full of fish.

"Kharlia, the healer," Liam answered.

"Mmm," Gabby said. "Someone had better get through to him. That scepter he has is dangerous."

"How so?" Bakari asked.

"It is one of the most powerful dragon artifacts ever created. It gives the user the power to unify, but its pull is strong, and only the most powerful can withstand being overcome by its hold. In legend, the golden scepter is tied to the golden dragon—their goal is the same; to make someone the most powerful wizard in the land and to rule everyone under a banner of unification."

"That surely fits Roland's goals," Bakari mumbled, then perked up. "But isn't that what being the Dragon King was, also? I became high king over all the lands."

"It's not the same," Liam said. "The prophecies of the dragon riders and dragon kings are fulfilled when peace is once again established in the land. You did not take power from others; you just helped to keep them safe."

"Liam's right," Gabby continued. "A wizard under the influence of the scepter wants total control and dominion."

"Then we need to stop him." Jaimon turned the fish on a spit he had built over the fire. "That's our job as dragon riders, isn't it?"

"Yes, it is," Bakari said. "But first we need to get our dragons back. Speaking of dragons, what's in that sack of yours, Jaimon? We've been riding so hard the last two days we haven't heard your entire story."

Jaimon handed the roasted fish to each one of them and then, after setting his down on a clean log to cool, reached back behind him and dragged the bag over. He proceeded to dump the contents out in front of them on the ground.

At least a dozen artifacts tumbled out of the bag. Some were the size of a fingernail, while the largest was a bit bigger than Bakari's hand. A few were carvings of dragons, and one was only a dragon head. One looked to be some type of fingerless glove, another, a necklace, and one looked very similar to the ring Gabby had given to Bakari.

Bakari stretched his hand out, and it brushed against the glove.

"No," Gabby jumped up. "Don't touch anything!"

But Bakari was already feeling its affects. Made of faded brown leather, the glove appeared to slip over the palm of his hand and then down a few inches past the wrist. He slid it on without thinking.

Whispers from long ago flashed through his mind. Creatures of magic popped in and out while a surge of power filled his soul. He found himself standing on the edge of the magic stream but didn't dare go in any farther. He had never fully realized the reservoir of power that flowed throughout the world. There were pinpricks of light, almost like he had seen on the dragon board, but these pulsed in and out.

Remembering his past times in the magic stream, he knew the pinpricks of lights were wizards all over the continent. If he ventured in he knew he would be able to discern individuals, but without the power of his dragon he might become lost. Staring out into the never-ending grayness, he suddenly became aware of lines crisscrossing and connecting the wizards together. Each of these lines ran to other flashes of light, some bigger, some smaller. These did look like the ones he had seen on the board and had represented the dragons and the Cremelinos.

Upon further inspection, he could tell the difference. For one, there were more Cremelinos than dragons. He could discern the four dragons all clustered together. He gazed around for Roland's dragon but couldn't find him. *Strange.*

After looking for a while, he realized there was another type of light. This one had a reddish hue, and in the vast expanse of his vision there were very few of them. What could they be?

There are more creatures of magic in your world, Dragon King. It was the voice of Flash, the Cremelino he had been riding.

Who are they? Bakari asked.

It is not time yet, Dragon King. Flash continued speaking. *Stay focused and pay attention. The magic of the spirit is the power to bind.*

Bakari looked around him again, trying to figure out what the Cremelino meant. But the voice faded from his mind.

Suddenly, he felt the evidence of another presence. One he had felt before.

To the east, the female voice said. *They travel east. I can sense them now through the dragon.*

Delia! Bakari knew that voice.

Find them! Delia commanded.

"Bakari!" another voice called. But this one was closer and more real.

"Dragon King," said another voice.

Bakari felt someone shaking him. He tried to push it away, but eventually his eyes opened. Liam sat on his knees in from of him, concern splayed across his features.

"What happened?" Liam asked. "Are you all right? Your eyes, they are… so blue."

Bakari knew that the whites of his eyes turned blue when he possessed a large amount of power. He had always thought it was in response to the powers of the dragon, but now he wondered if it was the…

The power of the spirit, Dragon King. Flash interrupted his thoughts. *That is what you felt.*

Bakari would think about that later. For now, he swiftly pulled the glove off. "Put them away. All of them."

"What's the matter?" Gabby asked.

"Jaimon, put them away now." Bakari jumped up and with his cloak began gathering up the artifacts and pushing them back into Jaimon's bag.

Jaimon complied, and soon all the artifacts were closed up once again in the bag.

"What's wrong, Bakari?" Gabby asked.

"Did you feel it?" Bakari asked.

Gabby shook her head.

"Feel what?" Liam returned to his sitting position next to Bakari. "You frightened me. Your eyes were closed, and you were mumbling something. We couldn't awaken you."

Bakari looked at Jaimon for a moment.

Jaimon only shrugged and looked down in a bit of disgust. "Don't look at me. You know I can't feel magic."

"Jaimon," Gabby pleaded. "Don't start that again."

Jaimon huffed but stayed quiet.

"It was Delia," Bakari stood up and waved his arms around. "She knows where we are."

"How?" Gabby asked.

"The artifacts," Bakari said. "Somehow with her connection with the dragons she can sense the artifacts."

Liam let out a long sigh and glanced around the dark night and then into the fullness of the forest in front of them. "We could move deeper into the forest."

They all looked at Bakari, awaiting his answer. He didn't want to travel farther that night, but it was the right thing to do. "They can find us quickly on the dragons. You're right, though, we should break camp and move farther into the forest. Maybe even travel all night and then rest in the morning somewhere out of sight."

There was no argument from the group. Though Bakari could tell they were tired, they quickly gulped down their remaining food, gathered their gear, and put out the small fire.

Soon they were back on their Cremelinos and heading east, deeper and deeper into the northern forest. Bakari knew the Mahli Mountains were directly north of them now. Thoughts of them brought back thoughts of home. *How are my people doing without me?* Bakari smiled at the thought, and a jolt of excitement filled him. They were his people, and it was his duty to keep them safe.

Even on the sturdy and quick Cremelino horses, the going was slower than Bakari would have hoped. Even in the wintertime the forest was thick—trees growing as big around as four or five men standing with arms outstretched. The muddy ground slowed their travel, and at some point during the night it started raining.

The four continued to push forward. Leaning over on their horses and pulling cloaks over their heads did little to alleviate the misery of it all. Early in the morning they crossed over a road that led from Alaris through a narrow opening in the Mahli Mountains and up into Mahli itself. At that time of day no one was on the road—a fact that the weary and cold travelers did not miss.

"We'll ride until daybreak and then find a cave or copse of trees to hide in," Bakari said from the front horse. He had taken over the lead from Liam now that they were heading toward the Elves.

The rest only nodded and trudged onward.

Bakari soon noticed a lightening to the air around them. The rain had reduced to a mere drizzle. He sat up straighter in his saddle and began looking around for a place to hide and dry out.

The horses seemed to know the direction to stay in as they plugged along without Bakari paying much attention.

Without warning, three men jumped out in front of them. Two had lighter skin, like most in Alaris, but one had dark skin, similar to Bakari's own. Bakari opened his mouth to say something when the lead man put a finger to his lips.

Behind them there was a rustling in the trees. When Bakari tried to turn around, a sack was pulled down over his head. He heard Gabby cry out, followed by grunts and yells from Jaimon and Liam.

"Silence," a voice said close by. "We will not harm you."

"Who are you?" Bakari whispered through the burlap sack.

A large growl sounded to their right, followed by a larger crashing through the bush.

"Let's go," said a man sternly, and Bakari felt his Cremelino being led forward. *It's all right, Dragon King. Trust them.*

Nice for you to say, since you can still see, Bakari snapped back at the Cremelino voice in his head.

A light chuckled sounded deep in his mind.

It was hard to trust someone who put a sack over your head. He heard the sounds of fighting and more growling and the roars of some type of beast, but Bakari continued to be led through the forest. After what seemed like another hour they stopped.

The sack was removed from his head, and he glanced around. His companions looked around also and with nods of their heads signaled that they were all right. Bakari looked in front of him and saw the early morning outlines of a village set up against a hill.

Bakari pulled up every map he knew about in his mind but couldn't figure out what town this might be. As they moved forward and the sun began to rise he realized the town was much bigger than he had first thought.

"Where are we?" Liam asked no one in particular. "Do you know who you have here?"

The dark-skinned man who led them turned around. "The Baron has ordered the whereabouts of our city kept hidden"

"This is the Dragon King you have captured," Liam said. "We are all wizards and could take down this village in a matter of moments."

The men who had captured them only smiled. The leader bowed to Bakari and moved a hand out in front of him, sweeping across the view of the village.

"We most certainly know who we have here. Dragon King Bakari, welcome to Hillside, the home of your birth."

CHAPTER NINETEEN

Roland ate his evening meal surrounded by fishermen who continued to toast to his good health. He had saved the small village from certain devastation—either to the losing of its children or to the wrath of Queen Esmaralda.

Rather than sleeping in the village that night, he slipped out and hurried back to where Orelia was waiting for him. With only a few minutes in the sky they covered a dozen miles and came to another fishing village, landing once again a few miles from the city.

First thing in the morning, Roland sauntered into the town and went to a tailor and purchased a different change of clothes and a wool cap to pull over his blond locks. Walking down to the docks, he noticed a few boats returning from a night run and others readying to go out at the next high tide.

As Roland expected, very soon the same official ship came into view. The water wasn't as deep at the shore here, so the ship anchored out a ways and let down a rowboat, in which the commander and a few men rowed in.

Roland hid at the back of the group once again and listened to a similar conversation from the day before. This village was quite a bit larger than the last, and Commander Luis looked a little more concerned for his safety as the crowd grew larger.

Arguing quickly broke out as the commander once again demanded the taxes to be paid.

"Tell the queen if she wants her taxes she can come and get them herself," said a robust man with tanned skin and graying hair. "We can't feed our families after paying her."

The crowd cheered the man, and the commander took a few steps back. He put his hands up in the air. "Now, Ricco, you know I'm just doing what I've been told to do."

"You're just a weasel, Luis," spat a woman twice Roland's age. She was thin and had a dirty apron tied around her waist. "You sold out your own people. What would your mother say, God bless her soul, working for the queen like you do and stealing our money?"

Luis's face turned red, and he floundered for what to say. "I have to feed my children too!" he finally spat out.

Roland began to make his way through the crowd. "What if the people had food and could pay their taxes, would that make everyone happy?"

The crowd turned and looked his way.

"Who are you?" asked Ricco.

Roland spread his hands to either side. "Just a man who wants to help." He turned to the commander. "The queen has storage barns somewhere, doesn't she?"

Luis looked at Roland carefully, but with the hat on and different clothes, Roland wasn't sure he recognized him.

"Well, yes," Luis stammered. "She has stores of food in case of an emergency."

Roland walked up and put his arm around the man. "Well, I would say the fishermen starving and not being able to pay their taxes would qualify as an emergency, wouldn't you?"

The crowd's voices rose as they talked among themselves.

The commander turned his head and looked at Roland. "I just can't take food from the barns. They're inland from here, and I'm on a ship as you can see."

Roland pulled the man in tighter and spoke softly. "Look, Commander, I'm trying to save you from a riot here. How would that look to your queen? If I get the people their food by tomorrow, can you wait a day to be paid?"

Luis shrugged his shoulders. "I guess I could. But how are you going to get the food?"

"You just leave that to me," Roland smiled. Then he turned to the crowd and quieted them down. "The commander has promised me that you will have food within a day. If you have enough food to feed your families, can you pay your taxes to the good man?"

Ricco thought for a moment and looked around. "Seems fair enough, but only the same amount of taxes that were due last year, not the increased amount."

The commander started to protest, but Roland put a hand up to stop him. "Sounds fair to me." He opened his pouch and poured out a few pieces of gold and handed them to the commander. "This should make up for the difference."

"You!" Luis said.

The man had recognized him now. Roland laughed and pulled the cap off his head.

"What's your name?" asked Ricco.

"Roland, sir. My name is Roland. And I promise you some food by tonight."

* * *

A few hours later Roland found himself once again flying on the back of his golden dragon. He was almost giddy with excitement. He loved seeing the looks on the villagers' faces when he made the deal with the commander and offered to pay for the difference in taxes. What was a few gold coins to him? He had kingdoms of treasuries he could now use.

Flying farther inland into the grassy heartland of North Solshi, he spotted Valencia, a good-sized city in which he was told much of the queen's food reserves were housed. Without any hills close by, Roland used the invisibility spell to mask Orelia's arrival. He landed a half mile away from the main road that led from Raleez, the capital city.

He grabbed a change of clothes he had purchased earlier. This outfit would mark him as more prosperous, but hopefully not call any undue attention to him until the time was right. He looked longingly at his golden cloak and fingered the smooth silk in his fingers for a moment before pushing it down in the bag. Making sure he had his sword and scepter, he let Orelia go back in the air. He didn't know if his dragon ate or not, and he didn't want to face what it meant if she didn't.

Roland moved out from behind the trees and joined some noon-time travelers walking toward the city. The gates stood impressively high.

"Quite a sight, isn't it?" Roland came up behind a family of travelers.

The man who walked beside a woman on horseback—Roland supposed it was his wife—turned toward Roland. Two smaller children huddled closer around their father as he looked Roland up and down, trying to determine his intentions.

"First time here," Roland said truthfully. "That gate is mighty impressive. Must be a great city to be guarded so well."

The man puffed his chest out just a bit farther. "Well, traveler, Valencia is renowned for its stores of grain and textiles."

Roland smiled broadly and winked at the younger children. "You have fine-looking children, sir. I see they get their beauty from their mother." Roland spread his hands out in front of him and chuckled. "No offense to you, sir." He gave a smile and short bow to the woman on the horse. She blushed slightly at the compliment.

"My wife is the beauty and the talent of the family," the man said. "We just got back from selling our wares in Raleez. My wife makes the finest and most colorful clothes." The man's demeanor dropped a bit. "Though prices are not what they used to be."

Roland shook his head in sympathy. "Troubles everywhere, it seems," he said softly.

"Aye," the man said, leaning closer to Roland. "The queen is making things difficult these days."

Roland looked around conspiratorially. "I understand." After a moment of silence, he put his hand forward to the man. "My name is Roland, by the way."

"Carlos," the man said, "and my wife, Marietta, and my children, Cecilia and Joca."

Roland nodded to all of them. The children looked to be around nine or ten, with only a year or so separating them.

They soon approached the city gates, and Roland looked up in mock wonder. He smiled broadly at the guards as they waved the family through.

"It was nice talking to you, Carlos." Roland took a few steps away. "Take care of that fine family of yours. I have some business to attend to."

"What type of business, if I may ask?" Carlos left his wife and children and walked closer to Roland.

"I need to procure some grain for some of the fishing villages," Roland said.

Carlos frowned. "The grain store here isn't for sale. It belongs to the queen. Her men guard it carefully."

"There are always ways." Roland lowered his voice. "Who controls the city?"

Carlos looked around, then back to Roland. "Well, the governor is the queen's ruler here, but the power really resides in the hands of the textile guild."

Roland almost laughed at how easy it seemed to be. He wondered if it was his training as a councilor wizard or just his own charm.

Or the help I am giving you, came a voice that made Roland jump.

"You all right there, Roland?" Carlos gave him a worried look. "Did I say something wrong?"

"Oh no, Carlos," Roland said with a calm smile. *Don't do that to me*, he said to the voice in his head—dragon or scepter, he wasn't always sure. The voices—male and female—seemed to blend together sometimes. "Would you be able to introduce me to this guild?"

"Carlos, we need to get home," Marietta called out from atop the horse. "My parents will be expecting news from Raleez."

Carlos looked at her, then turned back to Roland with a smile. "You seem like a legitimate fellow. Why don't you come home with us?"

Roland shook his head. "I have only a few hours to secure my business."

"But this is business," Carlos said with a wide smile. "My wife's father is the head of the guild."

Roland actually laughed at his good luck.

Or my ability to lead you, young wizard.

Roland followed Carlos and his family to their home. As he walked he wondered to himself how much of what was happening was really his doing, or if he was being manipulated and pulled along by something larger. The thought to unify continually pounded in the back of his head. Oh, he would use the scepter and dragon to their fullest promise, but in the end he would make sure he was still his own man—a ruler loved by all, but one who made his own choices.

As they walked through the rather substantial city they moved into an area with nicer and larger homes. Two- and three-story brick and stone buildings sat back a few dozen feet from the front of the widening street. Benches sat along the way, and front yards were enclosed by decorative fences. He imagined flowers filling the yards in the spring. Finally they turned a corner and went down a back alley to some stables.

After helping his wife dismount, Carlos led his family and Roland into the back of a nice brick home. White shutters sat to either side of many windows.

"You've done well for yourself, it seems." Roland clapped Carlos on the back.

"It's really my wife's designs," Carlos said as they stepped through the door.

Roland took a quick look around. It was clean and well-furnished by any standard. Neat piles of cloth and others of newly made pants, shirts, and cloaks sat around the house. Roland walked to one and fingered the material. It was the softest material he had ever felt.

He took a shirt from the pile and held it up. The cut was different than he had seen before. The bright fabric seemed to taper in at the sides and then flare out a bit at the bottom. "Exquisite!"

"But not selling as well in Raleez since the queen has increased the taxes on anything manufactured outside of Raleez and brought into the city," Carlos said.

"That seems unfair to you," Roland said.

"It is very unfair," said a deep voice coming in to the room.

"Grandpapa!" shouted the kids and crowded around the newcomer. Marietta walked over and gave the man—obviously her father—a peck on the cheek.

"Roland," Carlos said, "meet Tavio, my father-in-law and head of the textiles guild."

The man was a bit shorter than Roland and a little stockier. His dark hair was graying at the temples, and his brown eyes sparkled with intelligence.

Roland gave his best flourishing bow and upon rising said, "Pleasure to meet you, sir. I hear you are having a problem selling your wares in Raleez. What if I provided a new market for you?"

Tavio's bushy black eyebrows rose, and a few crinkled lines appeared across his forehead. He gave a booming laugh. "Raleez is our largest market. No other city in North or South Solshi could compensate for that."

"What about outside of Solshi?" Roland said and watched the calculations running through the man's mind.

"Let's sit and discuss." Tavio motioned Roland and Carlos into another room with him, while Marietta chased the children upstairs to change out of their travel-stained clothes.

A servant brought them refreshments. After a quick sip, Roland sat back in the plush high-backed chair and looked across a table at Tavio. He said nothing, waiting for the head of the guild to make the first move. It was one of the teachings from his days as an apprentice councilor wizard. Whoever spoke first in these types of situations lost the upper hand.

"What did you have in mind, Roland?" Tavio finally asked.

Roland smiled and leaned forward a bit to show his excitement. "For starters, Alaris and Tillimot."

Tavio's eyes went round, and Carlos sputtered a bit of his drink out in front of him.

"How many pieces?" Tavio asked.

"All of it!" Roland said with a wave of his hand. "I will take all you have in the city within the week; half paid up front, half once it's sold." Roland's mind moved with lightning speed on how he could accomplish this. He found his hand grabbing a hold of the orb on the scepter inside his jacket pocket and felt strength and intelligence racing through his mind.

Seal the deal now, the voice said to him.

But we aren't done negotiating, Roland pushed back. *We need to solidify the terms.*

Unify them. Unify them.

"Do we have a deal?" Roland stood.

Tavio frowned. "Well, it sounds all good and…" he stumbled on his words. "I… I need to have a contract drawn up and bring together the other guild leaders."

Roland drew the scepter out of his jacket and fondled it between his two hands. He pulled out one end, and it became its full length once again. Roland placed one end on the ground, and the other rested under the palm of his right hand.

"It's beautiful!" said Tavio, standing up. The glass scepter reflected the candled lamps of the room and splayed flecks of light around them.

"You are a wizard?" Tavio asked with a raise of his eyebrows.

Unify them.

Roland smiled but didn't answer directly. "Call for a meeting of the guild elders," Roland said. "I will address them all in one hour. Then the deal will be finalized."

Tavio appeared flustered and didn't quite know what to say.

"Now, Tavio," Roland said more firmly. "We must be unified. My offer expires in one hour."

Tavio nodded. "Of course, of course." He motioned for his son-in-law to stand with him. "Gather the guild, Carlos."

"Yes, sir," Carlos turned and quickly left the room.

Tavio stared at Roland for a moment and then tilted his head. "And what do you get out of this deal? Surely the queen and the people of Raleez will be angry to not have our textiles to sell."

Tavio waited Roland out this time. Finally, Roland caved.

"I want access to the food storage silos and barns by tonight," Roland said. "I have a promise to fulfill."

Tavio's eyes went wider than before, and he put a hand out against the wall to steady himself. "The… food stores belong to Queen Esmaralda," he stuttered.

"I know," Roland said with a wide grin. "Won't she be angry!"

Tavio nodded.

"But your city will be rich with my deal."

Again, Tavio could only nod.

CHAPTER TWENTY

Exactly an hour later Roland stood in front of a large room attached to the back of an inn. His stomach rumbled with the smell of stew and fresh bread. About twenty men sat in front of him. Most didn't seem too happy to have been summoned so quickly, but Tavio was the guild head, so they obeyed.

"Men of the textile guild, I must say I am amazed at your styles and colors."

"Who are you, and what do you want?" said an older man from the front. His tanned arms were crossed tightly across his broad chest. A thin mustache sat above his lip.

"Why are we here, Tavio?" shouted out another man from the group.

Roland put up his hand to quiet the group. "If I may… "

"It's not customary to bring strangers in here," said another man. "Maybe he's a spy from the other textile guilds."

"I am not a spy," said Roland, but no one was paying him attention. They were all turned toward Tavio, who seemed to have grayed since Roland had made his offer.

"The queen is giving us enough trouble," shouted a young man directly in front of Roland.

"Now listen here," Roland said, all but unheard in the bedlam of voices. He was getting frustrated. He had to get food back to the fishing village by nightfall. Maybe he should have promised the next day.

Unify them.

Roland grabbed the scepter tightly and took a deep breath. He took it up off the floor a mere inch or two, then slammed it back down. Lines of yellow and gold shot out from it and snaked across the floor. The crowd grew instantly quiet. Everyone sat facing Roland with eyes wide as they watched the last wisps of power fly from the scepter.

"As I was saying," Roland said, offering no explanation for the power of the scepter. "I have offered your guild master a deal of gigantic proportions. I have heard you are having troubles selling your goods in Raleez and have a lucrative solution, but if you would rather bicker, then I will leave and go to another town."

Roland knew they would bite at his offer. How could they not? But he waited for them.

"Continue," Tavio said.

Roland smiled and looked in the eyes of each merchant, then withdrew three pouches from his pocket and dumped them on the table in front of him. Money always worked.

"I am hurt to see you treated so by your queen," Roland began. "The woman who should be protecting you and helping you has turned her back on you."

A few men nodded but had a hard time turning away from the pile of gold in front of them.

"Valencia is the textile capital of North and South Solshi and produces the most beautiful and unique clothing I have seen in the southern kingdoms." Roland built them up and soon had more of them nodding and looking up at him. He had fudged the truth a bit; he had never been to many of the southern kingdoms outside of Alaris and Elvyn.

"You have to feed your families and take care of your city. The queen only cares about her coffers." Roland grew louder. He hoped there were no spies from the queen there—he wasn't quite ready for that confrontation.

"What if you didn't sell any of your wares in Raleez?" Roland asked. "What would happen?"

A middle-aged man stood up. "What do you mean? That's our biggest market."

"Just humor me a moment, what would happen?"

"Well," said the younger man up front, "the queen would not get her taxes, the people of Raleez would not get the clothes they want, and resellers in Raleez wouldn't have anything to sell so they would not have money to buy other goods from the other vendors."

"Chaos," said another man under his breath, "and economic disaster."

"Get on with it," said someone else. "All I hear is a lot of talk. You're wasting my time." He stood up.

"What if I offered you Alaris and Tillimot for a start?" Roland blurted out.

The man paled and lowered himself to his seat, nodding his head for Roland to continue. He pulled out a scroll from a pocket in his jacket—a document he had worked up in the past hour.

"This form authorizes me to sign an exclusive deal for you to sell all your textiles and goods in Alaris and Tillimot. I pay this now," he pointed to the pile of gold, "and the rest when the goods sell. I will pay for an agent in Cassian to keep track of it all. Your fashions and designs will now be the rage of all of the southern kingdoms."

Broad smiles began to cover the men's faces, and one by one they began talking among themselves and discussing the potential market that was now at their disposal.

"Valencia will be rich!" shouted a man from the back.

Roland put the scroll out on the table, where a pen and ink bottle sat, and he motioned them to come forward. One by one they came until only Tavio, the guild master, and Roland himself were left.

Roland looked at the happy crowd. "Congratulations, men, you now control your own destiny. The world is yours, and Valencia will become a center of textile trade for all the southern kingdoms."

The men cheered.

"The queen will no longer control your business," Roland shouted. "But there is one more thing I must ask you tonight before Tavio and I sign the agreement and make it official. I need to get some food from the queen's barns and silos and give to others who are in need of it. The fishermen on the coast have had a difficult time lately and need the food for their families, but the queen won't send it to them. But you men, men of Valencia, have the opportunity to help these poor families eat. What say you?"

As one, some men yelled out, "Tear the barns down!"

"Yes, feed the poor!" came a reply from others.

Roland let the cheers continue for a moment while he had Tavio and then himself sign the agreement. He then handed it to Tavio with a smile.

"Hail, men of Valencia!" Roland called out.

"Hail, Roland," the men echoed, and Roland laughed out loud.

Oh, this felt good.

* * *

Three hours later Roland stood next to a dozen wagons full of grain, potatoes, and other stored vegetables. He instructed men to take them as quickly as they could to the coast, while taking one wagon himself. He did have a promise to keep.

Thousands of townspeople had come outside the city to see what was going on. By now the city of Valencia was well aware of the deal that had been struck with the handsome blond stranger.

As the wagons pulled out one by one, the people cheered. Then Roland stood up on the front seat of his own wagon and waved at the people.

"Good citizens of Valencia. Thank you for your hospitality and kindness. I will always remember you."

The crowd went wild with cheers. A few younger women blew him kisses, and he laughed and waved back. Sitting back down on the wagon bench, he drove the team of horses forward and down the road.

Echoes of "Roland" drifted in the air behind him. *Orelia,* he called out in his mind as he drove off the main road and behind a small group of trees. Soon in the sky above him Orelia materialized and landed in front of the wagon. Roland had to calm the horses a bit. He undid their harnesses and let them go. He had no more use of them.

After tying thick ropes around the wagon, Roland climbed onto Orelia's back and then instructed the great golden dragon to pick up the wagon by the ropes. The cart tilted a bit, and a few vegetables fell out.

"Watch what you're doing!" Roland called out.

You didn't tell me I had to work today, came the reply.

You mean this little wagon is too big for your great, majestic body? Roland retorted.

The dragon let out a chuckle and let out a breath of golden fire.

Roland smiled. Even golden dragons were not immune to his charm and charisma. It was good to know.

Grabbing the ropes in its claws, the golden dragon struggled for a moment more, then lifted the wagon up high in the air. They began their flight back to the coastline as the sun began to set in front of them. Roland wrapped his jacket tighter around him and then remembered a spell he had learned. With the flick of his hand he was riding a thousand feet up, cocooned in a warm air pocket.

The landscape beneath them turned gray with the setting sun. In a matter of hours they came once again to the outside of the fishing town, and Orelia lowered the wagon to the ground. Roland jumped down and ran to the nearest farm he could find. With a few gold pieces he secured the use of two horses. The farmer, with lantern in tow, followed him out to the wagon.

"How'd you get here?"

"A dragon," Roland said.

The man laughed and waved a hand in the air. "No such things."

"You mean you haven't heard of the famed dragon riders?"

"Paw," the farmer said. "Rumors. Heard about dragons at a battle on the border earlier this year, but it's just men spreading stories. I have more wits than to believe that."

Roland chuckled.

After helping Roland hook up the horses the man frowned again. "How did you say you ended up with a wagon out here and no horses?"

"I told you," Roland chuckled.

The farmer seemed not to notice he hadn't got a clear answer. "What have you got there?"

"Food for the village, and more will be coming within the week from Valencia."

The farmer's eyes went wide with surprise. "You're that Roland fellow, aren't you? Been hearing about you."

"Don't believe everything you hear," Roland laughed.

The man nodded and waved at Roland as he moved off with the wagon. The moon shone bright, and in short order Roland came to the town square and stopped.

"Ricco!" he cupped his hand and called out. "Commander Luis!"

A few people out in the evening gave him strange looks. Finally one man stopped in front of Roland.

"You came back," he said with excitement. "I saw you this morning." He went running toward a simple home nearby. "Ricco, come out!"

Finally Ricco did come out. His wife walked next to him. From a nearby inn, Commander Luis also came out to the town square.

Roland hopped down from the wagon, and waved the people's attention to its contents. "Grain and potatoes for everyone!" he called out. "And more will be here from Valencia within the week."

The growing crowd grew quiet. In the back a woman burst out crying and walked forward. She knelt down at Roland's feet, bowing reverently. "You have saved my family, sir."

Another woman came forward, tears streaming down her face, and knelt next to the other woman. Then the men joined in. Soon, more than two dozen villagers knelt in front of Roland.

"Please rise, my friends," Roland said. "I just want to help."

"Hail, Roland! Hail, Roland!"

Ricco stepped forward. "I don't know how we can repay you, kind sir, for what you have done."

"Just seeing your faces is enough," Roland said. It wasn't an insincere compliment. Roland found that he was really enjoying helping them out. "You are my people," he added softly. "Esmaralda doesn't deserve you."

"What was that, sir?" Commander Luis walked up.

"Nothing, Commander," Roland said with a wave of his hand.

The commander grunted and grabbed Roland's arm in his tight grip. "Be careful what you say about Queen Esmaralda."

Roland twisted his arm from the commander. "A queen is only as good as how she treats her people. From what I see here, these people don't want Esmaralda as her queen."

Luis looked shocked at the statement. "That is treason, sir. I could take you in for that."

He took a step forward, and the crowd surged around him.

"I don't think they would like that very much," Roland said, his face growing darker. "Anyway, we all had a deal." He turned to Ricco. "You promised to pay that man your taxes if I brought the food. That, along with what I already gave him, should satisfy the queen."

Ricco nodded, left for a moment, and came back with a bag of coins, which he gave to Commander Luis.

"We are all honorable men here, Commander, aren't we?" Roland said.

"You tread dangerous ground," Luis said. "The queen will not stand for an uprising."

Roland took a step forward and glared hard at the commander. "Then tell your queen, when you see her next, that an uprising indeed is coming. I have done more in one day for this kingdom than the queen has done for anyone under her reign."

Luis took a step back, and a few of his men formed around him. His face turned red, and he shook his fist at Roland. "I will be in Raleez tomorrow morning. She will know about you then."

"I'm counting on it, Commander," Roland said. "I trust you to be honorable in your mention of events here and let her know the state of these people and what I have done to help them."

Luis snorted, then turned and began walking with his men toward their small boat.

"And, Commander," Roland called after him. "Tell her Roland Tyre will see her soon."

CHAPTER TWENTY-ONE

"Dragon king, welcome to Hillside," said a thin man with a stubble of a beard, blond hair, and a ruddy complexion. "I am Baron Curtis Dunst."

"Baron?" Bakari scrunched up his face. "I've never heard of this place or seen it on a map."

"We keep a low profile," the baron said, slapping Bakari on his back. "But I do remember you, Bakari. I was in my mid-teens when your mother took you to the Citadel. You were the last descendant of the ancient dragon king, Zahara."

"My mother?" Bakari glanced around. "Is she still here?" His heart beat with excitement.

The baron shook his head, and his countenance dropped. "I'm sorry. Your mother died a few years after that."

Bakari's gut felt hollow. "And my father?"

"Let's sit down," Baron Dunst said with a gesture toward a large table. "I'm sure you are tired and hungry, and there is much to tell you."

Upon mention of food, Jaimon's stomach growled, and those gathered laughed. Bakari and his party were shown to guest rooms where they could bathe and rest until the mid-day meal was ready.

Soon servants came and escorted Bakari and his group to the dining room. The baron, his wife, Angela, and a young boy about ten joined them at the long table. In quick order, servants brought food to the table. As the food arrived, Bakari introduced his company.

"Where are your dragons?" asked the young boy.

"Thomas, don't pester them," the baroness hushed.

"That is a long story, also," Bakari said with downcast eyes.

Soon plates of food were placed in front of each of them.

"Jaimon!" whispered Gabby under her breath. "Have some manners."

Jaimon looked up from the food he was wolfing down with hardly a breath and blushed. "Sorry."

The baron waved a hand in the air and laughed. "Don't worry, son. Growing young men need food."

Bakari and Liam took that as a sign to start eating, and with a snort from Gabby they all dived in. Roasted chicken with a tangy sauce, fresh bread, and a potato filled Bakari's mouth and eventually his stomach.

After emptying an initial plateful, the three young men finally slowed down. The baron called for more food, and they all smiled, but this time they enjoyed the taste a bit more.

"Dragon King," said the baron, "these must be dire times for you to be roaming this part of the land without your dragons."

"Delia, the new Oracle of Turg, has captured our dragons and one of my riders," Bakari said. "She intends to rule all of the kingdoms."

The baroness coughed loudly, and her husband turned to her. "Are you all right, dear?"

She stood up, and a servant helped her out of the room. "I just need a drink, Curtis. Go on without me," she said between fits of coughing.

The baron watched his wife with concern, then turned to his son. "You may leave, Thomas. Go and find your friends."

The boy smiled and jumped out of his seat. The baron looked at the door his wife had left out of and then back to the group.

"I see your son takes after you with his light hair," Gabby said, watching the young boy run out of the room.

"Ah, yes," the baron said. "His mother died from a grave sickness a few years ago. After the barrier came down last year, Angela arrived. She had gotten lost traveling across Alaris and decided to stay." The baron smiled broadly and blushed. "I'm glad she did."

"Sir, what can you tell me about my home here?" Bakari asked.

"Dragon King," the baron began as he shoved his plate away from him. "Your father was a descendant of Dragon King Zahara, through his son Malik. The story goes that a little over 150 years ago a minor wizard from Mahli by the name of Imari was studying at the Citadel and discovered a plot that the high wizard and king at the time were planning on invading the neighboring kingdoms."

"Rodrick Eckhart," Bakari said.

The baron looked surprised. "Yes, that was the king's name. At that time, Imari was asked by the Dragon King to save his last descendant and keep him safe. He brought the boy and a few other Mahlians here to Hillside, just south of the

Mahli Mountains. They intermarried with us and stayed. Of course, it was shortly after they came that the barrier was erected around Alaris, and they were never able to go back to Mahli. The prophecy of the dragon said that when the need was greatest a new dragon king would emerge and bring peace once again to the land."

The story was interrupted by the baroness returning. She, along with two cooks, brought trays of desserts into the room.

"I'm too full for any more." Gabby waved it away.

"Just a little piece then, my dear." Baroness Angela pushed a plate in front of her.

Gabby tried to give it back, but the baroness was insistent, so Gabby nodded, but didn't lift her fork.

Both Jaimon and Liam looked eager to dive into the sweet-looking chocolate cake. Angela placed a plate in front of Bakari herself and with a smile touched him on the shoulder.

Bakari looked up. "Are you feeling all right?"

Confusion spread across Angela's face.

"The cough from before," Bakari reminded her. The woman seemed to hesitate before she nodded. He noticed beads of sweat at the edges of her forehead. She still didn't look well.

"Oh yes, I'm fine," she said. "Thank you for asking."

The baron reached out and touched his wife's arm. She jumped and pulled it away quickly, then, realizing what she had done, laughed it off. "Maybe I am still not feeling well. If you will excuse me?"

The baron stood, but his wife turned quickly and with the escort of one of the cooks left the room.

Bakari caught Gabby's eye. She was worried about something, but Bakari only nodded for her to eat her cake. She picked up the fork and began to twirl it around while Bakari turned back to the baron.

"So how did I get to the Citadel?" Bakari asked.

"Well, shortly after you were born, your father, the last descendant of the dragon king, was killed hunting, and your mother always worried that something might happen to you. She didn't want to give you up, but after five years, when you began to show signs of remarkable mental abilities, she traveled south and left you at the doorstep of the Citadel. She thought they would be the best ones to care for you—a descendant of the dragon king. Your name, Bakari, means "promised." She had high hopes that you would be the prophesied one."

It was a lot for Bakari to take in. Noticing that Jaimon and Liam had both devoured their cake, Bakari took a few bites while thinking about his parents.

"So for 150 years you have protected the heirs to the Dragon King?" Bakari finally asked. "How does the rest of Alaris not know about you?"

The baron shook his head. "I do not know. Maybe it had something to do with the magic of having the dragon king's descendants here. We have always been a small barony—over 200 years old but with little contact with the outside world, other than a few brief travels for supplies. There is no direct road into our town—only trails—and the people here seem content that way." The baron paused for a moment. "Oh, but I have forgotten. There is a package here for you."

"A package?" Bakari asked.

"Something that Malik brought with him when they escaped from Mahli and that has been handed down from child to child." The baron stood and pursed his lips. "Now, where did we put it?" he said almost to himself. "It was given to my father's care when your father and mother passed away, and then to me when I became baron."

After a moment of thinking, the baron's blue eyes lit up again. "Oh, yes!" he exclaimed. "Follow me."

The four got up from the table and began to follow, but a loud crash behind Bakari made him turn around.

"Liam!" he raced back to his friend. "Are you all right?"

Liam's face was flushed with frustration. "Stupid foot again."

Bakari's heart lurched for his friend. They needed to get their dragons back! He and Jaimon helped Liam to his feet. Then the four followed the baron more slowly. They left the building and took a small pathway up the hill away from the village.

Finally Bakari spotted a lone building amongst the trees. He looked back and found Gabby directly behind him, but Jaimon and Liam were farther back. They stood next to a tree and held their stomachs.

Gabby laughed. "I told you not to eat so much," she scolded them. "And two helpings of cake? What were you thinking?"

Bakari smiled but noticed that he also was beginning to feel the effects of the cake, though he had eaten only one piece.

The baron knocked on an old wooden door of the small home, and soon it swung open. A very dark--skinned and thin elderly man opened it. A look of shock and surprise filled his wrinkled face. "I have seen the salvation of the land," the man said, falling to his knees. "My eyes behold the prophesied one," he looked up with tears streaming down his face. "It is true. Hail the Dragon King."

Bakari was touched by the old man's sentiments and reached out his hand to lift him back to his feet. "No need to bow to me, sir."

"Auni," the baron said. "I have come for the package. You still have it, don't you?"

The man's brown eyes went wide. "Oh, yes." He turned back into the home.

The baron turned to Bakari. "Auni is your great uncle, Bakari. He is a descendant from those who left Mahli with your ancestor."

"Uncle?" Bakari's heart surged. He had never had family before.

Auni came back and thrust a burlap-wrapped package into Bakari's hands. "This is yours. It was an artifact Malik had in his possession when he arrived in Hillside. No one knows what it does or if it means anything." The man's eyes sparkled with almost a boyish excitement.

Bakari turned it over in his hands, then he wiped water from his eyes. A soft groan came from behind him, and he looked back. Liam sat on a rock and wasn't looking well. Jaimon tried to comfort him, looking better than Liam, but still not well.

A sudden rumble split Bakari's insides, and he leaned over with a cramp.

"Bakari," Gabby stepped forward and took his arm. "What's wrong?"

"Cramps," Bakari said and then stood back up. "I'm sure it's just too much food."

The baron looked concerned but motioned to the package. "Open it, Dragon King. Maybe it's something that can help you."

Bakari pushed the pain away and slowly unwrapped the package, wondering what it could be. It didn't feel like a book. It was soft inside. Unwrapping three layers, he finally took out the item.

Gabby gasped beside him, and Jaimon took a few steps forward to see.

"It's one of the artifacts," Gabby said.

"It looks like the one I have," Jaimon said, then winced in pain but stayed standing.

Bakari turned it over in his hand. It was an identical match to the glove Jaimon had in his bag. Without thinking, Bakari slid a hand inside it and was transferred once again to the edge of the magic stream. Two bright lights, representing the Cremelinos, stood near him, and he could feel the wizarding powers of Gabby and Liam next to him. But then there was something else. Something not so good.

Bakari's stomach knotted up again, and his head began to throb. He moved to take off the glove—he didn't want to alert Delia again of their presence. As he began to slide it off he noticed another bright spot at the edge of the magic stream. It was far, far away to the south. He looked more carefully, but as he did so he felt his legs buckle.

"Bakari!" Gabby yelled out as he fell to the ground.

"Dragon King!" both the baron and Auni said with concern.

Bakari felt someone remove the glove from his hand.

Liam cried out and fell over. Jaimon moved over to him but screamed out in pain himself. Blackness filled Bakari's vision, and he struggled to stay conscious.

"Help," the baron cried out. "I need help!"

Bakari heard some distant shouts but found it hard to concentrate. Pain seemed to wrack his entire body. Gabby leaned down next to him and tried to talk to him, but her voice went in and out. Suddenly the voice of Flash, the Cremelino, broke through.

Dragon King, beware. There is evil here in Hillside.

Bakari's mind cleared for a moment as he remembered all that had happened since they had arrived—all in two beats of his heart. Gabby. Gabby was fine. Why was that?

"The cake," he mumbled out loud.

"What?" Gabby leaned down closer to him.

He wanted to tell her more but couldn't form the words. His brain wasn't working clearly. He fought against what was happening. His mind was the strongest part of him. He tried a myriad of spells, but to no avail. They all seemed to slip away like oil on water.

Poison. Bakari tried to make his mouth work. "Cake… poison… "

It was all Bakari could manage to say before he blacked out.

CHAPTER TWENTY-TWO

Alli sat looking out a third-story window of the castle in Thera. The sky was gray, and she could see the wind whipping up old leaves and litter in the streets beyond. Her life seemed like she was living in a daze all the time. She couldn't quite figure things out, and it bothered her.

The door behind her opened, and Alli turned around. In walked her new master, Delia. She never knocked. Going down automatically to her knees, Alli stared at the floor.

"Master, what can I do for you?" Alli asked Delia. She always felt inadequate around the woman. With long, flowing brown hair, and a commanding and powerful air, the new Oracle of Turg made Alli feel so plain and weak in her presence.

"Alli, get up." A frown crossed Delia's face. "Have some dignity. You are one of my dragon riders, after all."

"Yes, master." Alli stood up, hands behind her back, and awaited instructions.

"How is your dragon today?" Delia asked.

Alli shrugged. "Fine, I suppose. She doesn't speak to me much."

"You need to be more firm with her," Delia said. "Remember, you are the dragon rider—her master. She needs to know that. The bond is yours to command."

"Yes, master," Alli said automatically.

A quick slap stung Alli's face as her head snapped to the side.

Delia's mouth grew tight. "I almost wish you were like you were before. You are pathetic, Alli. Really, you are. When Constantine said he could break you, I had no idea you would turn into such a feeble mind."

"I'm sorry, master," Alli said. Her cheek stung with the slap, but she resisted the urge to rub her hand over it. "I don't understand what you mean, but I will do better for you. What would you like me to do?"

Delia grunted and threw her hands up in the air. "And to think you were once one of the most highly regarded wizards in the southern kingdom."

"Me?"

Delia laughed this time. "Do you really not remember anything, Alli?"

Alli thought hard for a moment, but like always when trying to think of her past, it made her head pound with pain. "I remember fighting in the arena and the doctor healing me each time I lost. I remember my master giving me more of my powers."

"But nothing before that?"

Alli knew there must be something before—there had to be. Some of the people that had come to the coliseum on the day of the new Oracle's coronation had seemed to know her. A man Delia said used to be the dragon king had called out to her—had even tried to command her. And the man in the golden cape wanted to take her away. Alli closed her eyes and shook her head. "Nothing, but a headache."

"Very well," Delia said. "No matter. We will just have to start from scratch. You are a dragon rider, correct?"

Alli did perk up at that. Flying on top of her dragon, Miriel, was the most amazing thing ever. High up in the sky, floating on the wind, she felt the most free. Her thinking was more clear, and she felt the bond with her dragon—but something wasn't right with it. She didn't know what it was supposed to feel like, but something told her it shouldn't be so hard to connect with Miriel.

"Yes, master, I am a dragon rider," Alli said.

"And do you know what dragon riders do?" Delia asked.

"They keep peace in the land."

"Right," Delia said with a smile.

Alli relaxed. She was pleasing her master with her answers.

"There are those who are trying to take away that peace, Alli," Delia continued. "I need you to be ready to fight them and to help me establish peace in the land once again. Can you do that for me?"

A rush of adrenaline filled her and the power inside pulsed. She knew what kind of fighter she was. She had beaten the champion at the coronation and was the best fighter in Turg. "I can fight."

"Good. Good," Delia purred. "But before we fight I need you to do something for me."

"Anything, master," Alli said. She felt something exciting coming on. Something that she could do to show her new master the type of person she could be. She had disappointed Delia with her earlier answers and didn't know why. But she could do better. She *would* do better!

"I need you to go to Raleez and to make friends with Queen Esmaralda there," Delia said. "We women need to stick together in this. She is a new queen and will need my guidance. Offer her protection and an alliance with me, the Dragon Queen."

Alli smiled at the challenge. "I can do that."

"And take your dragon with you," Delia said. "That should help convince them."

Alli nodded as she thought about flying on her dragon again.

"This is a test, Alli. Don't fail me."

Alli felt the threat in Delia's words and lowered her head. "I will not fail you, master. You can count on me!"

"Wonderful!" Delia said with a clap of her hands. "Our relationship has really taken a turn for the better. Maybe I do like you this way, after all. Much more easy to control."

"Yes, master," Alli said. "When would you like me to leave?"

"Soon," Delia said. "Why don't you go to the practice yard? You could teach the prince of Khazer some fighting skills. The man has been too pampered. You need to teach him how to be a true dragon rider."

Alli bowed deeply. "I would enjoy that." A small smile crept across her face. She loved fighting.

Delia turned and headed back to the door. Before exiting, she turned back around and with a smirk said, "Just don't hurt him too badly. I do need him for a bit longer to bring Khazer fully into my fold."

Alli nodded as the woman walked out and closed the door behind her. Finally she had something to do. Sitting in the castle for the last two days had been boring. Whether she remembered her past life or not, she knew she didn't like to just stand around doing nothing. Sparring with the prince of Khazer could be a pleasant diversion before she went off on her master's bidding to Solshi.

She reached out in her mind for her dragon. *Miriel?*

She knew the bond was there, could feel it, but her dragon was silent once again. She ground her teeth in frustration. She knew enough to know that a dragon rider's bond included communication with her dragon. *I am the master; you will listen to me!*

Again, nothing.

Alli grabbed her sword and fighting gear and stomped down to the training yard. A dozen men and less than a handful of women were sparring with each other. Prince Ender of Khazer stood off to one side, taking a drink from a servant. He looked to be twenty years old or so. His skin was darker than those in Turg. He saw her watching him and waved. A gracious smile ran across his thin lips as his brown eyes glanced up and down Alli's body.

As she came closer to the prince she bowed to him, not knowing the protocol between them.

"No need for that," Ender spoke with an accent that Alli was not sure she had heard before. "We are both dragon riders."

"But you are also a prince," Alli said.

Ender appeared uncomfortable for a moment but then smiled again. "I would rather be a dragon rider than a prince in Khazer. What can you tell me about the dragons and their powers? Are there more of them?"

For some reason Alli felt uncomfortable about his line of questioning and instead got straight to the point. "Master Delia wanted me to teach you a few things." She was uncomfortable talking about anything else.

Ender squinted his eyes at her. "All business, I see." He nodded and gave the cup back to the servant. "You are an interesting person, Alli, and very powerful if the rumors I hear about you are true."

"The Dragon Queen said you've been pampered in Jor." Alli went back to their task at hand as they walked to a corner of the practice yard.

"Oh she did, huh?" Ender laughed, but his eyes hardened. "Let's see about that."

Both dragon riders assumed a fighting stance, swords out in front, facing one another. Suddenly Ender lunged forward. He was quick, but Alli was ready—more than ready. With a swift sidestep, Ender fell past Alli. She turned and kicked him hard in the rear, sending him flying to the ground.

With a grunt he stood back up. Now he wore a mask of determination and this time circled around her, trying to find a weakness. Alli relaxed her muscles and went into fighting mode. She didn't have a weakness.

Without warning, she brought her sword around in a large arc and tapped the side of Ender's shoulder. He frowned and straightened up again.

"You're holding yourself too tight," Alli said. "Loosen up."

She moved in again and tapped his knee and side, then stepped around him and pushed him once again to the ground. This was all too easy. Something about the way Ender moved and fought didn't make any sense.

"Are you sure you've actually ever fought before?" Alli frowned down at Ender. "I would have thought a prince to have more training."

Anger mixed with fear flashed across Ender's eyes as he stood back up and resumed his fighting stance.

Taking a deep breath, Alli relaxed even more. This is where she felt the most clear-headed. Fighting was natural for her. Looking Ender straight in the eyes, she saw a flicker of movement in them. Instead of engaging him, which she could have done, she took three steps back. When Ender came in for her, she wasn't there.

Once he turned to find her, she took two steps and leaped into the air, summersaulting over his head and landing behind him.

"You cheated!" Ender said. Even in the cool winter air, sweat beaded his forehead.

"I did not," Alli said.

"You used magic," Ender argued. "No one can jump like that."

"It's not cheating to use all the weapons and power at your disposal," Alli said. After being without her powers for the first little while with Constantine she relished the rush it now gave her. She didn't blame Constantine. He had helped her to become who she was. It had taught her to hone her other skills even further and not to rely on her powers. But sometimes it was hard to separate one from another.

As if in response to her thoughts, Ender brought his other hand up in front of him and pushed a force of air toward Alli. At the last possible moment she realized what he had done and ducked low to the ground, then swiped a leg out and hooked the prince by the ankles. He fell hard, and Alli heard his head smack the dirt.

Standing back up she walked over to him. His eyes were closed. Leaning down, she shook him a few times. "Ender. Ender."

Slowly he opened his eyes and with a croak said, "You're a wicked fighter. Everything they say about you must be true."

There it was again—a reference to her past. It seemed everyone around her knew more about her than she did. "Are people talking about me behind my back?" Alli ground her teeth. "What are they saying?"

Ender stumbled on his words for a bit as if trying to decide what to say. Instead of answering her question he mumbled something instead. "Where I'm from our fighters are men and older and…"

Ender stopped as if caught saying too much. He shook his head and came up on his knees.

Alli helped him to his feet. He leaned on her for a moment for support, and she could feel the warmth of his well-toned body.

She opened her mouth to ask, but another voice spoke up first.

"Ender." It was King Abbas from Cyrene. "The Oracle wants to see you." He turned to Alli. "And she told me to tell you that you will fly south tonight under darkness."

Alli nodded. Excitement filled her as she thought about being able to please her master. She would secure Solshi for the Dragon Queen.

"Very well," Ender said as he finished dusting his clothes off. He turned back to Alli. "I will consider it a privilege to train with you, Dragon Rider Allison Stenos."

"If the master commands," Alli said, still thinking about pleasing Delia.

Ender gave her a strange look and tilted his head. "You mean the Dragon Queen? She is not our master. She is the Oracle and a queen."

Alli frowned. What did he mean? Of course Delia was her master. Her prior master had trained her and then passed her to Delia. She had to please her master.

Ender touched her shoulder, and Alli jumped back.

"You're so jumpy," Ender said as he followed King Abbas away from the practice yard. Over his shoulder he called back to her. "Now I can actually believe all the stories I have heard of the young battlemaster."

Battlemaster.

The word brought up flashes of memory that Alli couldn't quite grab a hold of. Her first master, Gorn, a battle in the southern desert, another in the forest at the edge of Elvyn, fighting for Alaris, and the Citadel. Bits and fragments flew past so quickly she almost imagined they were not real.

Almost.

CHAPTER TWENTY-THREE

Roland spent the next day and a night traveling through all the small fishing villages around the bay just north of the capital city Raleez. He provided relief and made deals for the fishermen and their families. Soon word travelled ahead of him, and the people of Sandy Cove greeted him by lining the streets on either side. Only an hour's walk from Raleez itself, Sandy Cove held a population that was more of a mix of people and trades.

Large warehouses sat just off the docks, holding wares from the kingdom of Arc in the north to Tillimot in the south.

The fishermen's guild was the first to greet Roland. And as he had done previously, he offered them help in paying their taxes and promised them relief from hunger, sending another messenger to Valencia and asking for more food.

Today he was dressed as a rich merchant. He had purchased new pants, which now tucked into new shiny black boots—boots that made him a few inches taller. A new red, wool-lined cloak hung over a frilly white shirt. It was not his usual look, but it got the attention he required now as part of his plan to unify the kingdoms of North and South Solshi under him.

Most everywhere he went now he heard people talking about him. He chuckled at who they thought he was. Some said he was a rich merchant's son and others a great wizard. There were even tidbits of him being a god come down to help them. *Well, not yet.*

Unify them!

The pounding words in his head became louder every day. He knew that the more time he gave Delia and her dragons to gather her army, the harder it would be to establish peace. But he had to unify the people first. *Then I will come for you again, Alli.*

"Sir," a well-dressed man approached him on the street. "Could we have a word with you?" He motioned Roland toward a group of men standing just outside of a nicely painted two-story building. The bright sign out front said *Dockmaster.*

Roland shrugged noncommittally. "I am a busy man, but I could make some time for such esteemed gentlemen as yourselves," he said with a wink.

The man led him to the building and escorted him inside along with three other men who had been standing outside. A young man at a counter nodded toward a nearby office door, and the five men, including Roland, headed in that direction.

Walking through the door, Roland quickly scanned the room. An older man with graying hair sat behind a serviceable desk. Roland's nose wrinkled at the scent of sweet smoke. The man picked up a rolled cigar and drew a long puff before releasing the smoke. Looking around at the rest of the room, Roland noticed a table and set of chairs standing over a worn rug. Old paintings of the sea sat askew on the walls.

While Roland was looking around, without warning one of the men moved around him and hit him hard in the gut. Power flared up inside him, and he was a breath away from using them to destroy the man, when the voice in his head whispered more loudly than ever, *Unify them!*

"What was that for?" Roland grunted in pain. He found his hand holding the collapsed scepter, but he kept his cool and waited for an answer.

"Just a test," the man at the desk said. He put down his cigar and stood up. "I am Ferdinand, guildmaster of the shipping guild for Raleez."

Roland tried to stand straight again, but it took a few deep breaths to do so. He hoped a rib wasn't cracked. "A test of what?"

Ferdinand's laugh was deep and followed by a few hacking coughs. "Some say you are a wizard or a god—personally I think you're just the spoiled third son of a minor lord, trying to stick their noses in business that doesn't concern them."

Roland grunted but followed it by as warm a smile as he could muster. He took a step toward the guildmaster and reached his hand out to shake. "I'm afraid we have started off on the wrong foot, Guildmaster Ferdinand. My name is Roland."

Ferdinand sat back down without shaking his hand, and Roland was pushed down into a chair opposite the desk by one of the other men. The first man who had greeted him in the street sat down next to him, while the other three moved back next to the door and stood awaiting further instructions.

Ferdinand waved a hand to the man on Roland's right. "This is my son, Joca."

Roland nodded at the man, then turned his attention back to Ferdinand.

"Now, what can we do for you, Roland?" Ferdinand asked.

Roland was perplexed. "I'm not sure, what you mean, Guildmaster. You are the ones who brought me here."

Ferdinand leaned forward in his chair, his fleshy jowls shaking with frustration. "What do you want from us in return for leaving us alone? We'll not have you messing in our affairs here closer to Raleez like you have been doing up the coast, and from what I hear also inland in Valencia."

Roland was surprised that they had heard about Valencia already; it must have shown on his face.

The guildmaster laughed again. "Ah, you don't understand the reach of my guild, do you? We run all shipping and transfer of goods in and out and through all of North and South Solshi."

Roland smiled at his good fortune. "Well, then I am glad we have met—though I would have preferred a better reception." Roland sat up straighter and ran a hand through his hair. "The question is not what you can do for me—for I fear there is nothing you can offer me that will deter me from my mission. The more pertinent question is, what can I do for you?"

"Did you not hear my father?" Joca said from the side.

Roland dismissed the comment with a wave of his hand. "Irrelevant to our conversation."

Roland looked over his shoulder as the scrape of boots signaled the three men moving closer behind him. Ferdinand stood and glared down at Roland.

"Boss?" asked one of the men behind Roland. "Should we take care of him?"

Ferdinand thought for a moment, and Roland took the opportunity to speak again. "Hear me out first, and then your goons can do whatever they want."

A hand boxed the side of Roland's head, and he snapped. "Will you stop that?" He turned back to the guildmaster with clenched jaw. He wasn't going to be able to take much more of this. How dare they treat him, the greatest wizard in the land, this way?

Unify them!

"Shut up!" Roland yelled out loud.

The men jumped with surprise. No one had said anything. The guildmaster looked at him like he might be crazy. Roland took a deep breath to try and calm his nerves.

"As you can see," Roland tried to speak more calmly. "I am no danger to you." *Ha!* These men didn't know how close they all were to having the entire building collapse on top of them. "Hear me out."

Ferdinand nodded and waved at his men. "Wait outside the door."

The men glared at Roland but left the room. As soon as they did, Roland stood, and Joco leaped from his chair and stood in a fighting stance.

Roland laughed. "Sirs, you are too jumpy." He walked to the window and opened one up. "Just getting a little fresh air in here." He tried not to wince from the pain of being hit earlier, but he noticed it was already lessening.

I have amplified your power to heal, wizard, came the voice in his head, and this time Roland knew it was from his dragon, Orelia.

He had heard the same thing from Alli and Bakari about the dragon bond strengthening the body as well as the mind.

Roland turned back around to the two men who were now standing. He waved them back to their seats. They looked annoyed at being told what to do but nonetheless returned to their chairs. Roland sat on his and draped a knee over one of the armrests.

"Now, sirs, I am here to make you very rich men," Roland said and then stopped and waited for them to say the next words. Ten seconds, thirty seconds, an entire minute passed, and Roland stayed quiet. He knew their minds were working. He knew they had to know more.

"And how is that?" Ferdinand finally said.

Roland had them hooked. He was now in control. "Stop collecting taxes on the goods you transport, and I will reward you double."

Joca looked from Roland and back to his father, his mouth hanging open. "Are you mad?"

Roland shrugged his shoulders.

Ferdinand slammed a hand down on his desk. "What game are you playing at, Master Roland? You know we cannot stop collecting taxes on transported goods. That money belongs to Queen Esmaralda and Regent Filipe."

Roland waved a hand in the air. "Regent Filipe of South Solshi is only a figurehead standing in for the young king. What will he do? You know as well as I that South Solshi follows the north."

"But Esmaralda?" Joca said.

Roland stood up and took a step away from his chair. "And I thought your guild the most powerful in Solshi. I guess I was misinformed. If you don't want my deal, I will find another."

Roland took a few more steps toward the door.

"Stop!" came Ferdinand's loud voice.

The door in front of Roland opened, and one of the men stuck his head inside. "Everything all right in here?"

"Everything is fine," Roland said and without touching the door pushed his hand forward and slammed it shut with a gust of air. He heard a loud shriek on the other side and then banging on the door, but he turned back around.

Both Ferdinand and Joca sat wide-eyed.

"Now, men, this is the plan," Roland began to state his terms. "The merchants, fishermen, and craftsmen all keep their tax money."

"But a portion of that money is given back to us by the queen," Joca said, still clearly not understanding how this deal was good for them.

"You will agree to transport anyone that I ask you to, and I will pay you double your transport fee—more than enough to offset your portion of the tax base," Roland said. "But you must agree to transport them across land or sea whenever I need them."

Ferdinand's eyes squinted inside his fleshy face. "I must say this is unconventional. Who will we be transporting, sir?"

"Troops."

"Troops?" Joca stood up in surprise.

Roland motioned him back in his seat, and he fell into it with a sigh.

"A war is coming," Roland explained. "A new Oracle in Turg has taken the dragons from the dragon riders and has set claim to all of the southern kingdoms. I intend to stop her."

Ferdinand placed his head in both hands and shook his head for a moment. "Madness. This is madness. The queen will be furious, and the people… the people… "

"The people will not stand for a queen who forces taxes on them or hides stores of food when they are hungry. Even as we speak her hold on the people is weakening. Textiles go east instead of west, the fishermen are enjoying her food, and now you will not be giving her the taxes she has demanded."

"Now, look here, sir." Ferdinand stood now and walked to the window. Roland looked out, too, and saw that dark clouds were rolling in from the west. A brutal storm was coming. Dockworkers scrambled around with ropes, securing ships and tying down loose articles. "I'm no fan of Queen Esmaralda, but she's the only queen we have. She is the rightful heir, and what you are asking me to do is treason."

Roland joined him at the window. "I see you are a loyal man. I honor that. But there are times when the people are justified in rising up and displacing their leader if that leader does not have their best interests at heart. A ruler has the responsibility to care for her people, to build them up, to support them, to love them. Rebels to one man, mean freedom fighters to another. Treason to one, can mean displacing a tyrant to another."

Ferdinand turned around and stared hard at Roland while Joca joined him. Roland stood once again in silence and looked out of the window. He hoped the storm would not last too long. *Orelia?* He called out.

Yes, wizard?

Are you close by?

Always .

Come for me! he commanded.

"What say you?" Roland turned back to the men. Which side will you be on, Guildmaster? Freedom or tyranny?"

Ferdinand shook his head a few times. "I still say it is madness, but yes, I will do as you ask. Your speech rouses my heart. The people deserve better, as you say. But who will be our new leader? Who can do all you say a leader should do?"

"Why, me, good sirs." Roland smiled broadly. "Tell the people that Roland Tyre, High Wizard of the Citadel, King of Alaris, Monarch of Tillimot, and Dragon Rider, will save them."

With those words, screams sounded on the streets as a beautiful golden dragon materialized directly in front of the dockmaster's building. Roland gave a quick bow of his head to the men, and to the amazement of the other guards opened the door without using his hands and walked through the lobby and out into the street.

"Citizens of North Solshi!" he called out, amplifying his voice with his powers. "Today begins the day of your liberation." Orelia knelt down, and Roland climbed up between her neck and wings and waved at the people. Opening a pouch at his waist, he threw out some gold pieces down on the ground. That is something the people understood—money.

The growing crowd scrambled for the coins. Ferdinand and Joca came out of the building. They were well known by the people, and some of the people now looked to them for an explanation.

Ferdinand knelt down, and his son joined him. "Hail, Roland Tyre. Hail the liberator of Solshi!"

The people still seemed confused about what was happening, but seeing the guildmaster bow to Roland, they began to echo his words.

"Hail, Roland. Hail, Roland."

As Orelia lifted off the ground, her wings soared over the people's heads. Drops of rain began to fall from the incoming storm, but Roland smiled down at the people—his people. "I will return."

CHAPTER TWENTY-FOUR

Roland knew that after revealing himself for who he truly was that the news would spread quickly across Raleez. Queen Esmaralda would soon know he was there. He had to hurry for the next part of his plan to work. He was driven to unify the people; to bring peace to the land once again was his aim. The Queen of North Solshi did not deserve her position.

He moved in disguise during the rest of the day, moving from the north side of Raleez to the south. South Solshi was a weak kingdom beholden to the north for protection and economic well-being. Hundreds of years before, the kingdom of Solshi had been split in two when a past king had died, leaving the kingdom to twin children—one a son and one a daughter. The two disagreed on how to run the kingdom; the daughter had taken the north portion, and the son, the south.

Now King Andre De Luz, a thirteen-year-old boy, ruled South Solshi. However, a regent, Filipe—an uncle—had been running the kingdom since the last king had died of sickness only a few months before. The circumstances were suspicious, and even though it wasn't said out loud, most agreed that the king had been murdered by someone close to Filipe. Andre's life was precarious at best.

Roland had discovered pieces of information about Filipe that made for quite a story—a story he now intended to tell Andre.

Waiting for the fall of darkness, Roland snuck to the back walls of the castle of South Solshi. Soldiers guarded the perimeter, but only at wide intervals. Standing outside of the twelve-foot wall, Roland placed his hand on the scepter and drew in its power. With hardly a thought he jumped and easily flew over the high wall, landing in a crouch on the other side. He listened carefully for a moment and then proceeded to move silently from palm tree to palm tree in the castle gardens until he came closer to the castle itself.

Hearing the sound of footsteps crunching on gravel, he ducked down behind a small bush and waited until the guard had passed. From the information he had gained, Andre's room was on the third floor, facing south. Looking up, Roland saw a large balcony around a room and figured that was it. He scooted toward the side of the building and once again called on his powers to leap up.

Over the rail of the balcony he went, landing a little harder than he had planned. He steadied himself against a small table outside before walking to the double door. Moving around until he could find a crack in the curtains, he peered inside. Inside, a boy slept in a large bed.

Roland took off his dark cloak and laid it on the balcony, then took out his golden cloak from a bag that he carried with him. Putting it on over a black shirt and pants, he smiled at his reflection in the glass door.

He turned the knob. It wasn't locked—who would think to lock a balcony door on the third floor? The door creaked as he pushed it open, but soon it stopped, and Roland crept inside the room.

This is going to be fun! He almost chuckled with anticipation.

He held his scepter in his hand and brought up a bright light. The boy—well he was only four years younger than Roland—stirred in his bed and sat up, placing his hand over his eyes to block the bright light.

"Shhhh," Roland said softly, not wanting him to wake up anyone else. He moved the light a bit, enough for Andre to see the light reflect off of Roland's golden cloak, but not enough to see his face clearly.

"Who are you?" the young king asked. "Are you a spirit?" The king's black hair was messy, with bangs hanging over his eyebrows. Using his fingers, he pushed them away from his eyes. His light tan skin was indicative of most among the western kingdoms of Quentis, Solshi, Turg, and Cyrene.

Roland smiled. "I am magic," Roland said in answer to the king's question. He would let Andre interpret that any way he wanted to.

The young king's eyes went wide. "I have magic," he whispered.

This Roland had not known. Things would be easier than he thought.

"Those with magic must stick together," Roland said. "A war is coming, and I need your help."

Andre nodded with excitement, now fully awake. "What can I do?"

"Early tomorrow morning Regent Felipe is meeting with Queen Esmaralda," Roland said, letting his voice carry to Andre in a loud whisper. "They plan your death."

"No!" Andre sat up even straighter, moving so his feet hung over the side of the bed. His eyes hardened, and he shook his head in disgust more than disbelief.

"I can see you are not surprised," Roland said.

"I know what they say he did to my father," Andre said. "I am not unaware of what goes on around me. I have studied the histories."

"Ah, a scholar wizard," Roland said. Thoughts of Bakari raced through his mind, and he pushed them away.

Andre smiled. "That is what I have been told, but… " his face fell. "I am untrained. My uncle keeps me from going to the wizard sanctuary in Quentis."

"Because he is afraid of you becoming too powerful," Roland said.

"Yes," Andre said. "That is what I thought also."

"But you would be welcomed at the Citadel."

"I would be?" Andre said. Then he squinted. "How can you be sure of that? Who are you?"

"A friend."

"What kind of friend doesn't show his face?" the king said. "You are aware that I could scream and guards would be here in a matter of moments."

Roland's nostrils flared. "And I hope that you are aware that with a snap of my fingers or a touch of my scepter I can have you killed and this castle crumbled to the ground." The scepter in his hand brightened. Roland took a deep breath and calmed his nerves. He was tired and had let the influence of the scepter get to him. He needed to be more careful.

King Andre paled and sat back farther on the bed. He shielded his eyes from the light of the scepter.

Unify!

Roland took a deep breath to steady his nerves. Yes, he needed to unify. With a softer voice he spoke. "I do not mean to scare you Andre; I am sorry. I'm not here to destroy you, only to warn you. Do what is right, and your kingdom will not only be saved, but will prosper in the golden light."

Andre appeared to relax, although he didn't come any closer. "How do you know about the meeting with Filipe and the queen?"

Roland laughed inside. *Because I arranged for it to happen.* Not that it wouldn't have anyway. Everything he said about Felipe was true; Roland just arranged to speed events up a bit. Without answering Andre's question, he continued. "In the courtyard between the two castles. Be there before the morning meal. You will learn the truth."

"But what do you have to gain from this?" Andre spoke.

Smart boy. "You will know when the time is right," Roland said. "Remember, I am your ally in this."

A light knock sounded on the door that Roland presumed led to another room in the king's suites.

"Is everything all right, sire?" a tired voice from the other side said.

"Yes. Yes, Paulo," Andre called out. "I am fine."

"I heard voices," Paulo said.

"I was just thinking and talking out loud," Andre said.

Roland smiled. The king was a natural. He would make a good wizard and a great king—if he was guided correctly. He nodded to the young man and stepped back onto the balcony.

"Is there anything you need, sire?" Paulo asked.

Roland heard the handle turn as he donned his black cloak again and leapt from the balcony. On the way down he heard Andre's voice.

"Yes, gather my personal guard. And Paulo," he paused, "don't let the regent know."

Roland hit the ground and took off running over the darkened grounds of the castle. Within a few minutes he was at the back wall and clearing it with one easy jump. Once out to the streets he slowed down. He stayed to the shadows and crept to the northern side of the castle complex. He had a note to deliver.

* * *

A few hours later, Roland sat with Orelia just outside of the city in a clearing of trees. He closed his eyes for a moment. He hadn't gotten much sleep that night. He might be a powerful wizard, but he hadn't found a spell yet that kept his body from having to sleep.

Wake me in two hours, Roland said to Orelia.

Yes, wizard, the dragon almost purred. *You are doing well.*

Mmm, Roland replied. Before noon tomorrow he would have the kingdoms of North and South Solshi added to his collection of kingdoms.

CHAPTER TWENTY-FIVE

Gabrielle von wulf paced back and forth in the healer's room. A local healer had arrived moments before and was examining Bakari, Jaimon, and Liam. All three lay unconscious on top of thick fur blankets on the floor.

She didn't know what to do. How could this be happening? First Alli, and now this. It was almost more than she could handle.

"Miss," the healer called her over to the three men. She was an old woman with skin color between Gabby's and Bakari's. Her eyes were dark brown and kind. "Do you have healing abilities?"

Gabby shook her head. "Not that I am aware of yet. I've only been training a short time."

The woman pursed her lips. "Either way, your powers could help. I can sense a great reservoir of power in the room."

Gabby nodded her head and knelt down next to the healer. "What can I do?"

"I am a relatively weak wizard, but I do know about healing," she said. "I am a distant cousin of the dragon king. With your powers and my guidance maybe we can do something."

Gabby hoped so. She didn't know what she would do without these boys, if she couldn't get them awake. She followed the motions of the healer and placed her hands on

Bakari's body first. Delving deep inside her mind, she brought up as much power as she could.

The healer yelped and gasped. "A little less, please."

Gabby let up but tried to maintain her concentration. She could feel the melding of her magic with the healer's deft touch. Moving through the body she could sense the poison there, but each time they tried to heal it, it seemed to move away from them and claim another part of the body instead.

Oh, Bakari! She couldn't bear losing him.

Finally, the healer lifted her hands off of Bakari, and Gabby followed suit.

"I don't know what's wrong," the healer shook her head. "This should be working."

The door opened, and Baron Curtis Dunst walked in. His eyes were heavy. "Anything?"

The healer stood up. "It's poison, Baron, but not any kind I am familiar with. It doesn't seem natural. The magic in his own body should be responding to my healing and dissipate the poison. He is the dragon king—his own powers should be strong enough."

The baron shook his head and wrung his hands. "What about the others?"

Both Gabby and the healer knelt back down, this time by Liam. They placed their hands on him, and Gabby cleared her mind. In her mind's eye she could see the poison swimming inside Liam's body. As parts of Liam's own magic flashed, the poison would only grow stronger—almost as if the magical powers they all held increased the powers of the poison, rather than decreasing it.

She sensed things from Liam that she didn't know if she felt comfortable about. She didn't know him as well as Alli, or even Jaimon, who was one of her kinsmen. She sensed a darkness in Liam, not one of evil, but one of frustration and doubt.

Gabby pulled away from Liam's mind. She didn't want to know his secrets or insecurities, especially while he was unconscious. The power of seeing—of reading ones thoughts was a unique power than ran through her family.

Soon the healer pulled away and shook her head at Gabby. They moved over to Jaimon and placed their hands on his body, and once again Gabby let her power flow into her friend.

This time it was different. She could feel the healer guiding her power toward the poison. Once again the poison seemed to feed off their powers, but there was no place for the poison to go. *Jaimon doesn't have magic!*

"Stop!" Gabby took her hands off of Jaimon and motioned the healer to do the same.

"But it was different this time," the healer said with a tired smile. "It might have worked."

Gabby shook her head. "I know this sounds strange, but the poison is feeding off of the magic. The more magic we infuse in their bodies as we try to help them, the more power we are giving to the poison. But Jaimon is different. He doesn't have any magical abilities."

The healer nodded, following Gabby's train of thought. "And so if we leave him alone, the poison should dissipate on its own, since it doesn't have anything to feed on."

Gabby smiled. "Yes. I think so."

The healer rummaged around in a bag at her feet and brought out a few jars of herbs. "Yarrow and peppermint should naturally help lower his fever and get rid of the poison in his body."

Gabby watched the woman mix the two together. She put a dab on Jaimon's tongue, and he automatically swallowed it. The rest she spread across his chest and then around his temples. After a few moments, both women leaned back against a wall to rest.

"You are very powerful," the healer finally said to Gabby.

"But not powerful enough to heal them." Gabby pointed toward Bakari and Liam. She wiped a few tears out of the corners of her eyes. Would she see the end of the Dragon King and his riders? She shook away the thought and took a deep breath.

The woman stood up. "You need some food and rest."

"I want to stay here," Gabby said.

"I understand," the healer said. "I'll have some food and blankets sent in for you."

Gabby nodded, pulled her knees up inside her arms, and tried to think of what she could do.

A servant brought food in—a plate of cheese and peppered beef—and Gabby ate it without even noticing if it tasted good or not. She knew she needed to maintain her strength, especially since using her powers, but she did so without any enjoyment.

With knees still pulled up to her chest, she laid her head down on her crossed arms and drifted off to sleep.

* * *

"Gabby," came a weak voice. "Gabby, what happened?"

Gabby opened her eyes and brought her head up off her arms.

"Jaimon!" Gabby crawled the few feet to his side. "Oh, Jaimon!" she reached down and hugged him.

Jaimon pushed up on his elbows and looked around. Then seeing Bakari and Liam lying still next to him, he frowned. "What happened?"

"You were all poisoned," Gabby said.

"But what about you?" Jaimon asked, then wrinkled his nose. "What's that smell?"

Gabby laughed, though at the same time she rubbed a tear from her cheek. She was so happy that Jaimon had woken up. "Yarrow and peppermint."

Jaimon nodded as if understanding. "Help me sit up." He moved slowly while Gabby steadied him. They moved back to sit against the wall.

"The cake!" Gabby said. "I'd forgotten. Right before Bakari passed out, he told me that the cake had been poisoned."

"Then why are you all right, and why are they still unconscious?"

"I never ate any cake," Gabby said. "I was too full."

"But why am I awake now and they aren't?" Jaimon shook his head with worry. "They will be all right, won't they?"

"I don't know, Jaimon. When the healer and I tried to heal all of you, the magic seemed to do more harm than good. Since you don't have magic… "

Jaimon's face soured.

"But it's a good thing, Jaimon." Gabby laid a hand on his arm. "Since you don't have magic we were able to remove the poison. But their own magic and my magic just seemed to feed the poison."

Jaimon sat quietly for a moment. Gabby knew he liked to process things out. He pushed his hands against the floor and then stood up. He wobbled for a moment, but Gabby joined him and kept him steady.

"We need to find out who poisoned us," Jaimon said. "Then maybe we can find an antidote."

Gabby nodded. She hated to leave Bakari and Liam alone, but they needed answers.

"One of the servants, maybe, or the cook," Jaimon said as they walked down the hallway.

"But why?" Gabby asked, knowing that neither of them had any answers.

They found the kitchen in full swing in preparing the evening meal. Gabby tried to talk to the cook, but he just pushed them aside as he worked.

"I've known all the baron's servants and kitchen helpers my entire life," he mumbled. "I've run this kitchen personally for twenty years and… " He paused and looked around. "Where is Dree?" he called out to the rest of his staff.

The cook was met with blank stares and shrugs.

"Haven't seen her since yesterday," said one of the other ladies. "I heard she wasn't feeling well."

Gabby looked at Jaimon, and he shrugged.

"Who is Dree?" Gabby asked the cook.

He poured a boiling pot of noodles through a strainer, and Gabby waited until he had replaced the pot on the counter for an answer.

"Look, you two, I have a meal to prepare for the baron and baroness." He scowled at them. "Dree is… " he thought for a moment and then shook his head. "Dree is very close with the baroness. Maybe you should talk to her."

"I thought you said you knew all your people?" Gabby pointed out.

The cook growled, then sighed. "I forgot about her. She keeps to herself. She came to Hillside with the baroness last year. Now, get out of my kitchen." The man raised a large wooden spoon at the two of them, and they backed away.

"Come on, Gabby." Jaimon pulled her away.

They left the kitchen and walked down a hallway to try and find the baron. Rounding a corner, they bumped into the baroness herself.

The woman put her hand over her mouth, and her eyes widened. She looked down the hallway past them and then back at the two with a dark look. "What are you two doing here?"

Gabby took a step back. "We're looking for Dree. We heard she was a friend of yours."

Baroness Angela's mouth grew tight and she turned and looked behind her. When she turned back she moved closer to Jaimon and Gabby. "Why would you be looking for her?"

Gabby opened her mouth to say something, but Jaimon jumped in first. "The cake was sure delicious yesterday," he said.

The whites of Angela's eyes stood out against her bronze skin.

Gabby picked up on Jaimon's line of questions. The baroness's reaction was too suspicious to ignore. "We heard that Dree prepared it, and we wanted to thank her," Gabby said.

Angela looked from Gabby to Jaimon and then back to Gabby again. "Where is the Dragon King and the other rider?"

"Back relaxing in their room," Gabby lied.

"I… I… well, I thought I heard they were sick," Angela said, her face going pale.

"Oh, nothing to worry about," Jaimon said. "I think we were just exhausted from our journey. But we would love more cake."

"Cake?" Angela said, "Oh yes. I will be sure to tell Dree for you."

"Angela," called out the baron from behind her. "Oh!" he exclaimed as he walked up. "Jaimon, you're feeling better?"

Gabby didn't want the baron to spoil their story. So she jumped in. "Oh yes, thank you, Baron. We were just telling the baroness how much we enjoyed the cake last night and that we were looking for more. But we couldn't find Dree, the cook's helper. The baroness was just hurrying off to find her."

The baron gave them a strange look.

"It really would make us feel better," Jaimon said. "I'm sure the Dragon King would be very thankful."

At the mention of the Dragon King, the baron's lips opened to a full grin. "Well, if the Dragon King wants more cake, Angela, get him some more cake."

Angela stammered a few moments and then turned and walked down the hallway. Jaimon leaned around Gabby and watched her walk down the hall and then turn right at the end. She turned around and glared at the two of them just before disappearing.

"Baron, how long have you known Dree?" Gabby asked.

"Why, as long as I've known my wife," Baron Dunst said. "They came to Hillside together last year—looking for a new life. Angela told me that Dree had been beaten by her father."

"And you said they came just after the barrier came down?" Jaimon said.

"Well, yes," the baron thought. "She's been so wonderful for Thomas. Ever since my last wife died, he's needed a mother."

"And where did they come from?" Gabby asked.

The baron turned from one to the other and then back again as the questions fired off at him. He was beginning to look flustered.

"Well, Angela never really said for sure," the baron offered. "It seemed they didn't want to talk about their past much, so I didn't pry. I was just happy to have met her." He paused for a moment. "But…"

"Yes?" Gabby continued to push, with a quick glance at Jaimon. She was sure they were on the same line of thinking.

Two servants came down the hall. Nodding to the baron, one of them spoke. "Dinner will be ready soon, sir. Should we tell the baroness?"

The baron nodded and motioned them down the hall the way his wife had gone.

"Baron?" Gabby prodded.

Baron Dunst's face flushed. "I don't know where she is from, for sure, but I've heard the two talk about one place more than others. I didn't think anything about it until now. With the barrier down, it was just exciting to have someone from another kingdom around."

"Baron, where did they talk about?" Gabby asked.

"Turg," the baron's face fell as if he realized something at the same time.

Alarm spread across Jaimon's face. The same alarm pounded in Gabby's chest.

"Hold on," she yelled out to the two servants that had just passed them in the hallway.

They turned with questioning eyes.

"We're going that way," Gabby said. "We'll inform the baroness for you."

The two servants looked at their baron, and he nodded and waved them away.

Jaimon looked up at the baron. "You might want to accompany us, sir."

The baron's face darkened, and he looked like he might be sick. "It can't be. It can't be," he whispered as he shook his head and followed Jaimon and Gabby down the hall. "It just can't be."

CHAPTER TWENTY-SIX

Baron Curtis Dunst took the lead as he joined Gabby and Jaimon in running to his living quarters. Coming into an open-area sitting room with light streaming in through two glass doors, Gabby saw a woman quickly fleeing outside to a patio and garden area. The baron's wife turned around from pushing the other person out, and surprise ran across her face.

"Angela." The baron's voice sounded as if it was torn from his soul. "What have you done?"

"Curtis," Angela said. A smile quickly replaced her surprise. Her chest heaved with exertion. "What do you mean?"

Jaimon ran to the door, jerked it back open, and ran outside. His energy seemed to be returning quickly.

Walking up to her husband, Angela put a hand on his shoulder. The baron's body seemed to slump a bit, but he looked at Gabby and seemed to regain a bit of his resolve. He took a step back, and her hand dropped to her side.

"Was that Dree?" The baron pointed his head in the direction of the door.

Angela's eyes darted to the same door. Gabby saw a vein throbbing in the side of her neck.

"What's wrong, Curtis?" Angela looked back at the door once again. "You know that Dree and I are longtime friends. She was just here for a visit."

"The cook said she was sick today," Gabby said.

Angela's eyes went wide, and she stumbled on her words. "Yes, yes, she wasn't feeling well. That's why she came here. She wanted my help."

The door opened back up, and Dree came stumbling in, with Jaimon pushing her from behind. The woman had a dark hood over her head and a bag slung over her back.

Jaimon moved out in front of her. "She doesn't look sick to me," he said. "It looks like she was going somewhere."

Gabby turned to Angela. "You and Dree put something in the cake last night. What was it?"

Without any warning, Dree pushed Jaimon to the floor, grabbed Angela's hand, and tried to run back outside.

"Angela!" The baron took a step forward and tried to grab his wife, but she slipped through his fingers.

Dree wrenched the door open, but before the two women could escape Gabby flicked a hand out in front of her, and the door slammed shut. Rattling the doorknob, Dree tried to pry it back open. But Gabby's spell was too strong.

Angela turned, and suddenly a small knife appeared in her outstretched hand. She jumped toward her husband, her eyes wild and crazy.

"Mama!" came a voice a few yards behind them.

Thomas walked into the room, and everyone turned in his direction. Everyone but Gabby. She reached over and used the distraction to disarm the baroness. Then she wrapped a spell of air around the woman, keeping her still. Gabby smiled at this show of power. What kind of wizard was she? Being from the royal family, she had been studying to be a counselor wizard, but it seemed she had more of an affinity for battle. Her mind went to Alli, and she sighed and turned back to the room.

The baron grabbed a hold of Thomas's hand, then called out for help. Soon two guards and a servant arrived. The baron handed the boy off to them.

"Take Thomas to his room, please," the baron said. "I have something to take care of."

"Papa!" Thomas yelled out. "No, Papa!"

"Thomas!" Angela said, her voice pleading, but when Thomas looked at her she didn't say anything else. The tears in her eyes showed her affinity for the boy.

The baron took a few steps and faced his wife. She stood still, not being able to move against Gabby's invisible cords of air. "Was this all an act?" His voice was heavy with emotion.

A tear slid down Angela's face. "No, Curtis. No. I… I… " She lowered her head.

Gabby and Jaimon moved Angela and Dree to a set of chairs and had them sit. Dree gave Angela a worried look.

"It's all my fault," Angela said. "Don't punish Dree. She was just following my orders. Let her go."

"No, no, Baroness," cried out Dree. "Don't take the glory from me. I did it willingly. I put the poison in the cake."

Baron Dunst paced the room, then turned back to his wife. "But why? I don't understand. How could you have known the Dragon King would come here?"

Angela's face up until now held regret and sadness, but now it hardened, and she glared at Jaimon and Gabby. "Why didn't the magic affect you two? The others are still dying aren't they?"

"I didn't eat the cake," said Gabby, without saying anything else about Jaimon.

"But the Dragon King, he is still dying?" Angela asked with a glow on her face.

"Angela!" the baron said again, this time his voice booming. "Tell me why you would do such a horrendous thing."

Angela stared up at her husband in defiance. "It was my mission, Curtis. We've all heard stories of the dragon riders and the prophecy of the Dragon King. When the magical barrier around Alaris fell, I, among others, was sent from Turg to find him."

The baron dropped down into a seat across from his wife. Jaimon poured him something to drink and handed him a glass.

"There were rumors when the barrier fell of a dragon orb and of a boy who was now a dragon rider. We knew that if he would become the Dragon King that Turg would not be able to rise to its glory." As Angela told the story her voice became stronger and her eyes brighter.

Gabby shook her head and looked at Jaimon. This was incredible. "Who sent you?"

Angela smiled. "My cousin, Delia, now the Oracle of Turg. She was powerful even back then and had begun to plan her rise as the next leader of Turg. And now you bring us news that she has been proclaimed as the Oracle and stolen the dragon bonds. It's more than we could've hoped for."

"But what brought you here?" The baron said, his face pale. "Did you ever really love me, Angela?"

Angela clapped her hands together once. "It was quite by accident. My intention was to travel to where we heard the Dragon Orb had hatched, and the shortest route was through these forests. When we stumbled on the town that freely spoke about the descendants of the Dragon King we decided that someday he would have to return here. I just bid my time until he did."

The baron opened his mouth to say something but then closed it again and dropped his head.

"Curtis… I… " Angela stumbled for a bit, and the baron looked up at her. "I did love you and Thomas, Curtis. I still do. We can still be happy together. I've done nothing to harm you or Thomas."

The baron's eyes went wide, and his face grew red. "Done nothing to hurt me?" He stood up, and his voice roared. "You might have killed the Dragon King! My family has kept each descendant of the Dragon King protected and alive for over 150 years, Angela! And now, on my watch, a traitor from Turg comes in and tries to kill him! You have destroyed everything this small barony has stood for. You and Dree might well have destroyed the hope of the western continent and plunged it into darkness."

Dree sat with a wide smile on her petite face. "Not into darkness, Baron; into a new age. Delia, the new Dragon Queen, will reign over all, and our names will be honored forever!"

"But what if you fail?" Jaimon said softly. "What then? Was it all worth the betrayal of good people here?"

The baroness looked like she had been slapped in the face.

"But we have not failed," said Dree with conviction. "The Dragon King is dying."

"But what if he doesn't die?" Jaimon said, shining doubt on their plans.

Dree glanced at Angela, and Angela looked at her husband, who stood glaring at them with tight lips and tired eyes.

"Was it worth it, Angela?" The baron echoed Jaimon's question.

A lone tear dripped down Angela's face. "Being with you and Thomas this past year has been wonderful." She paused. "But I will not regret what I have done for my kingdom and my Oracle."

"Guards!" The baron called out.

Three guards came forward.

"Confine the baroness and Dree to their rooms. Guard all exits, and await my further instructions."

"Wait!" Gabby yelled out and turned to Angela and Dree. "Is there a cure?"

Dree laughed. "A dose of the poison was given to each party that left Turg to find the Dragon King. There is no cure."

"You mean there are others?" Gabby gasped.

Dree laughed. "Oh yes, little princess. You will never know who was sent out to find the Dragon King. If we fail, others will succeed."

The guards took the two ladies away. Then the Baron returned his attention to Gabby and Jaimon.

"I'm so sorry," he said. His eyes were hollow, and he fell back down in his chair. "I had no idea."

Gabby only nodded; then she and Jaimon left the room.

"What now?" Jaimon said. "We are just one young wizard with a former dragon rider that doesn't have any magic. Once again I'm worthless to help."

"No, Jaimon," Gabby said. "If you had magic you would be lying there with Bakari and Jaimon. Not having magic saved you."

"Some saving," Jaimon said. "How will we tell the world the Dragon King is dead?"

"He's not dead yet," Gabby said. "We need to get to Elvyn. They can help him."

They ran back to the room where Bakari and Jaimon lay. The healer, who had been kneeling in front of Bakari, turned and looked up at them. Her face was ashen.

Gabby raced over to Bakari's side and gasped. His lips were pale, his skin drying up, and he barely looked alive.

"He isn't... ?" Gabby couldn't let herself say the rest of the question.

The healer shook her head. "No, they are both alive. But not for long. They need a stronger magic."

"I am stronger," Gabby said.

"But you don't have the knowledge, and neither do I."

Jaimon paced the room, then sat down on the ground. Gabby covered her face and tried to think.

"Gabby!" Jaimon erupted, and Gabby jerked her head up. He was holding his bag of artifacts. "Something here might help."

Jaimon was right. She ran over to him and grabbed the bag, dumping its contents on the floor. She spied the glove, and an idea came to her mind. She ran back over to Bakari and fished through his belongings until she found the glove Auni had given them. "They match!"

"What does it mean?" Jaimon asked.

Gabby shook her head. "I don't know. But I can try to use them."

"But you aren't a dragon rider," Jaimon said.

"You are."

"But I don't have magic." Jaimon threw his hands up in the air.

"I do," Gabby said. "We can do it together. We each put on a glove and hold on to Bakari and Liam and… and… "

"And what?" Jaimon said with exasperation. "Hope for a miracle?"

Gabby's eyes filled with tears, and she brushed them angrily away. "Yes, Jaimon. We hope for a miracle. It's all we *can* do!"

Jaimon nodded, looking a little taken aback at Gabby's outburst, and stood back up.

The healer looked at both of them and nodded. "I will guard the door so you are not disturbed. Good luck."

Gabby and Jaimon moved over next to Bakari and Liam. After they were settled they nodded to each other. Gabby motioned for Jaimon to put his glove on first. He did, then grabbed onto Liam with his other hand. Gabby put hers on and, with her gloved hand, held Jaimon's gloved hand, and with her other hand grabbed ahold of Bakari.

The Dragon King's skin felt cold and dry.

Gabby took a deep breath and drew upon her magic. Nothing happened.

"Jaimon, can you feel your dragon at all?"

After a moment, Jaimon whispered, "No."

"Try harder, just a spark," Gabby said. "You are still a dragon rider."

Gabby pushed more magic into herself and into the glove. Finally she felt a spark of Jaimon next to her and grabbed onto it.

"I can feel you, Jaimon."

"I was thinking about flying on Cholena. How beautiful she is." Jaimon's voice caught.

A bright light flared inside Gabby's mind, then settled into a dull grayness.

"I see it, Gabby," Jaimon said with excitement. "It's what Bakari calls the magic stream."

Gabby looked around and saw specks of light, some brighter than others. She thought of the Elves and wondered how she could get there. Suddenly in front of her were brighter lights.

Great Wizard, we will guide you, came a soft male voice.

Who are you? Gabby asked.

The Cremelinos. We will guide you to a place where the Dragon King and Liam can be healed. But we must hurry.

Suddenly in the corner of her mind she saw a bright light racing toward her.

It's Delia. She's felt us here. Hurry! one of the Cremelinos said. *Follow us.*

In Gabby's mind she saw hundreds of small lights racing by them. How could she know where to go?

Concentrate, said Flash. *Think of Elvyn.*

But I've never been there, Gabby cried out in her mind. Suddenly she felt something pulling her another way.

Found you, came Delia's voice.

"I've been there, Gabby," Jaimon said. "Look into my mind. Delia can't see me; I don't have magic. Look at me, Gabby!"

Gabby turned her attention away from Delia. Using her special *seeing* ability she looked into Jaimon's mind and saw the pain he felt from not having magic, his frustration at not being as good as the others. So much pent-up pain.

"Gabby!" Jaimon growled. "Concentrate on Elvyn, not me."

She looked deeper and saw the times Jaimon had been to Elvyn. She saw his memories of meeting King Lanwaithian and Breelyn. Suddenly a bright light flared up in her mind. *Breelyn!*

Go! The Cremelinos said.

Will you take us? Gabby asked.

No, even at our speed it will take too long, said one of the magical horses, *You must travel the magic stream. Hurry!*

Delia's light grew brighter and she soon joined them inside the magic stream, glaring triumphantly at Gabby.

Such weak children—you not even a dragon rider and Jaimon with not an ounce of magic in him. And poor Bakari. I see he has been poisoned. I will reward the person who did that.

Gabby thought about Angela and Dree, and it seemed that Delia read her thoughts.

Ah, so my cousin has succeeded.

Get out of my mind, Gabby bellowed in pent-up frustration.

Suddenly Gabby felt a different kind of magic surge around her. The Cremelinos. The same power the dragons had—the power of spirit—the power to bind. And they wrapped their power around Delia.

She screamed and tried to break through, but it did no good. Gabby thought about Breelyn and Elvyn again, and Delia faded into the distance.

Go and save them! Flash and Liberty said. *Go and find Kharlia!*

A bright light erupted in front of her, and she stumbled to a hard, wooden floor. She opened her eyes and looked around. Jaimon, Bakari, and Liam were with her in a different room, a large room with a throne up front and a multitude of benches and chairs. The wooden walls were shined to perfection, and the room seemed to sing to her.

Gabby stood up and glanced at Jaimon, who was struggling to get up himself. He leaned over and threw up with a loud groan.

"I'm never doing that again," Jaimon said, putting one hand against a wall to keep his balance. He held his head up with his other hand. "What did you do inside my mind?"

"I'm so sorry, Jaimon." Gabby didn't like *seeing* into people. "We had to get away from Delia. I... I..." She didn't know how else to apologize.

Jaimon glared at her a moment. "I don't want you in there ever again, Gabby. You promise?"

Gabby only nodded and hoped she could keep that promise.

Jaimon glanced around the room, and his eyes widened in apparent recognition. "You do know where we are, right?"

Gabby walked to a window. She looked out and placed her hand on the windowsill to keep from getting dizzy. She looked around the forest at the strange treehouses and people and let out a long sigh. "Elvyn."

CHAPTER TWENTY-SEVEN

With the sun still an hour away from cresting over Raleez, Roland was nudged awake by his dragon. Finding a nearby stream, he washed his face and smoothed down his hair. He really needed a good, warm bath and meal—and promised himself the reward once the morning activities played out.

Roland left his dragon outside the city and snuck back inside himself. He made his way to the twin castles, where both South and North Solshi ruled from. Guards patrolled both sides of the border but at this time of morning were tired and ready, too, for a warm meal. After watching two such guards pass, Roland ran to the wall and leaped over. Connecting the two castles of North and South Solshi was a giant courtyard garden. Roland paused just outside of the courtyard. Standing behind a large, leafless tree, he wrapped his golden cloak tighter around his body. His breath frosted the air a bit in front of him as he listened.

The distant sounds of gulls off in the bay and a slight breeze filled the early morning air. Slowly he slunk out from behind the tree and walked through a gate into the courtyard itself. Finding an evergreen bush, he moved behind it and waited to see how his plan would unfold. With winter taking most of the greenery away from the garden, he had a good view of the gazebo that stood in the center.

He didn't have to wait long. Soon from the North Solshi side came a group of people, led by whom he supposed was

Queen Esmaralda. Roland had never seen her in person before, and he had to admit she was quite striking. A dozen years or so older than he, she carried herself well. Long, wavy brown hair fell down a few inches past her shoulders. A warm winter cloak covered what appeared to be a fitted silk gown. Two men and a lady walked just behind her. All three were older than she and had similar scowls on their faces.

The four of them entered the gazebo and stood looking toward the southern castle. After a minute, the queen began to pace.

"This is dangerous, Your Highness," said one of the men with her.

"So you have already warned me, Minister Vasco," the queen said.

"The people were more restless last night," Vasco continued. "There is talk of a man helping the fishermen up the coast and paying their taxes for them."

The other lady stepped up to the queen and bowed her head. "Vasco is right. Someone is trying to undermine you. It is said that he convinced Valencia to open the food barns."

The queen's head whipped around. "Why wasn't I informed of this, Miranda? Why is this the first I have heard? Why would they do this?"

Miranda wrung her hands. "They were promised exclusive contracts with the other kingdoms for their textiles. I just heard about this last night, Your Highness."

Queen Esmaralda turned quickly to the third person with her retinue. "And Cristofer, do you also have bad news to tell me this morning?" The queen's eyes were dark and cold.

Roland had a hard time not smiling. He shifted a bit behind the bush to more fully see the four in the gazebo. Where was Regent Felipe? He should be here by now.

Cristofer bowed his head low, and when he brought his head back up he looked like he was sick. "My Queen, it is just an unsubstantiated rumor. You know how these things are. I'm sure it's nothing at all. I was going to check into it first thing this morning, but then you called us here."

"Quit babbling," Esmaralda snapped. "What are you talking about?"

"Well… " Cristofer paused.

A sound from the southern castle caught Roland's ears. Someone was coming.

"Cristofer!" the queen hissed at him.

"It is said that Guildmaster Ferdinand has stopped collecting taxes for shipping and returns the money back to the people." Cristofer said it with a wince and backed up a few steps after saying it.

Esmaralda's face turned red. "How dare he? What does he think he is doing? I'll have his head for this before the noon meal."

"It's said that a blond man in a golden cloak is behind it. The people are talking about him everywhere," Cristofer continued.

The other two nodded their heads.

"Roland," Vasco said. "They say his name is Roland. He is quickly gaining the people's hearts."

The queen looked about ready to strike her three ministers when, from the south, walked Regent Felipe with only one escort—a man dressed all in black, a hood over his head. The escort stood off to the side, watching the area carefully as the regent approached the queen.

Felipe bowed low before entering the gazebo. When he stood, his eyes sparkled as they looked at the queen. "Looking as beautiful as ever, Esmaralda."

"I'm not here at this time of morning for compliments, Felipe." The queen held her lips tight, and her cheeks flushed. "Why did you call this meeting?"

"Me?" Felipe said. "I was called here by you."

The queen looked back at her ministers, who only shrugged and looked ready to run at any moment.

"Someone is playing games here," Felipe said. "However," he looked around the garden area a moment.

Roland slid farther back behind the tree, careful not to make any noise. He wiggled his fingers around to maintain the circulation in the cold morning air.

"However," the Regent continued, "if we could speak alone?" he nodded his head toward her ministers.

"Yes, they're worthless anyway," Esmaralda snapped and turned her head to the side. "Ministers, you may leave me. Find me this Roland character and bring him to me."

The three cowed and bowed and soon walked off quickly back to their castle. Back behind the bush, Roland grinned widely.

The man with Felipe began to walk around the perimeter of the garden, as if sensing someone else's presence. He mustn't be found too soon. Oh, he wasn't afraid of the man— Roland could best him with the flick of his hand and a quick spell—but he wanted to wait until the right time to introduce himself.

The sun was now just beginning to crest, and a glow from the east pierced through the morning fog, bathing the courtyard in orange. Felipe walked closer to Esmaralda, looked around to make sure they were indeed alone, and took her hands softly in his.

"Esmaralda, you seem frustrated this morning," Felipe said. "What's wrong?"

The queen sighed and let out a deep breath. "Someone is trying to undermine me. A man, who seems to be everywhere at once. It's not possible, but the people are talking."

Felipe looked at her tenderly. He was at least ten years her senior. His hair was short and dark, and he sported a thick mustache. A dark cloak hung over his broad shoulders as he moved in and gave the queen a kiss.

Roland couldn't believe his luck. He rubbed his hands with glee. He hadn't known that the two were also a secret item. A sound to his left alerted him of Felipe's dark companion moving closer to him around the perimeter of the courtyard.

Felipe drew back. "It's time, Esmaralda. It's time to put the plan into action. I will take care of the boy tonight. The evidence will point to Quentis. An attempt to take advantage of a young king. You will pretend outrage, and the people of Solshi—both North and South—will rally behind us. We will raise taxes and gather an army to protect us against everyone."

A broad smile spread across Esmeralda's face, and she leaned in a bit closer to speak. Roland pulled upon a spell to hear them better. "The plans have changed, Felipe. I will rule Solshi under a larger banner."

Felipe's eyes looked troubled. "What do you mean, Esmaralda? I don't understand. The plan was always for us to be together and rule a combined Solshi."

Before Esmaralda could answer, the young King Andre burst out of the nearest castle doors; a half a dozen guards marched behind him.

"Felipe!" Andre called out, his young voice cracking just a bit.

Felipe turned around, and guilt flashed across his face. He bowed low. "My Lord."

"What treasonous actions do you plot behind my back with Queen Esmaralda?"

Felipe was not good at holding back his shock. The man that had come in with him suddenly moved through the courtyard and positioned himself behind Andre and his guards. Roland moved behind a smaller, closer bush to view the action. This had to play out just right.

Esmaralda took a few steps back and looked over her shoulder. Roland saw a glimpse of someone on the far side of the courtyard whom he hadn't noticed before. Dark hair moved closer behind a clump of bushes. He was sure it wasn't anything he couldn't handle.

"Guards, arrest Felipe for planning my death and conspiring with Queen Esmaralda," commanded Andre.

Two guards moved forward, but the man in the dark clothes moved swiftly and cut them off. He stood in front of them with a broad sword in his hands.

"The queen and I were just discussing business of the kingdoms, Andre," Felipe said, waving a hand for Esmaralda to join him. "There is nothing to worry about here. This is all just a misunderstanding."

Queen Esmaralda took another step back.

"Esmaralda?" Felipe called out.

Her visage grew darker. "I'm sorry, Felipe. I don't know what you mean."

"But… " Felipe stuttered. "You and me?"

Queen Esmaralda laughed. "You and me? Ah, Felipe, I have had a better offer."

Felipe ground his teeth, and his face flushed a bright red. "A better offer? I was giving you a kingdom, Esmaralda."

A few of the guards hissed and moved closer to Felipe. The man standing between them looked torn for a moment.

"Now you do speak treason, Felipe," Andre said. "Guards!"

Felipe's assistant brought his broad sword high in the air, but instead of attacking the guards he turned and threw the sword toward Esmaralda instead.

Roland gasped but stayed hidden. Maybe they would do his work for him.

Half of Andre's guards rushed the dark-cloaked man and took him to the ground. The rest grabbed Felipe and held him tight. But over behind Esmaralda, a person moved with such speed that it was only a black blur that pushed Esmaralda aside and grabbed the broadsword right out of the air.

Esmaralda's savior was hidden from Roland's view by a pole from the gazebo, but something in the way the person moved tickled Roland's mind.

The person, in dark leather clothes, leaned down and helped the queen back to her feet. Roland leaned out from the bush farther to get a better view.

Queen Esmaralda turned back to Felipe. "I'm sorry, Felipe, but I have been offered protection and help from a much greater power."

Felipe's eyes widened. "But who?"

Stepping forward, the person with Esmaralda came into full view. The alabaster skin, shoulder-length black hair and fighting stance was as familiar to Roland as his own reflection. Waves of nausea wracked his entire body with shock as he stumbled out from his hiding place.

"I am Allison Stenos, Dragon Rider, and representative of Dragon Queen Delia Marinos."

Roland groaned. This was definitely not part of his plan.

CHAPTER TWENTY-EIGHT

With the sound of Roland's groan everyone turned and looked in his direction. He straightened up, trying to regain his dignity, and did all he could do to stride forward. With the scepter extended in his right hand and the early rays of the sun catching on the edges of his cloak, he shone like the morning sun.

"Who are you?" Queen Esmaralda said with a stern look.

Stopping a dozen feet away from the others, Roland took a moment to gaze at Alli. Her full lips held firm, but her eyes darted around, trying to figure out what was happening. He turned and winked at Andre.

"I am Roland Tyre," said Roland, purposefully leaving off all of the other titles he had assumed.

The queen's eyes narrowed. "You are the one causing me so many problems."

"I am."

Alli took a step forward and cocked her head to the side almost as if remembering something; then she turned to the queen. "This man is in league with the Dragon King and fights against the true Dragon Queen, Delia—the Oracle of Turg."

Roland put a hand up in the air. "Now look here," he said. "I am definitely not in league with the Dragon King. I am my own man and make my own rules."

"But you know him," Alli said slowly.

Roland glared at her. "As do you, Alison Stenos. Or don't you remember leaving me as my battlemaster and scampering off after your beloved Dragon Master Bakari?"

Alli blinked a few times, obviously surprised at Roland's outburst. He snapped his mouth shut, berating himself for losing control.

"You are the man from my dream last night," said King Andre De Luz, stepping away from his guards, who still held his uncle Felipe and his companion tightly.

Roland smiled and raised his scepter slightly in greeting. It blazed a bright gold.

Unify them.

Roland smiled at the voice in his head. Orelia was waiting invisible just outside of the outer castle walls. The pounding in his head was the one thing he was now sure of. He had to unify all the nations to beat Delia.

"King Andre," Roland bowed to the boy. "I see you have caught your uncle and Queen Esmaralda in treachery."

Andre nodded. "Yes, Felipe will be stripped of his regency and await trial."

"But you are too young to make such decisions," Queen Esmaralda said, her voice softer now. "Join with me, and we can make Solshi strong gain. The Dragon Queen has offered us much."

Roland snorted. "The Dragon Queen—if she can actually use that title—has nothing to offer here. She stole the bonds of the dragons and is not a rightful ruler of anything more than Turg. And even that ruling is tenuous."

"Delia will sweep the nations under her," Alli said with a broad smile that never reached her eyes. "Turg, Cryrene, and Khazer already bow to her. Solshi and Alaris will be next."

Roland coughed, and Queen Esmaralda frowned.

"No one rules Alaris but me," Roland said. Then he turned to Esmaralda. "Is this what you want for your people, Esmaralda, to be ruled under a lady mad for power and caring little for her subjects?"

The queen pursed her lips and looked at Alli. "The man has a good point, Dragon Rider. What do I get out of this?"

"You get to live," Alli said without pause.

Esmaralda paled with the apparent realization that her choices were becoming more and more limited by the moment.

"Alli!" Roland said in exasperation. "Come to your senses." He took a step closer, and she moved into a battle-ready stance. "I won't fight you."

"Then you will die also," Alli said evenly and ran toward him.

It was all Roland could do to twist out of the way. Alli's outstretched arm hit his shoulder hard, knocking him off balance, but after a stumble he stayed standing.

"Now, look here, Alli." Roland was getting mad now. "I don't know what Delia did to you, but you are still my battlemaster. I command you to stop. I am your High Wizard."

Alli hesitated a moment.

"Remember, Alli," Roland pleaded with her now. Maybe he could reach her. "Remember when we met for the first time in Cassian. I felt something for you that first moment. Then our travels, the war, and now the last six months in the Citadel.

Do I mean nothing to you?" Roland's voice cracked at the question.

"I would never fall for the likes of you," Alli said, but her eyes looked wide and a bit uncertain. "You are arrogant, egotistical, and too powerful for your own good."

Roland laughed. "Yes, yes, you do remember me," Roland tried to lighten the mood. "Well, I take offense to your third point; I can never be too powerful. You see, my task is to unify all the kingdoms." He held up the scepter.

Alli flipped a hand out in front of her and threw a bolt of fire at his staff. It hit the glass orb on the end, and a bright light almost blinded all those in the courtyard. When Roland could see again, the scepter didn't look any different.

"This dragon artifact belongs to Delia as the true Dragon Queen," Alli spat.

Roland was getting tired of this. He would eventually rescue her and bring her to her senses, but first he had to get back to his plan.

Outside of the castle walls, the day was beginning, and noises of the people could be heard in the streets. Chanting began to sound, getting louder and louder. All present tilted their ears in that direction.

"What is all that noise?" Queen Esmaralda asked.

"That's your people revolting," Roland said with a wave of his hand. "Your food stores are being given out to the poor, taxes are being reduced, and new opportunities of trade have opened up to your people."

"Join us, Esmaralda," Alli said with a flourish of her hand. Suddenly, rising high in the sky behind Alli was her dragon,

Miriel. "Join the Dragon Queen's empire and rule a united Solshi under her banner."

Esmaralda's face lifted in thought. She glanced at Andre and a wicked smile spread across her face.

The crowd's noise picked up, and a loud crash echoed off the courtyard walls. Minister Vasco came running out of the castle doors. "My Queen, the people have taken down the front gate. They are running through the castle grounds!"

The crowd grew louder. Suddenly the chant became discernable. "Roland! Roland!"

A generous smile spread across Roland's face. With a wave of his own hand and a silent command to his dragon, Orelia suddenly appeared in the air above them. Those in the courtyard gasped. With flapping of wings, Orelia lowered herself into a bare spot not too far from Roland, his long tail knocking over a statue.

"Esmaralda, do something!" Felipe yelled out. He struggled and pulled free from the guards and ran to her. "We can still make this work. You and me. We can rule Solshi together."

"You have no authority, Uncle," said Andre.

"I am the regent still," Felipe said. "You are not old enough to be king and cannot command me."

Suddenly, through the castle doors emerged six men and women. Andre waved an arm in their direction. "By my recommendation and by the vote of the majority of the council, you are relieved as Regent officially. Guards!"

The guards moved toward him, but Felipe ran to Esmaralda's side. He pulled a knife from his waist and held it to the queen's throat.

"Stay back!" Felipe said.

"Felipe, what are you doing?" The queen tried to move her hand up to her neck.

"Stay still," Felipe said. Then turning to the others, he said, "You will let me leave, or I will kill the queen of North Solshi."

Andre's guards didn't appear too concerned. Roland took some steps back and rested his hand on his dragon. Taking a deep breath, he felt the power throbbing there. He shook his head at the scene in front of him. Such a waste. So many people obsessed with ruling, for the sake of ruling itself. They cared little about the law, and less about the people they should be protecting.

Felipe dragged the queen backwards toward her castle doors. Suddenly, over the walls of the courtyard climbed the people of North Solshi. Guards tried to pull them back down from the other side, but there were too many.

"Stay back!" Esmaralda cried out and waved a hand at the people, but they paid no attention to her. Their eyes were on Roland and his golden dragon.

Circling over their head was Miriel. Alli looked up and then back to the group around her. She glared hard at Roland. He only smiled back and raised his scepter to her.

"Dragon Rider," Queen Esmaralda said, "If you save me, I will side with the Dragon Queen. My people will be her people. She can have whatever she wants from them.

Alli gave Roland a smug look and took a step toward Felipe. Roland knew this wasn't going to end well for the man. A lone man holding a knife was no match for Alli. He recognized her stance, and in the blink of an eye she had Felipe's knife hand in her own and was pulling it away from the queen. She bent his wrist, and Roland heard a loud snap.

Felipe cried out in pain but tried to kick at Alli. With a push of her hand, she threw Felipe a dozen feet in the air, crashing against a courtyard wall. The man's head hit with a thud, and he slumped to the ground.

Without any weapons in hand, Queen Esmaralda then dove for Andre. "You little brat! You did all of this! Solshi is mine, you hear me? All mine!"

The dark-cloaked man who had been with Felipe twisted in the arms of his captors and grabbed a sword from one of them. In a move hardly faster than Roland could see, he jumped between Andre and Esmaralda.

His movements startled Esmaralda, and she tripped and fell forward into the point of the sword. A loud scream, then a softer gurgle, and the queen of North Solshi sank to the ground. The chanting crowd cheered around her body.

Roland winced; he surely hadn't planned on her dying. But he wouldn't lose sleep over it.

CHAPTER TWENTY-NINE

Alli gasped as Queen Esmaralda tripped and fell into the sword held by the man with the hooded cloak. A flash of her master's displeasure swept through her mind. *Delia will not be happy with this.* But maybe she could still salvage what was left and hand over Solshi to the Dragon Queen.

Cheers behind the man named Roland caught her attention. The walls of the courtyard were filling with men and women of the city. Guards stood nearby, but the overwhelming numbers, and now the death of their queen, gave them pause.

Without thinking about it, Alli's eyes went to Roland. Standing there in his golden cloak he did look arrogant but grand. Something tickled the edge of her mind as she thought about what he meant to her.

Roland took a step forward, but Alli snapped back to her task and in the moment of confusion turned and jumped toward the man who had killed the queen. He brought up his sword against hers, and they circled around for a moment. When Alli sliced her sword in, the man slithered to the side. When he came around with an arc of his sword she side-stepped, and the sword only caught air.

The man seemed content to stay on the defensive. Alli jumped in the air, ran up a column of the gazebo, and flipped over, coming down behind the man. This would be it.

But somehow the man ducked low and slid on the ground in as smooth a motion as Alli had ever seen. His moves seemed familiar to her, but like everything else in her life, she couldn't remember anything prior to her master, Constantine.

Alli grunted and hardened her face as she thrust out her hand toward the man and tossed him to the side. He obviously didn't have the powers she did.

He stood back up, and the cowl fell off his face. Alli wasn't the only one who gasped. The man, a few years older than Alli, could only be described as beautiful. His olive-skinned face was flawless, and his brown, almond-shaped eyes sat under the darkest lashes. When he smiled his teeth were a brilliant white. Recognition flickered at the edge of Alli's mind.

"Alli," he said, and his voice was as smooth as honey.

It was enough to stop Alli in her tracks. How did he know her? She lowered her sword and took a minute to get her breath.

"Alli," he said again. "It's me, Kas."

Kas? The name meant something to her, but she couldn't place it. But why was he trying to kill her? But was he really? As she thought over their short fight, he had never been the aggressor.

Roland took another step closer, and she quickly glanced at him. He, too, was staring at the man. Then recognition washed over his face.

"Kasper Von Wulf," Roland said under his breath, then louder. "What is the heir of Quentis doing here in disguise?"

The man named Kas smiled at Roland as if he shared a secret, but then looked back hopefully at Alli.

"I do not know you," Alli finally said to him.

Kas's face fell, and he turned to Roland again—this time with questioning eyes.

"Her memories have been erased, or at least suppressed," Roland said.

Alli tried to follow what they were saying about her. It was infuriating to have people talking about her and pretending to know her when her mind was only a large hole!

Alli screamed with the frustration and charged toward both of them. She would take care of them both, and then she could get back to Delia.

"What have you done to me?" Alli yelled, as much to Constantine, Delia, and herself, as to the two men in front of her. Sword in one hand and a ball of fire in the other, she jumped high in the air, preparing to destroy them both.

Before Roland or Kas could react, the Golden Dragon let out a deafening roar and spit fire from his giant mouth. Sparks and flame of gold, orange, and red shot forth, racing toward Alli with unbelievable speed. Suddenly from above another roar sounded, and Miriel swooped down with her own fire. A feeling of awe and pride filled Alli's heart. The two flames met between Roland and Alli, exploding into a bright light, then extinguishing.

Roland ran and jumped up on a rock a few feet away, then slammed down the golden scepter he always seemed to have at his side. "Enough!" His voice echoed across the castle and courtyard walls, and silence fell. Miriel landed behind Alli, knocking down part of the gazebo as she did. Alli stepped back closer to her dragon.

Roland took the scepter and raised it high above his head. He swung it around, and a bright, golden light spread out from him across the courtyard, over the castle and the outside walls, through the city of Raleez itself.

Birds stopped their morning song, babies ceased their crying, venders closed their mouths, and all went quiet. In the courtyard itself, Alli, along with Kas and Andre with his guards, stood staring in turn at each other.

In the quiet of the morning air Roland spoke, and his voice was clear. "King Andre, it seems you need a new regent." Roland glanced at Filipe still on the ground and not moving. He was either dead, from Alli's attack, or very injured. In either case, he would be regent no longer. "Who will you name?"

The young king didn't even hesitate. "I name Roland Tyre Regent of South Solshi."

The group of councilors took a step forward behind Andre, and one of them took an additional step. "Sire," he bowed low. "We will take your suggestion into advisement, but we don't even know this man."

Roland cleared his throat and looked down at the man. With a nod and then a flourishing bow, Roland spoke again. "Master Councilor, it is good to see you have the good will of our young king in mind. I, too, wish him well. Let me introduce myself to you."

With another wave of his scepter, Roland's cloak began to glow as if the golden sun itself fell into the courtyard. Alli and others close by had to shield their eyes. Alli's mind thumped with the power that crackled in the air around her. She needed to find a way out of there.

"I am Roland Tyre, High Wizard of the Citadel of Alaris, King of Alaris, Monarch of Tillimot, and rider of the golden dragon," Roland said. At that, his dragon lifted his head up in the air and roared. Golden light flew up into the sky and exploded over their heads like fireworks in the sky. The crowd cheered.

"I assure you," Roland continued, "my credentials are impeccable."

A little over the top, Alli thought. *So much like Roland.* The thought surprised her, and she moved back closer to her dragon. Bringing her hand up, she rested it on her dragon. Did she really know the man in front of her?

The councilor paled, looking back over his shoulder to the other counselors. They nodded to him, and he turned back around and bowed low to Roland.

"In light of the circumstances," he said, "we accept King Andre's suggestion to have Roland Tyre named regent of South Solshi."

The people cheered and began to chant Roland's name. With each utterance of his name something clicked inside of Alli. Flashes of recognition—mostly jumbles of past events— jumped in and out of her mind. She glared at Roland as if daring him to call to her once again.

Roland cleared his voice. "Ah, there is one other piece of business. It seems that North Solshi's queen is dead and she has no heirs. If I remember my studies of history correctly, if this circumstance ever happened to either the north or the south, that kingdom's rule would be dissolved, and North and South Solshi would become one again under the existing ruler—which, for now, would be me, and then Andre's on his sixteenth birthday."

King Andre's eyes went wide, but after conferring with his counselors he turned back to Roland.

"Be it known," King Andre said in his young voice, "that Roland Tyre is now regent of all of Solshi, and I at the age of sixteen will assume the throne for both kingdoms—Hail Solshi. Hail Roland Tyre."

"Hail Solshi!" yelled a lone man in back.

"Hail Roland Tyre," said another.

"Roland. Roland. Roland." The crowd swelled forward with a loud cheer.

With each iteration of Roland Tyre's name, walls seemed to crumble down inside of Alli's mind. With her hand still on her dragon, a new feeling surged within her.

Dragon Rider, came the voice of Miriel, and tears came to her eyes. She had finally spoken to Alli.

Roland called to her. "Alli, it is your choice. Return with me. Rule by my side. Be not only my battlemaster, but be my queen."

Alli gasped in surprise. *A queen?* One foot moved toward him. Scenes of the Citadel flashed through her mind. "Roland?" she whispered.

"Yes, Alli!" Roland jumped off the rock and began to move toward her, but suddenly the crowd swelled around them, and he couldn't reach her. "Alli!" he yelled out.

Suddenly she saw him again, standing on the remains of the gazebo, now a pile of debris. Alli watched him carefully, not knowing what to feel or do.

But then Miriel roared, and the voice of Delia, her master, came crashing through her mind, wiping away any last thoughts of Roland.

Come back to me, riders. The Dragon King is with the Elves, Delia said, the vibrations of her voice loud and clear in her mind. *We prepare for war!*

"Master?" Alli said both out loud and in her mind. Her master called, and she must leave. She climbed up the side of her dragon and settled down between her neck and wings. She glanced down at the crowd once again.

Roland caught her attention once more. What had they been talking about before? Something lingered in the back of her mind, but insistent calls from Delia turned her attention back to her. Alli was the Dragon Queen's rider and was sworn to respond in time of need.

"Alli, where are you going?" Roland yelled out.

She looked down at him, and something in her mind bade her to answer. She put a hand to her head and groaned with frustration. The crowd was loud, and Alli could hardly hear her own thoughts.

She looked down into his pleading eyes and for some reason felt drawn in once again. She rose higher in the air, and his golden form grew smaller below her.

"Where, Alli, where are you going?" he shouted again, his voice growing smaller in the crowd.

His blue eyes bore into her. Commanding, yet compassionate at the same time. For a moment she broke and knew she had to tell him something.

"Back to my master," came a soft whisper.

Tears filled Alli's eyes, knowing she had hurt Roland. She mentally commanded Miriel to fly faster. She really didn't care where at the moment. Anywhere but in a direct line of sight of Roland Tyre's eyes.

Fly, Miriel. Fly.

The dragon picked up speed, but once again there was no answer. Alli hardened her heart. Once more she flew to her master.

CHAPTER THIRTY

Gabby turned away from the window in Elvyn and joined Jaimon, who was looking over Bakari and Liam.

"They don't look well," Jaimon said.

"I know," Gabby whispered and shook her head. "The Cremelinos said to find Kharlia."

"I hope she is nearby," Jaimon said. "I'm not sure they can last much longer. The Dragon King's breath grows shallower." His voice caught for a moment, and then he continued. "And Liam barely looks alive."

"Hold!" commanded a voice from the door to the room. Within a matter of moments, a dozen Elvyn warriors filled the room. Each of them, but one, had a bow trained on Jaimon and Gabby.

The eyes of the man without the bow swung quickly around the room. Seeing Bakari on the ground, he gasped and moved forward.

"King Lanwaithian Soliel," Gabby said quietly and bowed to the obvious leader of Elvyn.

On the way there the king looked at Jaimon and smiled in acknowledgement. "Dragon Rider," he nodded his head. "Normally I would say it is nice to see you, but..." he knelt down next to Bakari and ran his hand over the Dragon King's braids.

The king, like most Elves, was tall and slender. His dark hair fell straight down his back, and Gabby could see one of his tipped ears poking out as he studied both Bakari and Liam. A shiny silver knife was tucked into his clothes.

"King Lanwaithian," Gabby began. "We need to see the healer, Kharlia."

"Please call me Lan," Lanwaithian said as he stood back up. His eyes gleamed with intelligence. "We are not so formal here."

Gabby looked back at the men with the king. They still held their bows taut and scanned the room for trouble. She cleared her throat to get the king's attention.

Lanwaithian noted her sign, nodded to his men, and they lowered their bows but still looked ready to pounce at a moment's notice.

"The Dragon King and his rider have been poisoned with something that feeds off of their magic," Jaimon reported to the king. "We are afraid they might not make it much longer."

"The Cremelinos told me to find Kharlia, the healer," Gabby said.

King Lanwaithian let out a deep sigh. "Kharlia is not here. She went with a delegation to Alaris ten days ago, and we have not heard from them since."

Gabby glanced at Jaimon, and his face fell.

The king appeared in deep thought; then his eyes brightened as he turned to Jaimon. "Dragon Rider, with your dragon you could find Kharlia and bring her back. Where is your dragon?" Lanwaithian had moved to the window and looked outside. "I do not see her at the bay."

"She is not here," Jaimon said, his lips tight. "She took them."

"Who took what?" said a new voice.

Gabby turned to the newcomer and saw the most beautiful Elf she had ever seen and knew at once it was Breelyn, the wife of the Elvyn King. She was a famed Elvyn guardian and had been a dragon rider for a short time. Gabby had heard both Alli and Bakari mention her at times. Her long blonde hair parted at the middle and hung down to her waist. Her skin was pale, and she had light blue eyes. Gabby instinctively moved her hand up to her own hair, sure it was a mess.

Gabby, following Jaimon's lead, bowed to the queen before answering.

"Delia Marinos, the new Oracle of Turg, has stolen the dragon bonds," Gabby said. "She now calls herself the Dragon Queen."

The king and queen's eyes widened as they regarded first each other, and then Gabby and Liam.

Breelyn cocked her head at Gabby, and then her eyes sought out Jaimon. He blushed but held her attention a moment before speaking.

"This is Gabrielle Von Wulf," Jaimon said, motioning to Gabby. "She is princess of Quentis."

"Ah, Princess," the queen said. "I am Breelyn."

"Bakari and Liam are dying, and we need a healer," Gabby said. It was rude, she knew, but they had no time for formalities.

"Get the healers." Breelyn snapper her fingers, and a guard took off running. Gabby heard a few yells outside, and within the matter of moments four people entered—one woman and three men. They carried two stretchers. The men laid Bakari and Liam on each one, and the woman proceeded to kneel over the Dragon King. She closed her eyes and ran her hand over his body, then jerked and pulled back.

"The poison feeds off of magic and makes the poison work quicker," said Gabby. "We were told to find Kharlia, that she could help."

The healer nodded and took out a few vials from her robe. She mixed them together with a small amount of water and then brought the cup to Bakari and Liam's lips. The liquid slid over their parched lips, and Gabby saw them swallow.

"Kharlia may indeed be able to help," the healer said. "She saved our king. But she is not here."

"Halleema," said the king, "take them to the healing room and gather all the healers in Elvyn. We must not let the Dragon King die."

The healers gathered them up and out of the room. Gabby and Jaimon stood together and watched. The queen came up behind them and put a hand on each of their shoulders. "We will care for them. Come and have a meal with us and tell us your story. We don't always keep up with all that happens among the race of men."

Gabby and Jaimon followed the king and queen of Elvyn down the tree and to the ground. Gabby peered up through the trees and marveled.

"First time here, huh?" Jaimon said with a wistful smile.

"Yes," Gabby said. "It's as beautiful as they say." They walked along a soft patch of rich brown soil. Ferns and other broad-leaf bushes filled both sides of the path. Colorful birds flitted around between the tops of the bushes and the branches of the wide trees. Gabby caught glimpses of houses and other beautiful structures between the leaves. The sun sparkled down between the breaks in the leaves.

"Smell that?" Gabby asked Jaimon with a deep breath.

"Just like home," Jaimon said with a sigh.

The salty air reminded her of her homeland, and she blinked away a few stray tears as she thought about her family. Her brother, Kaspar, had been gone for the last month on what her father said was a secret mission. With her father's ability to *see,* and as the head of the followers of the dragon in the south, Gabby wondered if he had had a premonition of what would happen with Bakari and the dragons.

They were led to another tree. Other Elves stood there and bowed to their king and queen. "Dragon Rider," they said with a smile, and Jaimon nodded back. The four of them stepped onto a platform, and the two other men began to pull a series of pulleys to lift them up in the air.

"Hold there!" yelled a man who came running out of the forest. "My King and Queen," he said as he tried to rush a bow.

The men lowered the platform, and the king stepped off to greet the man. "Ambassador Rassdurthian." He looked behind the man. "Where are the others?"

"I am not sure, Sire," Rassdurthian said, still trying to catch his breath. "I came as fast as I could. I have ill news."

The king's eyes grew troubled, and he motioned Rassdurthian to join them on the lift. "It seems ill tidings are the words of the day. Come and dine with us and tell us what has happened."

It was only then that the ambassador seemed to notice Gabby and Jaimon standing there. He bobbed his head to Jaimon.

"This is Gabrielle Von Wulf, princess of Quentis," Jaimon said in introduction.

Ambassador Rassdurthian bowed his head to her, and his eyes squinted with confusion. He looked back at the king, but no one spoke further.

The group was pulled up a hundred feet in the air, passing multiple platforms, until they finally stopped. Gabby put her hand on her stomach for a moment to steady herself.

"Are you all right?" Queen Breelyn said.

Gabby nodded. "Yes. It's just been a long day. Only a short time ago we were in Alaris."

Breelyn placed a soft hand on Gabby's arm and laughed lightly. It was as if music filled the air. Gabby's tension and apprehension faded away, and she regarded the queen in wonder.

"It will be all right," Breelyn said. "I've known the Dragon King for quite some time. He has a way of getting out of impossible situations."

Gabby hoped so. She was worried that Kharlia wasn't there and that the Elves, although concerned, seemed to not be moving around with much sense of urgency.

An hour later they finally finished eating and started discussing the business of the other kingdoms. The news that Gabby and Jaimon brought about Delia taking the dragon bond was met with obvious anxiety. And the news that Rassdurthian had brought about Tillimot invading Alaris and Roland's subsequent grab for power fit in with what Gabby and Jaimon had seen of Roland.

"What about Bakari and Liam?" Gabby finally said. "How do we find Kharlia?"

"The last I saw of Kharlia was in Corwan in southern Alaris." Rassdurthian shook his head. "Roland mentioned that he had seen her there after its destruction, but I do not know where she has gone hence or how to find her."

"If we just had our dragons," Jaimon said under his breath, "or even the Cremelinos, we could find her."

Gabby wrung her hands. "Is there nothing else you can do? By the time we find her they will be dead!" She stood and turned her back on the group.

She tried to be strong. She was the daughter of the Wolf and sister to Kaspar, both highly respected men in Quentis, but she was young and unprepared. She couldn't let Bakari die; at the same time, she felt utterly helpless. Her fists clenched, and tears trickled down her face.

The room behind her grew quiet, and soon she felt a soft hand on her shoulder. She looked up. It was Jaimon. He smiled at her, but his eyes held pain, too. In the midst of her pity she had forgotten that besides all that they were dealing with, Jaimon had also lost the bond with his dragon.

"I'm sorry," she whispered to him.

He only shook his head and put his arm around her. "It's all right, Gabby. We'll find a way. We'll find Kharlia."

They stood that way for a moment. Then she straightened quickly.

"That's it, Jaimon," Gabby said. "*We* will find Kharlia. We'll use the gloves again. The dragon artifact allowed us to see the sparks of magic. We can find her and bring her to us."

King Lanwaithian called to them, and they turned around and returned to the table. The worry in his eyes was obvious. They waited for him to speak. When he did it was not what they wanted to hear.

"From what you have told me, Delia could follow you through the magic stream," the king said. "If you used the gloves again you could pull her right here. I'm sorry; I cannot allow you to do that. You cannot bring your war here."

"But Bakari…" Gabby sighed. "He might die."

The king only shook his head. "He's my friend, too. I would do anything for him."

Jaimon took a step forward. "Anything but get involved in the affairs of men, you mean."

A gasp filled the room, but no one stopped him from talking.

"The Elves have sat too long on their own," Jaimon said. "The dragon riders saved the kingdoms once already. It is only a matter of time until evil reaches your shores; until Delia arrives with her dragons and an army. What will we do then? Will men leave you to your own devices?"

"Jaimon!" Gabby said.

Rassdurthian stood up quickly, but his face did not hold anger. "Dragon Rider," he bowed to Jaimon. "We recognize the wise words of the dragon riders. For thousands of years our race and your riders have held only the highest esteem for one another."

"Then do something about this!" Jaimon said.

The ambassador looked over at the king and spoke freely. "Roland Trye had recently spoken similar words to me. We have indeed hidden ourselves away for much of our existence. I was sent as the head of the delegation to begin establishing relationships once again with the other kingdoms. If what Jaimon says is true, we may have need of them someday. And if that day comes and we have not shown our willingness to help them we may indeed not receive any help."

This time it was Lanwaithian who stood back up. He looked at his wife, who nodded.

"You know my thoughts on the matter, Lan," she said to her husband. "I was the first one to enter Alaris as the barrier went down."

The king turned to Jaimon and Gabby. "I am not angry at your words, Dragon Rider. You do indeed speak the truth, as our Ambassador has said. But it is a hard thing you ask of us."

"What would Bakari do for you?" Gabby whispered.

Silence filled the room for a solid minute. The birds outside even seemed to quiet down. Only the rustle of the wind through the trees and the distant break of the waves on the shore drifted through the room.

The king offered a grim smile and nodded.

The queen joined her husband and interlocked the fingers of her left hand with his right one. Tears glittered in her pale eyes. "We will do everything in our power to save the Dragon King. You have our promise."

"But don't expect it to be easy," Rassdurthian said. "With Roland Tyre involved, who knows what may happen."

CHAPTER THIRTY-ONE

The crowd surged around Roland, still chanting his name, but all he could think of at the moment was Alli. It tore at his heart to see her like she was. She had always been a feisty one, full of spunk, but her loyalty and compassion were as strong as her battle skills. He gritted his teeth at what had been done to her—and all in the company of the Dragon King. It was his fault! *His fault!* Bakari should have looked after his riders better.

Roland held the scepter tight, letting the orb dig into the palm of his hand. And let the anger build.

"Curse him!" he spat out.

"Who?" Kaspar Von Wulf walked up next to him.

Roland turned his direction. He had seen the man before, and it irked him to see someone so perfect. He glared back.

"The Dragon King," Roland said. "He should have protected her better."

"From what I know of Alli, she usually does not need protection," said Kaspar. "She can hold her own."

"Then what happened?" Roland roared and others near him backed away. "Can you explain that to me? She doesn't remember who she is."

Kaspar's eyes flashed in surprise, but Roland cared little for what the man thought of him.

"Surely the Dragon King didn't do that to her," Kaspar said with smooth tones. Even after his battle with Alli, his dark hair sat perfectly combed on his head, and his clothes looked hardly dirtied. "It's this woman—Delia, the one who calls herself the new Dragon Queen. She is the one to blame, the one we should be going after."

"We, Prince of Quentis?" Roland asked. With the hand not holding the scepter he snatched Kaspar's arm in his grip.

Kaspar flinched but did nothing to get away. He only gazed into Roland's eyes, and Roland felt something pushing against his mind.

"What are you doing here as an assassin, Prince of Quentis?" Roland could barely control another outburst.

Kaspar glanced around at the people. King Andre stood off at a respectable distance, but Roland could tell he could hear the exchange.

"I could ask the same of you, Roland Tyre," Kaspar pushed back. "What is the High Wizard of the Citadel doing collecting kingdoms?"

Unify. Unify. Unify. Roland took his hand from Kaspar and put it to his throbbing head.

"It's the Scepter of Unification, High Wizard," Kaspar said. "It's affecting your ability to think clearly. You are being torn up inside. You want more power and the adoration of the people, but conquering all the nations is not going to accomplish what you want. You will never have enough." He whispered this, so only Roland could hear.

Roland tapped the scepter on the ground in frustration. "What do you know of what I want or need?" He felt a pressure on his mind and realized it was the Prince of Quentis trying to see into his mind. "Get out of there!"

Roland used his considerable powers and mentally, then physically pushed Kaspar back away from him. The man stumbled but didn't fall. His eyes opened wide with surprise at Roland's apparent power.

Turning to King Andre, Roland took command. "Gather the councilors from North and South Solshi. I will meet with them before I leave."

"Leave, sir?" Andre came up closer to him. "So soon? Where will you go?"

Roland twisted his head around and glared at Kaspar. "The Prince of Quentis and I will be traveling to Quentis. There is work I have there to do to unify the people."

Kaspar narrowed his eyes and shook his head. "Sir, my father will not welcome…"

Roland threw his hand out, and Kaspar flew through the air, landing at the feet of Orelia. "Watch the prince for me, Orelia," Roland said out loud for the benefit of Kaspar. "He seems to think that I am making a request."

Kaspar had the good graces to keep quiet and only stood back up and glared back at Roland. Roland turned back to Andre. "And along with the councilors, make sure that Guildmaster Ferdinand is there."

King Andre gulped but bowed low. "Yes, Regent."

With that Roland jumped up on his dragon and lifted up into the air. "I will be back to meet with them in one hour," Roland shouted and flew up and over the city of Raleez.

The crowds below him yelled out in greetings. Their smiles softened his anger, and he lifted up higher and felt the freedom of the skies once again. He needed a few minutes to think before meeting with the councilors

* * *

Three hours later, Roland and Kaspar sat on the back of Orelia and headed southeast toward Margarid, the capital of Quentis. Kaspar's hands held on to Roland's waist—an awkward touch, to say the least, especially after the words they had exchanged. Through the help of his scepter's power, Roland had picked high-ranking ministers and councilors in both North and South Solshi that he could trust to run the kingdom in his absence. His thoughts turned back to Alaris now—with his quick exit there and direction to Daymian Khouri to handle Tillimot for him, he wondered who was running things there. He would have to check on that as soon as he was finished in Quentis.

"Why do you hate him so?" Kaspar said from behind.

"Who?" Roland asked, already knowing the answer.

"The Dragon King," came Kaspar's reply.

Roland sighed. "I don't hate him."

"Why are you so angry with him, then?"

"Because he doesn't realize the power that he has—or had." Roland wasn't sure of Bakari's status at the moment.

"Maybe he does realize the power he has, and that's why he doesn't use it all the time," Kaspar said.

Roland grunted. Why was he arguing with this man?

"Much of the potential in having power is knowing when to use it and when to not," Kaspar said. "More and more power does not determine greatness. It's how you use the power you have that brings distinction with the people."

Roland turned his head. "And what do you know of power, Kasper Von Wulf? I saw how Alli threw you back like a rag doll."

"You saw what I wanted you to see, High Wizard."

Suddenly the dragon dipped lower, and Roland cried out and grabbed on tighter. Out of the corner of his eye he saw Kaspar holding a strange object with one hand while the other hand stroked the golden scales of the dragon.

"What are you… ?" Roland couldn't even finish his sentence before the dragon did a nose dive toward the mountains of Quentis.

Stop. Orelia, Stop, Roland commanded.

There was no response, and Roland dug deeper in his mind for the connection with his dragon. Instead of finding his dragon he found Kaspar in his mind.

High Wizard, Kaspar spoke to his mind. *As I said, powerful people know when to use power and when to not.*

Roland growled in frustration. *You'll kill yourself along with me if that's the purpose of this little demonstration.*

Light laughter filled Roland's mind, and the dragon leveled off. Kaspar's presence disappeared from his mind, and once again Roland could feel the magic of his dragon and the scepter.

Nothing was said for a few minutes as they flew over the peaks in the northern part of Quentis. After a few deep breaths, Roland was back in control.

"So you could have bested Alli," Roland grumbled.

"Yes," Kaspar said. "Oh, don't get me wrong. She is very, very good. But I am a better fighter than she. I lost to her once in a sparring match and vowed to never lose again."

"And the dragon?" Roland asked.

"I hold a dragon artifact that, along with other abilities I possess, allows me to do many things, Roland Tyre."

"That's not fair," Roland said under his breath. Why should someone else have that kind of power?

"And that scepter of yours?" Kaspar asked. "Is that fair? Do you even know what it is?"

Roland twisted his head around. "Yes, I know what it is. It's a constant pounding in my head. It's the Scepter of Unification."

"And you intend to keep using it?"

"Of course," Roland said. "Why do you think we are flying to Quentis? It's the last kingdom for me to unify before I take on Delia and her dragons."

Not the last, came the voice of the scepter.

Roland wasn't quite sure how to take that. He would have five kingdoms under his control once he left Quentis. Wasn't that enough?

There was no answer.

"Why were you in Solshi, anyway?" Roland changed the direction of the conversation.

"Ah," Kaspar sighed. "As you knew, Queen Esmaralda was getting out of control. Her people were suffering, and there was a growing instability in the region that was not good for Quentis."

"But you were with the regent, and his plan was to get rid of the king and merge the kingdoms under him and Esmaralda. What good would that do?"

"Actually, we had heard of the plan, and my job was to make sure that didn't happen," said Kaspar. "My actions there were to help King Andre gain a more firm footing, but…" he coughed for a moment. "It seems you had the same idea. But a different approach."

"I don't have time for a more subtle approach. I must unify the kingdoms."

Unify them. Unify them. Roland pushed the constant pounding to the back of his mind.

"Well, flashing that golden scepter around and bringing in the golden dragon surely wasn't subtle," Kaspar mumbled. "I don't know how you will be greeted by my father, Roland. But I will stand up for you."

The last statement surprised Roland. "And why would you do that?"

Kaspar shifted a bit behind Roland and leaned closer to his ear. He could smell the spicy breath of the prince of Quentis and tried to move away.

"I have seen into your heart and mind," Kaspar said softly. "I may not agree with your means, but your heart is in the right place. That is where greatness is defined. You are actually quite a good person, Roland Tyre, High Wizard."

High Wizard. Hah! Roland thought. *The least of my titles now.* Did Kaspar use that title on purpose? The prince shifted farther back in his seat as off in the distance Roland spotted Margarid, the capital city of Quentis. Darkness was just descending, and lights around the city highlighted domed roofs and palm trees. The tips of the turquoise waves in the Bay of Ghazi picked up the last rays of the setting sun.

"Beautiful, isn't it?" Kaspar said.

Roland only nodded. He had never been this far south before. Since the barrier around Alaris had fallen last year, he had been busy trying to clean up the pieces of a civil war and run the Wizard Citadel. He hadn't had time to travel, and he hadn't had a dragon to do it on. He rubbed his hands lovingly over the hard scales of Orelia.

CHAPTER THIRTY-TWO

Kaspar directed Roland to a place to land just outside the city walls, and soon the two of them were being escorted by an honor guard through the city and toward the palace. The air was warmer and drier here, and Roland found himself instantly liking the capital city of Quentis. His mood lightened, and he quickened his pace. He was anxious to bring another kingdom into the fold.

Unify them!

I know. I know.

The people of Quentis were beautiful. Olive complexions, shiny black hair, and friendly smiles met them at every turn. They waved at Kaspar, and he smiled back and commented to many of them.

"Do you know them all?" Roland asked.

"No, not all." Kaspar waved at an older lady and told her he was excited for her next grandchild.

"But they treat you like a friend," Roland said. "You know about their children, work, and families."

"It's what a good ruler does," Kaspar said. "Ruling is a privilege, and it is our responsibility to protect and serve the people. They should be happy—not like in Solshi."

Roland nodded his head. "I agree."

"I know," Kaspar said with a twinkle in his eye.

"You're not rummaging around in my mind again, are you?" Roland glared at the prince.

"No," Kaspar shook his head. "I can just tell. You are a good ruler, Roland," he paused a bit.

"But?" Roland prompted.

"But, I just don't know if you can handle all you've taken on."

"I don't have a choice."

They passed through the palace gates, and Kaspar directed them down a path to a side door of the castle.

Roland gave him a questioning look.

Kaspar laughed. "A grand entrance is not always the best way. Today we will see my father in private."

Roland grunted but supposed the prince might be right. This was a kingdom at peace and not a conquest that he would win through power and might. These people didn't need to be saved by him, but they needed him just the same. He wasn't sure why, but the thumping in his head was insistent. And he had learned to trust the voice that constantly reminded him to unify the people. It had grown more urgent of late and Roland was anxious.

The grounds of the palace were like a garden of paradise. Even in the winter sculpted trees lined the pathways, and flower beds surrounded broad green lawns that were manicured to perfection. Glancing up, Roland watched the silhouetted sway of palm trees in the sea breeze. Soon they came to a side door, where one guard nodded to the prince and let them through.

Roland was actually sorry to have not stayed longer in the garden. It made the one in the Citadel appear barbaric and untidy. He would have to do something about that when he returned.

The shiny marble floor of the palace reflected light from the hundreds of candles that lined the hallway. Large tapestries covered the walls. Suddenly Roland stopped and stared at one.

Kaspar turned his head, then stopped and headed back. "What is it?"

Roland gazed over the tall tapestry in front of him. It was of a man similar to the one in the Citadel tapestry. He was tall, with dark hair, and wore a crown. In his right hand he held the scepter.

"Come, the Wolf is waiting." Kaspar motioned with his hand and continued walking down the hall.

Roland started after him but turned his head and glanced at the tapestry once again. The man in the scene exuced great power, but then Roland saw the man's eyes. They bored into his own. They were dark and troubled and tired. He shivered and turned back around and followed Kaspar.

The scepter had promised him power and glory, but in return what would it require of him?

Two guards flanked a door, and with a nod of his head, Kaspar directed them to open it for them. Upon entering, Kaspar moved out in front and cleared his throat.

A man, Roland presumed the leader of Quentis, the Wolf, looked up at his son. His body stayed relaxed, but his eyes grew concerned for a moment.

"Sire," Kaspar bowed his head with hands clasped in front of him, "may I present to you Roland Trye, High Wizard of the Citadel of Alaris, King of Alaris, Monarch of Tillimot, Regent of North and South Solshi, Dragon Rider, and possessor of the Scepter of Unification." The last title he uttered as if it was the most important of all Roland's titles. "Roland, this is my father, the King of Quentis, Mathias Von Wulf, or just the Wolf for short." Kaspar grinned and looked back and forth between Roland and his father.

The Wolf stood up from his seat and moved around his dark mahogany desk and approached Roland slowly, his eyes never wavering from Roland's own.

Roland swallowed hard. The man's coloring was similar to his son's, but he stood taller. His shoulders were broad, but with all his size he moved in a smooth and distinct motion around Roland. But it was his eyes that bore into Roland.

Here was a man that knew things. The King, simply known to the nations around him as the Wolf, stopped about three feet in front of Roland. A power rose up inside him as if in automatic recognition of this king's power. Something tickled the edges of his mind, and Roland slammed it shut harder than he probably should have.

The Wolf swayed on his feet a bit, and Kaspar was quickly at his side.

"You are strong, Roland Tyre," said the Wolf. "But are you too strong or not strong enough? We shall see."

What did that mean? Roland wondered if the man was all there or not. How could Roland be too strong or not strong enough? The comparison made no sense.

"King of Quentis," Roland bowed his head slightly, trying to take control of the situation. "It is an honor to meet you. Your kingdom is beautiful, and your people are stunning. I have never seen gardens so colorful and elegant in my entire life."

"But then you haven't lived that long, have you?" the Wolf said with a twinkle in his eye.

Roland realized the man was toying with him.

The Wolf directed the three of them to a set of chairs off to the side. A small, rectangular table at knee height held an assortment of fruits, breads, and a chilled pitcher of something that looked refreshing—all set as if the Wolf had been expecting them. After sitting down, the Wolf poured a glass for each of them and leaned back in his high backed chair. Roland was surprised that there were no servants in the room.

Chilled, tangy pomegranate juice ran down the back of Roland's throat as he took a sip of the refreshing beverage. It had been a while since he had eaten anything, and he followed the Wolf's actions and grabbed a plate of oranges and fresh bread.

"You seem to have been expecting me," Roland said between bites.

"I like to keep abreast of what is going on," the Wolf said. "Your exploits over the last week or so have come to my attention. But I have not heard about the outcome in Solshi yet." He looked at his son.

"The queen is dead and the Regent has been incapacitated and released from service," Kaspar reported evenly. "King Andre has retained a stronger hand and now will rule a united Solshi upon his sixteenth birthday."

"I take it that Roland was named as regent?" the Wolf peered back and forth between the two.

Roland nodded. "Sir, I am driven to unite the kingdoms. Delia, the new Oracle of Turg, has stolen the bond of the dragons and names herself the Dragon Queen. She has designs to rule all the southern kingdoms, but I will stop her."

"And what about the Dragon King? Where is he?" the Wolf asked, his face grave. "His fate should be one of your greatest concerns."

Roland ground his teeth. "He has let some of this fall on himself. The bonds were stolen while his dragons slept, and Dragon Rider Allison Stenos has sided with the new Oracle."

The Wolf's eyes narrowed. He looked at Kaspar for confirmation.

"I fought her, Father," said Kaspar. "She remembers nothing. Somehow her mind has been altered, and she doesn't know who she is. The High Wizard is right."

Roland bristled a bit at still being referred to as only the High Wizard.

"That is ill news," the Wolf said.

The three took bites of food and stayed deep in their own thoughts for a few minutes. Roland finished his orange and licked his fingers.

Finally the Wolf pointed to Roland's scepter, which was tied next to his waist. "You realize the responsibility you have with this scepter, young man?"

Roland felt like a student again in the Citadel under the Wolf's chastising tone. But he was Roland Tyre. He was magic.

Placing his hand on the orb of the scepter, Roland stood. Power flared through him, and the scepter brightened.

"Sir, I assure you, that I know what this is and what I am doing," Roland said. "I am not some new student playing with magic for the first time. I am a level-four wizard—with the power of the scepter, even more. I have powers of the earth, heart, and mind; I am magic!"

The Wolf stood and even from a few feet away looked down on Roland. "Don't be sure you know everything. Once you think you know it all and have all power, that is when you will make your mistake."

Roland opened his mouth to argue, but the Wolf pushed through.

"I assume you are here to unify my kingdom," the Wolf paused and glared deep into Roland's eyes.

Roland held his gaze. It was as if the Wolf was measuring the kind of man he was. Even though Roland locked the man out of his mind, he knew that the Wolf was still stripping him bare and *seeing* him for who he really was. It was not a comforting thought.

Roland did not say a word. The next person to speak would be the loser.

Kaspar stood up next to his father and had the same look on his face. After a full minute, the Wolf turned to his son. Kaspar offered an almost imperceptible nod. When the Wolf turned around he lowered his eyes and went down on one knee.

"Roland Tyre, as holder of the golden Scepter of Unification, I bow to you as the Protectorate of Quentis. In this I do not offer my crown as king, but so do swear to unite with you in the battle that is yet to come. May your power be strong enough to ensure victory, but your benevolence as a balance so as not to destroy the kingdoms in your hand at the moment of triumph." The Wolf stood back up and took a step closer to Roland.

Roland didn't comprehend everything the king was saying, but he let out a slow sigh. He had secured the final kingdom and this time without any bloodshed.

The Wolf stuck out his hand, and Roland took it in a firm handshake. The king's dark eyes bored once again into Roland's lighter ones. "And may you not be enticed by the scepter to become more than you are meant to be."

Roland felt a shock of power flash from his hand to his heart. He pulled away quickly and glared for a moment at the Wolf. There was more power there—and a different kind than Roland was used to.

"There is one condition," the Wolf said.

Roland grinned. "I thought this was too easy."

The Wolf raised his eyebrows. "In return for my unwavering commitment to you and a declaration that my people will follow you I ask one favor."

"Only a favor?"

"Well," the Wolf paused with a smile. "More of a show of fairness and kindness on your part to the people that I have willingly given to you."

Roland smiled and relaxed. This would be easy.

"Save the Dragon King," the Wolf said with eyes that brokered no argument.

Roland raised his hands in the air, his right one still holding the scepter. "What? I don't have time for this."

"This is a minor thing to ask of such a man in your position," the Wolf said. "With all your power we only ask you to help one man. Is that too much for you? Are you not powerful enough for that simple task?"

Roland put his head back and laughed out loud. "Oh, now I know why they call you the Wolf. You, sir, are one shrewd negotiator. Of course I have the power to do that. And as a favor to you and your people, I will find the Dragon King and make sure that he is all right."

"The artifacts have spoken," the Wolf grew more grave in his tone. "The Dragon King lies at death's door in the company of Elves."

Roland stood with surprise on his face.

"You know my family leads the followers of the dragons in the south. Over the years we have gathered stray artifacts." The Wolf pointed to the scepter. "They are not as powerful as yours, and many we have given to the Dragon King, but we do hold a few in our family still." He reached into his pocket and drew out a small glass replica of a dragon. It was clear and flawless.

Roland breathed in quickly. He could feel the power from the beautiful artifact. The Wolf handed it to Roland, and power flared up inside of him and Roland was transported in his mind to another room. The smell of trees and salty air filled his nose. He looked around the wood-paneled room and saw two men lying lifeless on the floor. Blankets had been propped around them. Gabby and Jaimon stood nearby and looked down with fear written across their faces.

Peering down himself, Roland sucked in a breath. Bakari and Liam were the men on the floor. Their skin was dry and lips chapped. Bakari's dark hair had lost its luster, and his face was void of emotion.

"We need to find Kharlia," Gabby said through the vision. "We must go into the magic stream again."

Jaimon nodded. "It will be dangerous, but it is our only hope. There is no one else to call on."

Another man walked into Roland's view. It was Lanwaithian, King of Elvyn. He put his hands on the shoulders of the two young people from Quentis. "Our healers will watch over him tonight. You must regain your strength before entering the magic stream again. Get a good night's sleep, and we will watch over you in the morning as you find Kharlia." Lanwaithian paused and looked down at the two still men.

Suddenly Roland was swept away and stood back in the presence of the Wolf and Kaspar.

"You felt it didn't you?" the Wolf asked. "You know he is in danger."

Roland shook his head, still struggling with his current feelings for Bakari. "I did not feel it as you say. I was there. I saw it."

The Wolf put his hand over his heart. "Your powers are great indeed."

"Your daughter is with him, as is the dragon rider Jaimon."

"And they are well?" the Wolf asked.

"As far as I could tell," Roland said. "The Dragon King and Dragon Rider Liam are sick; dying. Kharlia is their only hope."

"Kharlia?" Kaspar asked.

Roland smiled. "A dear friend of Bakari's, an Elvyn-friend, and a healer of some renown."

"And do you know where this Kharlia is?"

Roland nodded. "Actually, yes, I do."

Within the hour, Roland was back on his dragon. As he passed over Margarid, the people cheered for him.

He would get Kharlia and bring her to Bakari. He would do, once again, what no one else could do. He would show them all his benevolence, and then he would gather his armies and crush the Dragon Queen and be hailed as the savior of the southern kingdoms.

Soon it would be over. Within a few weeks all would be peaceful again. He was sure of it.

CHAPTER THIRTY-THREE

The last time Roland had seen Kharlia was in the city of Corwan in the southeast corner of Alaris. She had stayed there to help heal those hurt when Queen Ameena Shabon from Tillimot had invaded. He now flew east and slightly north from Margarid to Corwan, passing a portion of Tillimot.

He looked down over the land and wondered if Ambassador Khouri had arrived there yet. He had left the man to rule in his stead until he returned to settle things. As he flew, Roland's head spun with the area he had covered in barely more than a week. From Cassian in Alaris, to Thera in Turg, to Raleez in Solshi, then to Margarid in Quentis. It was dizzying to think of all he had accomplished in the last week.

Unify!

Ahead of him, high in the sky, bright stars poked out between clouds. He wrapped himself once again in a spell of warmth and settled in for a few hours atop his dragon. He turned his mind inward.

Are you real, Orelia?

As real as you want me to be.

Are all dragons as secretive as you?

Are all wizards as inquisitive?

Roland chuckled. *Ah, a dragon with a sense of humor.*

I am as real to you as your magic is.

Roland thought about that for a few minutes. He and his power were as one. He couldn't separate the two. Did that make his magic more or less alive than he himself was? Now he was sounding as cryptic as the Wolf. Roland wondered what the man meant about making sure the scepter didn't make him more than he wanted to be.

I want power and fame. I want to be the greatest wizard the world has ever known.

And are you willing to pay the price?

Roland was now distinguishing the voice of the scepter from the dragon. It was different. The dragon was female with a more quiet voice; the scepter was deeper.

What do you require of me?

To have all you want, you have to give up all you need.

Roland was getting frustrated again. *Riddles. Is that all you give me? What do you want from me?*

Unify them!

Roland was tired of the circular argument and concentrated on the land around him instead. Besides the periodic flapping of his dragon, it was eerily quiet. The type of quiet you could get lost in. And for the next few hours that's what he did.

Finally in the distance, at the convergence of the Dunn and Corwan rivers, Roland spied Corwan. This time of night there were torches periodically set on the portion of the outer wall that was still standing after the battle. A few random candles flickered throughout the city. It was approaching the middle of the night, and the city would be quiet.

He brought his dragon down on the broad road leading into the front gates of the city. The gates were down, but a small guard patrolled the entrance to the city. Upon seeing the dragon a cry went up, and additional men gathered around. Roland dismounted and walked forward. His scepter was strapped to his waist, and he held his hands out in front of him.

"Men and women of Corwan," Roland said. "It is I, Roland Tyre."

One man stepped forward, older than the rest. He walked slowly toward Roland, his sword out by his side.

"General Guyason," Roland said with a smile.

The general responded grimly and waved the other men back with his hand. "High Wizard."

Roland did nothing to correct the man for not bowing. Corwan had been through a lot.

"What of the city?" Roland asked.

The general shook his head. "It's in shambles. The governor's mansion was totally destroyed and, much of the outer wall down. The docks are also in ruins."

"Mericus?" Roland had to ask.

"We have not found his body yet," the general shook his head. He looked exhausted. "I have heard you have assumed command."

"I have," Roland said. "Have you seen the healer Kharlia?"

"That woman was remarkable," the general's eyes opened wider. "She healed hundreds of men and women. And the three elves were no less serviceable. The kingdom owes them a debt of gratitude, my Lord. But they left day before last, heading to Mallek and a ship to Lor'l."

Roland groaned. He didn't have time to waste. The vision of Bakari lying almost dead came unbidden to his mind. *What did you do, Bakari?*

"I must find her," Roland said. "The Dragon King needs her help. What can I do for the people?"

General Guyason thought for a moment and then shook his head. "I truly do not know," he said. "Many lost their loved ones, and their city has been destroyed. We are still finding people buried under the rubble. It will take some time to rebuild the city. I need more men."

Roland nodded. "More men you shall have, General. I will send the best artisans and builders to Corwan. The city will be rebuilt and will be a beacon of brightness along the river." As he spoke he noticed men and women crowding in. He guessed some of the guards had told the people about the golden dragon. Many began walking out of the broken-down gate in their night clothes. They held on to each other, afraid to lose more than they had already lost.

The general turned at the sound, then glanced back at Roland. "I'm sorry, sir. I will send them away."

"No, General," Roland said with compassion. "The best thing I can give these people is hope."

Roland walked within about twenty feet of the closest person. Hundreds of men and women crowded behind. He raised the scepter up in the air, closed his eyes, and drew upon his significant powers; Earth: and the walls at the front of the city began to rebuild themselves; Mind: the people were infused with clarity of thought and how best to rebuild; Heart: he gave people hope. He hit the scepter on the ground hard, and a bright light spread out toward the crowd.

A collective gasp sounded in his ears; his eyes remained closed. He thought about each individual there and spread healing into them. Finally he opened his eyes, and everyone, including the general knelt on one need.

"Hail Roland Tyre!"

"Hail The High Wizard!"

"Hail the King of Alaris!"

The crowd stood and cheered to Roland's opened arms. He looked up at the sky and felt euphoria fill his breast. *This is what power felt like.*

"People of Corwan and Alaris, welcome to my kingdom of unity," Roland said in a loud voice.

"Hail the Golden Empire!" someone from the crowd yelled.

The Golden Empire. The sound of it felt good to Roland.

Unify them!

A slight frown marred Roland's moment of joy. *Why do you keep saying that?* He had more than enough to fight against Delia now.

"I must go," Roland said.

"Thank you, Sire," the general said. "If I had listened to you at first, we might not have lost the city."

Roland tilted his head with a questioning look. But if they had listened to him, Mericus might still be alive, and Roland would not be king. Everything was working out as it should be.

Mounting his dragon to the cheers of the people, Roland lifted into the sky and flew due east. The pounding in his head and heart was growing.

Unify them, thumped with every heartbeat.

Melding with his dragon, he looked out of Orelia's eyes for signs of Kharlia and her party. The dragon could see much better in the dark. Another advantage that Bakari now didn't hold over Roland anymore. He smiled at that.

Early in the morning, just before sunrise, Roland spotted a campsite just west of Mallek. Orelia brought him down and over the group. They were up and packing.

"Kharlia!" Roland called out as he brought the dragon back around again.

Orelia skidded to a stop at the edge of a copse of trees, and Roland hopped off. Kharlia, along with Ambassador Maerwen and guards Gloron and Keryth stepped out. Kharlia's face held a big smile, her eyes wide looking at the golden dragon. Maerwen's lips held tight in a frown, and Gloron and Keryth laughed and slapped each other's backs.

"Roland! What are you doing here?" Kharlia squealed as she reached him and gave him a big hug. "And where did *you* get a dragon?"

"Kharlia," Roland tried to speak, but Kharlia jumped back in.

"Bak? Is Bak all right? Where are the other dragons?"

Roland shook his head. "Delia, from Turg, has stolen the dragon bonds, and Bak lies ill with Liam in Lor'l. I have come to take you to them."

"What happened?" Kharlia asked.

"I'm not sure." Roland kept his face stern. "He tried to stop me, and we had words, and he left."

"I can't imagine someone having words with you, Roland Tyre," said Maerwen. Her long, blonde hair lay silky and perfect down her back—even at this time of morning.

"Maerwen, nice to see you are in a good mood," Roland said. The lady was a junior ambassador for Elvyn and had never been friendly to Roland. She was a younger sister of the queen of the Elves and treated everyone as inferior to her.

Gloron laughed, and Maerwen gave him a dark look. He tried to compose himself, but Keryth smiled.

"I see you still carry that thing," Maerwen said, indicating the scepter.

Roland smiled and grabbed it. Power filled him once again, and he relished in its bath of glory. "Yes, I do."

"And have you used it?" Maerwen asked, still stern.

"Yes, Maerwen, I have used the scepter to unify the kingdoms," Roland said. "I must gather an army and defeat Delia—who now calls herself the Dragon Queen. She has turned the heart of Alli and declares to subject all the kingdoms to her."

"But the Dragon Riders," Keryth said. "They are meant to keep the peace."

"As I said, she stole the dragon bonds. The Dragon Riders have no power." Roland was getting annoyed at their questions. "The Dragon King has no power. I, Roland Tyre, must save the land. I am your ruler. I am your savior."

"Roland, don't say such things." Kharlia's brown eyes turned darker. "The power of the scepter has gone to your head."

"You are not my ruler, High Wizard," Maerwen said firmly, "and don't you ever assume such. The Elvyn kingdom will stand against whatever comes—and without your help, I am sure. We have stayed safe for thousands of years, while your kingdoms squabble and fight."

Unify them. Unify all of them! The words came louder and with more urgency than Roland had felt before. He put his hand to his head and growled.

"Roland, are you all right?" Kharlia stepped forward. She stood on tiptoe to touch her hand to Roland's face, but he pulled away.

"Save your power for the Dragon King," Roland said more harshly than he intended. But he was tired of it all. Of people not taking him seriously. "Get on the dragon, Kharlia."

She gave him a questioning look and then looked at the others.

"Now, Kharlia. Now!" Roland put the scepter back at his side and grabbed Kharlia's arm.

"But… what about them?" Kharlia tried to pull away.

"They can take a ship," Roland said.

"But my bag," Kharlia yelled up at him. "I need my bag of herbs, Roland."

"Fine, Kharlia, get it and let's go now! There is no time."

Kharlia ran back, while Roland hopped up on Orelia. He lifted up in the air and flew the short distance back to where Kharlia now ran back from the camp. The dragon skimmed over the ground, and Roland reached down and grabbed Kharlia and threw her up behind him.

"Hold on, Kharlia. We don't have much time if we want to save the Dragon King."

CHAPTER THIRTY-FOUR

Roland pushed the dragon as fast as they could go toward Elvyn. The sun rose and bathed the day in golden rays of light. He directed the dragon to turn north, but instead she continued east out over the Blue Sea and toward a darkening storm cloud.

"Where are we going, Roland?" Kharlia asked, holding on tightly.

"I don't know," Roland yelled into the increasing wind. "Sometimes she has a mind of her own."

Unify them!

He was tired of that command. He was tired of people telling him what he could or couldn't do. He thought of Delia and how she had used Alli to try to take Solshi right out from under his nose. It wasn't hers to take. It was his now. All of them were part of his golden empire—well, there was still Elvyn. He wasn't sure how that would go. Elves were a stubborn race, known for staying out of men's affairs. They hid behind their magic and large trees with their smug, long-lived lives, and moved at a snail's pace.

Dark clouds billowed up farther in front of him.

Orelia, stop. We need to go north to Elvyn!

Unify them. All of them!

But his dragon wouldn't turn; only sped faster and faster out over the churning sea.

"Roland!" Kharlia yelled. "I can barely hang on."

He had never been this far out to sea; in fact, he had never been out to sea at all. Having grown up in landlocked Alaris behind the barrier, he had only seen the sea recently. At this speed they would end up beyond where most had ventured. Well, the Eastern Kingdoms were far to the east, and periodically large trading ships did make the venture. But many of them were lost, from what he had heard.

Cranking his neck to the back behind him, he could barely see the shoreline of Elvyn anymore. He thought of Delia once again. With the might of all the southern kingdoms behind him, Delia couldn't stand long in the united territories. Four dragons wouldn't be enough for the combined might of all he was gathering.

Lightning flashed ahead of him, and the wind pushed back against them. They flew farther and farther out, faster and faster. There was nothing he could do to stop his dragon. She was out of control. He could feel Kharlia holding on for dear life, and he himself hugged Orelia's neck.

They flew past the point where a ship could get to in a day, three days, two weeks. Turning around, he could see the western continent no more.

He held up his scepter and screamed into the wind. Light flashed out in front of him. Maybe he could banish the storm and force Orelia to turn around. Fire and lightning sizzled off the end of the scepter and joined with the lightning in the dark sky around him. He cast the spell he had seen Maerwen use, and while it continued to rain, it now slid around them and they stayed dry.

"Are you all right, Kharlia?" Roland yelled behind him.

"I'm scared, Roland!" She pushed into his back and grabbed on tighter. "Where are we going?"

The storm raged, and Roland's frustration grew, but he felt the power of the storm filling his reserves. It was almost intoxicating. He breathed deeply and felt it all inside him. The power of earth, mind, and heart swirling through his breast. Only the power of spirit was missing—but that was held in the dragons and other magical creatures. He could harness it when the time came. With his mighty army of five kingdoms, he probably wouldn't need it.

Unify them! Unify them!

I am! He shouted back at his mind. It seemed that both dragon and scepter spoke to him now.

All of them!

All of them? he asked. He had Alaris, Tillimot, North and South Solshi, Quentis, and would ask the elves for their aid.

The storm blew them sideways, and Kharlia began to slip.

"Help!" Kharlia yelled as she began to fall.

Roland grabbed around the neck of his dragon with one hand and grabbed Kharlia with the other and moved her back up behind him. The scepter almost fell from the hand that held the dragon's neck. They were now in the midst of the powerful storm. Thunder boomed, and lightning struck every few seconds.

He rode the storm but now relished in its force. *Such power, such strength!*

Unify all of them! came the voice again; more insistent than before. *Unify them!*

The pounding in Roland's head threatened to overwhelm him. Five kingdoms was surely enough to destroy Delia, find Alli, and restore peace. Why was more needed?

His scepter grew bright, and a blinding light shot out from the orb. It sped toward the clouds and parted them with its power.

Look! came the forceful command.

The air wavered in front of him and daylight streamed through a hole in the clouds. Roland couldn't tell if what he was seeing was truly below him or if through the magic he was seeing a vision of what was farther out in the ocean.

"Roland!" Kharlia yelled. "Turn around. The storm's going to kill us."

"Don't you see it, Kharlia?" Roland said, his voice barely carrying the few inches back to Kharlia.

"See what?" Kharlia replied.

"The ships!"

Below him, for as far as he could see were ships—hundreds of war ships, maybe even a thousand if he would guess. Their numerous masts were lowered as they tried to maneuver the raging storm. He could hardly understand what he was seeing. No one would believe him. "Don't you see them?"

Unify them, the voice now came as almost a whisper, but it pierced every corner of Roland's soul.

Now he understood the urgency. Now he truly knew what he was up against.

His Citadel, Alaris, Delia, even Bakari were minor considerations and complications compared to what he was seeing below him. With one more flap of the wings, his dragon finally turned around and headed west, back into the storm and back toward Elvyn.

Fear gripped Roland's heart for a moment, but then a feeling of destiny came over him. He was not meant to rule the Citadel, or save Alaris, or even fight Delia with his five kingdoms. He had been given the Scepter of Unification to save all of them from the might of the Eastern Kingdoms.

Unify them. Unify them. Unify them.

The thumping continued as power filled Roland from head to toe.

The elves would soon bow to him.

All would bow to him and his golden empire.

And then he would save them all.

#

Read THE GOLDEN EMPIRE
Book 3 in THE DRAGON ARTIFACTS and discover the
stunning conclusion of Bakari, Alli, and Roland's
grand magical adventure!

How much power does one wizard need?
Some may say he is overstepping his bounds.
But who else can stop the war from coming?

With the Dragon King on the brink of death and Alli and the other dragon riders falling by the way, Roland Trye tries to unify the kingdoms against the threat coming from the east. Both arrogant and charming, Roland's thirst for power has no limit. But will it be enough?

But in the end the magic needed to win may require the ultimate sacrifice. Who will take up the cause and give up all they have to save the people?

Will the Dragon King survive? Will Alli and the other riders rejoin their dragons, and will Roland Tyre become what he has always wanted to be—the most powerful wizard alive?

Other Series By Mike Shelton
The Alaris Chronicles

Read about how Roland, Bakari, and Alli first met

A magical barrier. Civil war. Power-hungry Wizards.

The fate of a kingdom rests on the shoulders of three young wizards who couldn't be more different.

As the magical barrier protecting the kingdom of Alaris from dangerous outsiders begins to fail, and a fomenting rebellion threatens to divide the country in a civil war, the three wizards are thrust into the middle of a power struggle.

When the barrier comes down, the truth comes out. Was everything they were taught about their kingdom based on a lie?

Will they all choose to fight on the same side, or end up enemies in the battle over who should rule Alaris?

Sign up on Mike's website at www.MichaelSheltonBooks.com and get a copy of the prequel novella e-book to The Alaris Chronicles, Prophecy of the Dragon.

Protect the youngest heir of the Dragon King. That is the mission given to Imari in this prequel novella to The Alaris Chronicles.

The Cremelino Prophecy

About 15 years prior to The Alaris Chronicles and a few kingdoms to the north.

A Prophecy. A Powerful Sword. A reluctant wizard.

Darius San Williams, son of one of King Edward's councilors, cares little for his father's politics and vows to leave the city of Anikari to protect and bring glory to the Realm.

When a new-found and ancient magic emerges within him, he and his friends Christine and Kelln are faced with decisions that could shatter or fulfill the prophecy and the lives of all those they know.

Wizards and magic have long been looked down upon in the Realm, but Darius learns that no matter where he goes, prophecy and destiny are waiting to find him.

Sign up on Mike's website at www.MichaelSheltonBooks.com and get a copy of the prequel novella e-book to The Cremelino Prophecy, The Blade and The Bow.

Follow Darius and Kelln in one of their more fantastic adventures prior to The Path Of Destiny.

The TruthSeer Archives

On an island far out in the Eastern Sea join a new adventure of magic through the stones of power.

Everyone lies.
What if you could tell when they did?
What if this knowledge caused you immense physical pain?

Given a rare TruthStone, Shaeleen suffers immense agony with every lie she hears or tells. While struggling to control her new power and curb the pain she learns a powerful truth that could thrust an entire continent into civil war.

The stones of power protect the five kingdoms of Wayland - and have done so for two hundred years. Now those stones are failing and a dark power threatens to take control. With the help of her brother, and a young thief, Shaeleen sets out on a dangerous journey to gather and restore the power of all the stones.

The lies could kill her, but the truth could destroy a kingdom.

Will she succeed before the endless lies destroy her?

About the Author

Mike was born in California and has lived in multiple states from the west coast to the east coast. He cannot remember a time when he wasn't reading a book. At school, home, on vacation, at work at lunch time, and yes even a few pages in the car (at times when he just couldn't put that great book down). Though he has read all sorts of genres he has always been drawn to fantasy. It is his way of escaping to a simpler time filled with magic, wonders and heroics of young men and women.

Other than reading, Mike has always enjoyed the outdoors. From the beaches in Southern California to the warm waters of North Carolina. From the waterfalls in the Northwest to the Rocky Mountains in Utah. Mike has appreciated the beauty that God provides for us. He also enjoys hiking, discovering nature, playing a little basketball or volleyball, and most recently disc golf. He has a lovely wife who has always supported him, and three beautiful children who have been the center of his life.

Mike began writing stories in elementary school and moved on to larger novels in his early adult years. He has worked in corporate finance for most of his career. That, along with spending time with his wonderful family and obligations at church has made it difficult to find the time to truly dedicate to writing. In the last few years as his children have become older he has returned to doing what he truly enjoys – writing!

mikesheltonbooks@gmail.com
www.MichaelSheltonBooks.com
https://www.facebook.com/groups/MikeSheltonAuthor/
http://www.Twitter.com/msheltonbooks
http://www.Instagram.com/mikesheltonbooks